THE GHOST
AND THE BIRTHDAY BOY

HAUNTING DANIELLE

THE GHOST
AND THE BIRTHDAY BOY

BOBBI HOLMES

The Ghost and the Birthday Boy
(Haunting Danielle, Book 28)
A Novel
By Bobbi Holmes
Cover Design: Elizabeth Mackey

Copyright © 2021 Bobbi Holmes
Robeth Publishing, LLC
All Rights Reserved.
robeth.net

ROBETH
PUBLISHING, LLC

ISBN: 978-1-949977-66-0
(A)

To my narrator Romy Nordlinger. Thank you for bringing my characters to life.

ONE

Blood stained Molly's nurse's uniform. She stood alone at the battered chain-link fence, looking out at the street and the car that had just pulled up and parked. Overhead, tree limbs swayed with the afternoon breeze, and she could hear the surf in the distance.

Molly watched as two people got out of the vehicle, the driver, a woman—and her passenger, a man. After slamming the car door close, the woman walked toward Molly, but stopped when she reached the front of her car, some twelve feet away. She looked to be in her forties, with short, curly brown hair, wearing a fitted A-line, pale blue dress on her slim frame. The woman folded her arms across her chest, frowned, and stared Molly's way.

Molly glanced to the male passenger, who had walked to the back of the vehicle. He wore a gray suit, but no hat on his shortly cropped dark hair. He opened the trunk and pulled something out. It looked like a sign, approximately eighteen by twenty-two inches, attached to a metal stake.

Awkwardly, the man rested the cumbersome sign on one knee as he slammed the trunk hood shut.

"Who are they?" a male voice asked.

Molly turned her head slightly and saw Waylon now standing at her side, a concerned frown furrowing his brow. "It's the same ones who were here the other day." Molly looked back at the couple, who now walked their way, the man still carrying the large sign. She noticed one of his hands holding the edge of the sign also held what looked like a hammer.

"JENNA, WOULD YOU TAKE THIS," Ray grumbled as the hammer fell from his hand. It landed in the dirt, barely missing the toe of his right shoe.

Jenna paused a moment and looked back at Ray, who continued to fumble with the sign. She walked to him, leaned down, and picked up the hammer. He scowled when she offered it back to him. With a sigh, she held onto the hammer and turned to look at the property. An aged chain-link fence encircled its perimeter.

"This place gives me the creeps," Jenna said, now absently fidgeting with the hammer, passing it from one hand to the other and back again.

Ray set the tip of the stake against the ground, while resting his palms along the sign's top edge to keep it standing. With Jenna by his side, he inspected the property at a distance.

"It's a splendid piece of real estate. I can't believe the city decided to list it. And they gave me the listing!" Ray beamed.

"That's because no sane Realtor wanted it," Jenna snarked.

"Don't be ridiculous. Certainly, you don't believe in ghosts."

Not smiling, Jenna stopped fidgeting with the hammer and looked at Ray. She had lived in Frederickport her entire life and had been a real estate agent for just six months. After her divorce, she needed a job, and she didn't want to leave town. There was no reason to. Her ex had already left Frederickport with his new girlfriend. Jenna had never had a real job before, but she knew all about Frederickport, was good at math, and enjoyed looking at open houses. It seemed like the perfect job. Perfect, until she agreed to be Ray's assistant, and he took this listing.

"How long have you lived in Frederickport?" Jenna asked.

"A year. You know that. Why?"

"It's not about ghosts, Ray. Anyone who's lived here for as long as I have has heard all the stories about this property. And I'm not saying it has anything to do with ghosts. But there is seriously some bad energy here. Can't you feel it?" Jenna looked back at the property and shivered. "It's like the place is cursed."

"What I feel is a big fat commission in my future. I've been in this business for over twenty years. There's no such thing as cursed property, just crappy real estate agents."

"It'll be a cursed listing if you can't sell it," Jenna argued.

"I will."

"Who's going to buy it? Why do you think the city hasn't sold it yet? They've tried listing it before. No one in Frederickport will touch this place."

"I don't imagine the buyer will be a Frederickport native. Lots of Californians with more money than brains looking for beach property. It's not right on the beach, but it still has a splendid view, and it's within walking distance to the ocean. That's why I need to take lots of pictures. I plan to have this listing online before nightfall. Did you remember the camera?"

Jenna let out a sigh. "Yes. It's in the car. You plan on selling this to some unsuspecting person from out of state?"

"Oh, stop. There's nothing wrong with this property."

"WHAT DOES IT SAY?" Waylon asked Molly. Not that he couldn't see the bold words printed on the sign, but Waylon had never learned to read.

"The same thing that was on the other signs. Remember them?" Molly asked patiently. "Look at the words. See if you can figure it out. You're not stupid, Waylon. I don't care what those other people said about you. You don't give yourself enough credit."

Waylon studied the sign. The letters meant nothing to him. But he considered her words, and he remembered the other signs. Angrily he turned to Molly and asked, "Is that another one of those For Sale signs?"

"Yes. But the way those two are just standing there talking, I wonder if they're changing their minds."

Waylon studied the man and woman through narrowed eyes. The corners of his mouth curled into a smile. *I can make them change their minds*, Waylon told himself.

"ENOUGH OF THIS CURSE TALK." Ray lifted the sign. "I want to get this up and take those pictures."

Before Ray could take a step, the For Sale sign slammed against his chest, knocking him off his feet, sending him tumbling backwards. He fell to the ground, landing on his backside in the dirt. The runaway sign kept on moving for a few moments until it landed unceremoniously in the middle of the road.

"Ray!" Jenna gasped. She dropped the hammer, leaned over, and offered both hands to help him stand back up.

Taking hold of one of her hands, Ray stumbled back to his feet. Once standing again, he let go of her hand and looked to the sign some six feet away. With the palms of his hands, he brushed dirt from his slacks. "Where did that wind come from?" Ray muttered.

"There was no wind," Jenna insisted.

Ray turned another scowl to Jenna before reaching down to the ground and picking up the hammer she had dropped. He handed it to her. "Then what knocked that sign out of my hands, a ghost?" he asked with a snort before turning from Jenna and lumbering to the street to retrieve the For Sale sign.

Jenna did not reply but looked uneasily from the sign back to the property in question.

"And get that camera!" Ray called to Jenna.

EN ROUTE to their lunch destination, Melony Carmichael drove the car. Adam sat in the passenger seat and blurted, "What do you think of the Winterborne engagement ring?"

Taken aback by the unexpected question, considering they had been debating lunch destinations, Melony glanced briefly at Adam before looking down the road.

"Where did that come from?" she asked.

Adam shrugged. "I just wanted to know if you like it. You told me before you thought it was gorgeous, but would it be something you'd wear?"

Arching her brows briefly, Melony again looked at Adam and then back down the road. "Ahh, you're finally getting ready to sell it. I was wondering why you held on to it for so long. But it's a little out of my price range. I think you're going to need to look somewhere else for a buyer." She snickered.

The Winterborne engagement ring was a priceless piece of jewelry its previous owner had hidden in a novelty frame in hopes someone would someday find the treasure. Technically, Danielle had found the treasure, yet since the frame held a vintage photograph of Adam's great-grandfather, Danielle had given it to Adam the previous Christmas. Danielle knew she was giving away the valuable ring along with the frame and photograph. Since she had no use or desire for another treasure to store in her bank safe deposit box, she rather liked the idea of giving it to Adam. Seeing his expression when the ring fairly flew from the frame's hidden compartment when liberated by Adam was worth more than the ring's value to Danielle. She also imagined it was the reaction Eloise Winterborne had envisioned from the ring's new owner when she had hidden it in the frame.

Adam scowled. "I wasn't asking so you could buy it."

"Yeah, right," Melony scoffed under her breath before making an unexpected right turn.

"Hey, where are you going?" Adam sat up straighter in his seat.

"Hold on, Adam, you are perfectly safe in the car. See, I'll lock the doors." The next moment, Melony hit the door lock. It made a clicking sound.

"This is not the way to Pearl Cove," Adam argued.

"I just want to see something."

Adam grumbled under his breath.

"Oh, come on. I know you hated riding your bike on this street when we were kids. Surely you aren't still afraid of the Marymoor ghosts?" Melony teased.

"I just don't like going down this way," Adam muttered.

"I wanted to see if it's true."

"What, you didn't believe me?" Adam snapped.

A few moments later, Melony pulled up along the opposite side of the street from the Marymoor property. At one time it had been the site of the infamous Marymoor Sanatorium, which had been more insane asylum than sanatorium. The building had burned down years earlier, leaving behind a large piece of property, now owned by the city, separated from the rest of the residential neighborhood by chain-link fence. Today a newly erected For Sale sign stood in front of the property, and a man walked around the grounds, taking photographs. Nearby, a woman sat alone in the driver's seat of a parked car.

"That's Ray Collins," Adam said with a snort. "Thinks he's God's gift to real estate."

"Wow, they really are trying to sell it again." Melony's hands rested on the steering wheel as she studied the property. "Maybe you can find a buyer."

"You know, Mel, sometimes I ask myself why I want to marry you."

Adam's unexpected words startled Melony. She froze a moment and then turned to stare at Adam. "What did you just say?"

"I wasn't trying to sell you the damn ring. I just wondered if you'd like the Winterborne engagement ring or would rather pick something else out."

"Are you asking me to marry you?" Melony fairly choked out.

Adam shrugged and glanced from Melony to the Marymoor site and then back to Melony. He grinned and said, "Yeah, well, considering our history, I guess it's only appropriate I propose in front of what used to be an insane asylum. So, what do you think, Mel? Wanna get married?"

TWO

"Does this mean you're pregnant?" Lily asked in a conspiratorial whisper. She sat in the side yard of Marlow House, sipping lemonade and visiting with Danielle. Across the street her son, Connor, napped in his crib, while her husband, Ian, worked in his home office next to the nursery. Sadie, Ian and Lily's golden retriever, had come over to Marlow House with Lily but had immediately raced inside to visit with Walt, where she stayed.

"Not sure," Danielle said with a shrug. "I should start any day now, but I don't feel like I normally do right before I start my period."

"It blows my mind your mother-in-law was the one to tell you, you might be pregnant!" Lily laughed.

"Yeah, considering she's been dead for over a century." Danielle shrugged before taking another sip of lemonade.

Walt's mother hadn't told Danielle she might be pregnant, but her spirit had suggested it to Walt during a dream hop days earlier. After Walt had shared his dream with his wife, she hadn't mentioned it to anyone until now.

"So is this the reason for the switch from iced tea to lemonade?" Lily asked.

Danielle glanced briefly at the half-filled glass of lemonade she held and back to Lily. The two sat on patio chairs on the side porch, each dressed casually, enjoying the late summer weather. The outside temperature hovered just under seventy, without a cloud in the sky.

"Yeah, I suppose. I haven't had coffee or tea since Walt told me. Although, I wonder how bad the sugar in lemonade is for a baby, compared to caffeine."

"Oh, a baby!" Lily squealed. "I hope your mother-in-law knows what she's talking about. A little less than two years age difference between Connor and yours won't be that much. They will be play-mates! Will it be a boy or girl?"

Danielle laughed. "We don't even know if I'm pregnant yet. And it is entirely possible Walt's mother was talking about a child in our distant future."

"No way. Didn't she mention your craving for chocolate?" Lily reminded her.

Danielle laughed again. "I'm always craving chocolate."

Lily let out a sigh and set her glass on the side table. "I suppose. When are you taking a pregnancy test? I assume you haven't taken one yet. Why not?"

"I'm going to wait. If I don't start in the next week, I'll take one. Perhaps I'll wait until after your family leaves."

"Why would you do that?" Lily frowned.

"If I know for sure, it would be hard to keep it to myself. And I don't want to tell people so early in my pregnancy. Do you understand?"

Lily nodded. "Yeah. I waited a while before I told anyone but you about Connor. What about Eva and Marie? Are you telling them?"

"No." Danielle shook her head. "Marie will cluck around me like a protective mother hen once she knows. Let's delay that, shall we? Anyway, we all have enough going on right now. What with Connor's big birthday bash, and don't you have a wedding anniversary coming up?"

Lily groaned.

Danielle arched her brows. "You don't want to celebrate your wedding anniversary?"

"I'd love to do something special. But everyone will be here. Feels weird for Ian and me to go off and do something by ourselves. Ian and I talked about it, and we both agreed we would celebrate our anniversary later."

"I don't see why you guys can't go do something, just the two of you. Heck, you'll have tons of babysitter options. Both sets of grandparents…"

Lily groaned again and slumped down in her chair, folding her arms across her chest.

Danielle arched a brow. "You don't seem too excited about your family coming for a visit."

"This was my idea. But now that it's almost here, well, I'm starting to wonder if it was such a terrific idea, having Ian's parents and mine at the same time. I like Ian's parents and everything, but…"

"But what?" Danielle asked.

"Ian's mom is just like Kelly," Lily said.

"How so?" Danielle asked.

Lily sat up straighter in the chair and considered the question a moment before answering. "I'm not saying they don't like animals; they do. But they feel dogs belong in their place. Remember when we got married, how Ian's mom about had a fit when she found out Sadie was going to be in the wedding?"

"In fairness, she didn't know Walt was there to help Sadie understand what we needed of her."

Ignoring Danielle's comment, Lily added, "And remember how Kelly locked Sadie out of Connor's room when she first babysat him?"

"Babysitting someone else's child is a tremendous responsibility, and some dogs—"

"Oh, stop, Dani! You asked how they were alike."

Danielle grinned sheepishly. "I'm sorry, go on."

"They are both kinda in everyone's business."

Danielle nodded. "Yeah, I see that with Kelly."

"Kelly is Ian's mom's mini-me. And Ian adores both his sister and mom—which he should. I try to keep my mouth shut. So please, say nothing."

"I understand. Families are complicated," Danielle said.

"And then my mother…" Lily began.

"I love your mom." Danielle grinned.

"So do I. But when she and Ian's mom get together, it's like this mother competition. Or should I say grandma competition? They each have their own way of doing things—which is fine. I do too. But having some distance between them just makes things a little easier. As it is, I have to deal with Kelly practically every day. But put both the moms together with us for two weeks, each telling me how I'm doing it wrong—how I should do it." Lily groaned again. "This sounds awful, but I'm really glad none of them live in Frederickport."

"It's only for two weeks. You can do this. And just be grateful you have them," Danielle gently reminded her.

"That is one thing I hate about you, Dani."

Danielle frowned. "What?"

"You always make me feel so guilty when I complain about my family, when you don't have a family to complain about." Lily slumped back in the chair again.

Danielle laughed. "I'm sorry, Lily. You can complain to me, and I'll try to keep my Pollyanna, count-your-blessings comments to myself."

HEATHER DIDN'T MEAN to spy on her crabby neighbor Pearl. She was looking for her calico cat, Bella, and was afraid the mischievous feline had slipped next door to visit Pearl's flower garden. But when she peeked over Pearl's fence, she saw her neighbor doing her own bit of spying.

Pearl's backside faced Heather as she crouched by the side fence separating her property from Marlow House. It tempted Heather to say something, but pressure on her right foot distracted her.

Glancing down to her feet, Heather saw Bella weaving in and out around her ankles. Leaning down to pick up the cat, Heather heard the purring. "How did you get outside?" Heather whispered to the petite feline. Now holding Bella in her arms, she glanced back over the fence. Pearl remained glued to the back fence, her backside sticking out like it needed to be smacked. Heather wished Marie was there to do it.

Curious to see what Pearl was watching, she refrained from calling out to her neighbor and instead continued down the street to the side gate at Marlow House, Bella in her arms.

THE SOUND of the side gate opening stopped their conversation. Both Lily and Danielle looked that way. A moment later Heather walked into the yard, carrying her cat.

"Hey, Heather," Danielle called out, followed by another greeting from Lily to Heather.

"Look out, you're being watched," Heather whispered loudly when she was in earshot.

"We are?" Danielle asked.

Heather glanced briefly to the fence separating Pearl's yard from Marlow House. A moment later she sat down in one of the empty yard chairs and told them what she had seen. Bella remained on her lap while Heather gently stroked the cat's back.

"Is she still there?" Lily asked, looking that way.

Heather shrugged. "I guess. I was hoping she was watching something exciting over here. She must be really bored if she has to spy on you two drinking…" Heather looked at the glasses. "Is that lemonade or margaritas?"

Danielle laughed. "No, lemonade. Want some?"

"No, thanks. I'm good." Heather looked at Lily and asked, "Where is my little buddy?"

"I assume you mean Connor. He's napping," Lily said.

"We were just talking about his birthday party," Danielle said.

"No. We were talking about my family descending on us for two weeks," Lily said.

"Aren't they all staying at Marlow House?" Heather asked.

"Yeah." Lily let out a sigh.

"Hey, not to change the subject, but guess what I saw Adam doing this morning," Heather said.

"You never know with Adam." Danielle grinned.

"What?" Lily asked.

"I think he took the Winterborne ring out of his safe deposit box," Heather began. "I went to the bank this morning, and Adam was coming out of the safe deposit area, carrying a small box. Like a ring box. I was standing in line, and he didn't see me. And then a few minutes later, when I went outside, he was sitting in his car, looking at something. I walked up to the car, knocked on the window, and he about jumped out of his skin. He was looking at whatever was in the box, and he immediately closed it, and from what I saw, it looked like the ring."

"I wonder if he found a buyer for it," Danielle mused.

"What did he say?" Lily asked.

"He said nothing, didn't even roll his window down. Adam just waved, gave me a goofy smile, and drove away. And then an hour later, you know what I saw?"

"What?" both Danielle and Lily chorused.

"Adam in the car with Melony," Heather said.

"It's possible Mel found a buyer for the ring," Danielle suggested.

Heather rolled her eyes. "Oh, please, the way he was looking at that ring, he was thinking something else."

"Something else like what?" Danielle asked.

"Like a man preparing to propose," Heather suggested.

Danielle frowned at Heather. "Why, because he was looking at the ring all goofy?"

Heather nodded. "Yep."

Lily laughed. "Heather, that is how Adam looks at anything that's worth a lot of money."

Danielle looked to Lily and said, "Exactly."

Heather let out a snort. "Brother, you two are so unromantic. Is that what happens when you get married?"

Danielle flashed Heather a grin and said, "Marie would be all over your scenario, but knowing those two, they're probably taking it to a buyer. Although, as much as Marie likes Mel, I imagine a part of her would be happy if some woman who wanted to have kids snagged Adam."

"Hey, I understand Mel and Adam not wanting kids. I don't want kids," Heather said.

Lily frowned at Heather. "But you're terrific with Connor."

Heather grinned at Lily. "I adore Connor. But it doesn't mean I want kids of my own. I mean seriously, do I really want to pass down serial-killer genes to a new generation?"

"I understand if you don't want kids, but I hope you're kidding about the serial-killer thing. I don't believe anyone is born a killer. It's how a kid is raised," Danielle said.

Heather sighed. "I'm kidding… a little. No, not really. Didn't you ever see *The Bad Seed*? The old movie from the fifties?"

Lily shivered. "Oh, I remember the movie. That little girl was creepy."

"And it was fiction," Danielle reminded them.

Heather shrugged. "Not a chance I want to take. And speaking of creepy, did you hear the city is trying to sell the Marymoor site? Chris told me this morning. Adam told him."

"Did Adam get the listing?" Lily asked.

"No. And I doubt he wanted it," Heather said.

"That's an enormous piece of property," Danielle said. "Are they going to subdivide it into smaller residential lots?"

"I don't think so," Heather said.

"Can you imagine someone building a house on that site?" Lily gave a shiver. "I remember the bloody nurse Dani saw over there. Sure, only mediums will likely see her, but what about little kids like Connor? I wonder if the kids in that neighborhood ever see anything."

THREE

June Bartley stood in the middle of the den, surrounded by moving boxes, her hands resting on her hips, while her husband, John, sat nearby at his desk.

Looking up from the laptop, John peered over his reading glasses, watching his wife as she glanced around the room. "You need to sit down," John insisted. "Rest. You've done enough today."

"But there is so much to do!" June insisted. "We leave for Frederickport in less than two weeks. I have the rest of this house to pack up."

John removed his reading glasses and set them on the desk. He rubbed his eyes briefly with his right thumb before saying, "The moving company will do that. Why do you keep insisting on boxing everything up yourself? That's why we're hiring them."

Reluctantly, June took a seat on the recliner, facing her husband. "But we've never used a mover before."

"That's because we've lived in this house forever, never was a need to hire a mover before. We're too darn old to move ourselves. We aren't kids anymore."

June cocked her head slightly and looked at her husband. "Are you going to be sad to leave this house?"

"This has been a good house. Lots of fond memories. But am I feeling sentimental and reluctant to move? No. You?"

June grinned. "I love this house, but I'm ready to move. Ready for a change. And the time is right."

"And the grandkids," John teased.

June's smile widened. "Especially the grandkids. I don't want to rush Kelly, but now that her and Joe are officially engaged, I assume they'll be starting a family. And when they do, I don't want to be so far from them. And I want to spend more time with Connor. As it is now, he knows that Heather girl more than he does me."

"I don't think a neighbor who babysits occasionally will replace a grandmother," John insisted.

June shrugged. "I don't want to be strangers to our grandchildren. Someone they just see a couple of times a year. I want to be part of their lives, go to Connor's baseball games. I want to be there when Kelly has her baby."

"They haven't even set a date," John reminded her. "Let's not get her with child yet."

"You know what I mean."

"I hope we don't regret not calling that Realtor friend of Ian's before we get there. He could have a rental all lined up for us," John said.

"I want this to be a surprise. He might say something to Ian, and that would ruin the surprise. Come on, aren't you excited to see the expression on Ian's face when we tell him we're moving to Frederickport?"

"You mean when we tell him we've already moved to Frederickport?" John asked with a laugh. "When we get there, we'll technically be homeless, with all our worldly goods in storage and someone else living in this house."

"He's going to be surprised. Ian never believed we would ever leave this house."

"We still should have a rental lined up," John said.

"What if we find a house to buy? It would be silly to move into a rental first," June said.

"I want to build our last house," John reminded her. "But even if we bought a house instead, it would take more than a month in escrow, and we can't stay at Marlow House that long. Either way, we're going to need a rental."

June let out a sigh. "I suppose. But it's only a couple of weeks now."

"I just hope he's going to be happy about it," John said with a snort.

June rolled her eyes. "Don't be silly. He's going to be thrilled. And Lily will finally have someone to watch Connor, so she doesn't have to rely on those neighbors. I'm sure she's eager to go back to teaching. This way she can do it without worrying about Connor because I can watch him. And since Ian works from home, I'm sure he'll be more comfortable having me there instead of some stranger. And I can always make Ian lunch and get dinner started for Lily."

"Who's going to make lunch for me?" John teased.

"I know you. If you end up building our house, you're going to be busy the next year. You can always stop by Ian's and have lunch with us."

"I'm looking forward to this next phase in our life," John said.

June let out a sigh. "Me too."

They sat in silence for a few minutes, each lost in his or her own thoughts. Finally, John asked, "What are you thinking?"

June looked up at her husband. "That tattoo."

John chuckled. "I assume you're talking about Lily's dragon tattoo?"

"I loathe that thing." June cringed. "It's going to be so embarrassing for Connor when he grows up, and his mother has that gawd awful thing on her arm. It's so tacky. I wish she'd wear long sleeves."

"It's hardly Lily's fault. Anyway, it seems like all the women their age have tattoos now."

"Kelly doesn't," June reminded him.

"I know. But like I said, it's not Lily's fault."

"She could have had it removed. Instead, she added another tattoo to the arm."

"Ian said removing it would leave a scar, something about the ink," John said.

"A scar would be more respectable than a huge tattoo. I just wish she didn't have it."

"I'm sure she wishes she didn't have it too," John gently reminded her.

June let out a sigh. "I'm being petty. Whatever you do, don't tell our son what I said about Lily's arm. He's so protective of her."

"Well, she is his wife."

June stood up. "I'm going to start dinner. I can do more packing in the morning."

16

John didn't bother trying to convince his wife to leave the packing to the movers. Instead, he picked up his reading glasses, put them on, and turned his attention back to the computer. After a couple of clicks on the computer, he opened the Realtor.com website and entered "Frederickport, Oregon." While his wife wanted to consider existing houses, he searched for residential lot listings. He had been looking every day for the past month, hoping something would pop up. Of course, it was always possible there were residential lots for sale in town by owner and not listed on the website. Those he would have to look for when they got to Frederickport.

Ten minutes later June returned to the den to ask John if he wanted salad or coleslaw with dinner, but before she could get the question out, he blurted, "You have to see this!"

"See what?" She frowned, walking to the computer.

"A new piece of residential property just went on the market today. This won't last," he said excitedly.

"Why do you say that?" She stood behind his desk chair, peering over his shoulder at the computer monitor.

"It's a great price," he began, enlarging the webpage so she could better see.

"That looks kinda expensive," she muttered, noting the price.

"Not for the size of the lot, it's huge. It's in a residential neighborhood. If we could subdivide, I could build a couple of spec houses."

"No. If you want to build our house, I'm fine with that. You said you were going to retire," she reminded him.

"I just suggested it might be a possibility. Here, look at the pictures." He started a slide show of the listing photographs. June leaned over his shoulder, looking closer at the monitor.

"Wow, that is nice," she muttered. Some photographs were of the neighborhood.

"Looks like a beautiful area," John said.

"Is it far from Ian's house?" she asked.

"According to the map, walking distance."

"Connor could walk to Grandma's house." June smiled at the thought.

"I think he's a little young for that," he teased.

June playfully swatted John's shoulder and said, "Hush." She looked back at the pictures.

"It's nice and flat. It won't need much grading, and it has a view," John said.

"We could make our own little park, where the grandkids could come and play."

"There is a nice tree on it. That might make an ideal spot for a tree house," John suggested.

"Let me see the pictures again," June said after the slide show finished playing.

John grinned at his wife and then replayed the slide show.

When it finished playing, June let out a sigh and said, "It really is nice. I think we should make an offer."

"It went on the market today. It's not going to last long. I imagine it'll be gone when we get to Frederickport."

"Then call that Realtor friend of Ian's. Make an offer on the property," June insisted.

John turned from the computer and looked up at his wife. "Are you serious?"

June grinned. "Yes. It's perfect. But you need to tell him not to say anything to anyone, especially our son. I want this to be a surprise."

"Do you still have his business card?"

"Of course." June dropped a quick kiss on her husband's cheek and said, "I'll go get it."

ADAM NICHOLS SAT ALONE in his office, his feet on his desk as he leaned back in the chair. In his hands he held a small ring box, its lid open. He studied the ring inside. The box hadn't come with the ring. When the Winterborne engagement ring had fairly flown from the frame's secret compartment, it hadn't been in a box. Adam glanced up to the wall and noted the framed photograph of his great-grandfather—the same frame that had once held the Winterborne engagement ring.

Just as he looked back at the ring in his hands, his phone rang. With a sigh, he closed the box, tossed it on his desk, and picked up his phone's receiver, his feet still on his desk.

"Adam Nichols here. How can I help you?"

"Hello, Adam, I don't know if you remember me, John Bartley, Ian's father," came the male voice on the other side of the line.

Adam sat up straighter and removed his feet from the desktop, setting them on the floor.

"Why certainly," Adam said. "How can I help you?"

"I'm interested in purchasing property in Frederickport," John began.

Adam smiled. "Ahh, I heard you were coming to town later this month. Are you looking for investment property or vacation property? If it's vacation property, you can always put it in my program and earn some income when you aren't using it."

"First, I need you to promise me something, Adam."

Adam furrowed his brow, still holding the receiver to his right ear. "Sure, what?"

"This transaction has to be confidential. I don't want Ian to know about it. Not that we're keeping it from him forever, but it's more of a surprise."

"You're buying property for Ian?" Adam asked.

John laughed. "No. But I'd rather he not find out until we're ready to tell him."

"I respect my clients' privacy."

"Good. I saw a piece of property in Frederickport; they listed it today. It won't last. I want to make an offer," John told him.

Adam's grin broadened. "Certainly. Can you give me the address?" Adam reached for his computer's mouse and quickly brought up the local MLS site on his computer.

After John gave him the address, Adam punched it in the search box. But before he finished typing in the address, he realized what property John wanted.

Crap, Adam said to himself. "Um… can I ask what you intend to do with it?" Adam choked out.

"Again, say nothing to my son—or to anyone. My wife and I intend to move to Frederickport. In fact, we've already sold our home here. The movers are coming in a few days to pack up our house and put everything in storage. When we arrive in Frederickport this month, we are moving there. We want to build our forever home on the property."

FOUR

Holding the phone to his ear, Adam momentarily closed his eyes and cringed. He took a deep breath and said, "I'm familiar with the property."

"Great. But unless the listing's wrong and I can't build a house on it, I'll want to make an offer tonight," John insisted.

"I'll tell you what I know about it. Marymoor Sanatorium was on that site. It was closed years before I was born, just boarded up and fenced. The buildings burned down when I was a kid. The city owns the property. Over the years there was talk of building a park on the site, but that never materialized, and a couple of times they tried to sell it," Adam explained.

"What was Marymoor Sanatorium?" John asked.

"My grandma used to say it wasn't really a sanatorium, it was an insane asylum. They named it for the guy who donated the property, but I guess he didn't want it called Marymoor Insane Asylum. But he had enough ego that he still wanted his name attached for posterity, so they went with Marymoor Sanatorium," Adam explained.

"Why do you think it never sold before? Is there some illegal fill on the property, some environmental problem that needs to be cleaned up?"

"Not that I'm aware of, but I would definitely recommend

inspections. But the reason for it not selling, probably the ghost stories."

"Ghost stories?" John asked.

"People say it's haunted," Adam explained.

John laughed.

"I'm serious. There have been numerous unexplained events on the site over the years."

"Do you believe it's haunted?" John snickered.

"I just know strange things have occurred over there. For example, after it burned down, it took over a year to clean up the site. Accidents kept happening. In fact, one guy who works for me—I've known him for years—his father worked on the site after the fire. He broke his leg when he was working. He said someone pushed him off a ladder, but he was alone," Adam explained.

John laughed again. "I've been in construction for years. Accidents happen. But I have to say, I never had a ghost show up on one of my job sites."

"Not saying it's actually haunted." Adam felt stupid. "But because of random events over the years, it's earned something of a reputation that it's cursed. I suspect that's why it hasn't sold. If you wanted to resell the property later, it might be difficult because of its reputation."

"I don't believe in ghosts. And this will be our last home. So resale value is not an issue. But I believe in inspections. I'm more concerned about someone illegally dumping on the site, or issues left over after the building burned down. I definitely want to include inspections in the offer."

"YOU READY TO GO?" a cheerful voice asked from the open doorway.

Adam looked up to find Melony smiling in his direction.

With a sigh, Adam said, "I can't leave. I'm writing an offer for someone. He wants to do it tonight."

Melony frowned and walked all the way into Adam's office. To a stranger, Melony might look like a fashion model as opposed to her true profession, a skilled criminal attorney. "You don't look thrilled about writing an offer. What's wrong, is your potential buyer lowballing?"

Now at Adam's desk, Melony sat on its edge instead of taking one of the empty chairs. While listening for his answer, she snatched the abandoned ring box off the desk and opened it.

When Adam saw what she held, he asked in a soft voice, "Have you decided?" His dark black eyes studied Melony as he ignored her initial question.

Before Melony answered, a third party entered the office. The spirit of Adam's grandmother, Marie Nichols, hovered over the desk, the image of the elderly woman wearing a floral-print dress and a straw garden hat. "What are you two up to?" Marie chirped to deaf ears. Neither Adam nor Melony could see or hear Marie.

"I already said I would marry you," Melony said with a grin. "Isn't that the important part?"

"You're getting married!" Marie exclaimed. "Oh, how exciting!"

"What about the ring?" Adam asked, his eyes still focused on her as she casually perched on his desk's edge.

"It is beautiful," she said with a wistful sigh.

"We can get it resized to fit your finger," Adam said.

"You're giving her the Winterborne ring!" Marie studied the ring.

Melony looked at Adam. "This is crazy. You should sell it. It's worth a fortune."

"Don't sell it," Marie said, now sitting on an imaginary chair nearby.

"If you don't want to accept an engagement ring that was given to me, I understand," Adam began.

"It's not that!" Melony insisted. "It's not uncommon to get a ring that was handed down in a family. And while this didn't come from someone in your family, it actually has a better story."

"So is that a yes?" Adam grinned. "You want to make the Winterborne engagement ring the Nichols engagement ring?"

"Adam, you could sell this and buy half a dozen beautiful engagement rings." Melony removed the ring from the small velvet-lined box and held it in one hand, inspecting it.

"I don't know about it buying that many engagement rings. But why would you want that many rings, anyway?" Adam teased.

Melony grinned at Adam. "You know what I mean."

"Oh, Adam, you're so sweet," Marie cooed.

Adam returned Melony's grin.

Melony studied Adam for a moment before saying, "We've

known each other for a long time. And frankly I'm surprised you'd want to give it to me."

Adam frowned. "What is that supposed to mean?"

Melony shrugged. "The Adam I know just wouldn't spend a fortune on an engagement ring."

Adam laughed. "I didn't spend anything on it. So I guess I'm exactly the Adam you know."

"Come on, you have to understand what I'm saying."

Adam let out a sigh and leaned back in the chair. He watched as Melony tried the ring on her left ring finger. It fit loosely.

"I guess I do," Adam admitted. "There was a time I would have been all about finding a buyer."

Melony looked from the ring to Adam. "What changed?"

"When Grandma died and I inherited most of her estate, I realized I wasn't wealthy like Chris, but I was doing pretty damn good."

Melony laughed. "Adam, you were doing good before your grandma died."

"Yes, he was," Marie agreed. "I don't think Adam ever gave himself enough credit."

"I suppose. But the thing was, after getting that big fat inheritance, it suddenly dawned on me how sometimes a windfall—or treasure—isn't worth it. It wasn't worth losing Grandma."

"Oh, Adam…" Marie wanted to cry.

"I suddenly understood Danielle a little better," Adam continued. "Heck, I was close to Grandma, but Danielle had all sorts of issues with her cousin Cheryl, yet after Cheryl died, I believe Danielle would have gladly given up the inheritance to bring her back. And when Danielle gave me that frame, knowing what was probably inside, she found value in something beyond its monetary worth. Maybe just whatever fun she would get watching me open it; I'm not sure."

"Wow, you are getting philosophical," Melony mused.

"You have really grown up in the last few years," Marie noted. "I'm so proud of you."

Adam shrugged. "Perhaps. But I figure that ring is outstanding. It's legally mine. Legally mine to give to anyone I want. And like Danielle, who felt there was more value in whatever pleasure she had in giving it to me than what she could sell it for, I feel the same way. But only if it is something you'd want."

Melony looked at the ring and smiled. "Oh hell, I really love it."

Melony leaned closer to Adam and kissed him. When the kiss ended, she jumped off the desk, removed the ring from her finger, and put it back in the box. After telling Adam she would get it sized before wearing it, she asked him how long he was going to need to prepare the offer. With that question, Adam groaned.

"What's wrong?" Melony asked.

"I almost forgot about the offer."

Melony glanced at her watch. "I can come back and pick you up. How much time do you need?"

"The problem is, I really feel uncomfortable about his offer."

Melony frowned. "What do you mean?"

"Promise not to say anything to anyone. This is about client confidentiality."

"Um, so does this mean you shouldn't say anything to me either?" Melony asked.

"Well, technically, the client said he didn't want me to tell Ian. He said nothing about not telling my fiancée."

"What does Ian have to do with it?" Melony asked.

Excited to share the news about Adam's engagement with Eva, Marie was about to leave when Adam began telling Melony about the offer he was supposed to write for a client. When he mentioned Ian's name, she lingered to hear the rest of the story.

Adam pointed to one chair and suggested Melony sit down. After she did, he told her about the phone call from Ian's father.

"I feel funny not telling Ian about this," Adam said after telling her about the offer. "If it were any other piece of property…"

"You can't violate your client-agent confidentiality. And he did expressly ask you not to say anything," Melony reminded him. "Is this because it's the Marymoor site?"

"Of course," Adam said. "I remember a conversation we once had at a barbeque at Chris's. You were there. I was teasing Danielle about all her *treasures*. Someone brought up the Marymoor property. I think it was Heather…"

"Ahh yes," Melony cut in. "Heather asked, if you won a prize and the prize was the Marymoor property, would you accept it?"

"Lily was the one who most emphatically said no way. She said if one of us won the property and built a house on it, don't expect her to visit. Ian agreed with her."

"I have to agree with her, too," Marie muttered. "Not a good place to build a home. And did I understand that correctly, Ian's parents intend to move to Frederickport?" With a frown, Marie disappeared.

"Unfortunately, you can't say anything to Ian," Melony said.

"Ian won't be happy."

"Adam, if it were any other property, would you have an issue selling it without telling Ian?" Melony asked.

"Of course not."

"Remember, those are just old stories. Ian's father was right. Accidents are common on construction sites."

"You don't think there's any reason for my concern?"

"I imagine you would feel different if you didn't believe those ghost stories yourself," Melony said.

Adam frowned. "I don't believe in the ghost stories."

"Come on, be honest. You still let that place get to you, and now it's impacting how you do business. I say write up the offer, submit it, and if he has an inspection contingency, he can back out. Your fiduciary duty is to represent your client to the best of your ability. And after you submit the offer, you and I can go over to the Marymoor site."

"Why would we do that?" Adam frowned.

"To readjust your perspective on the property. You can put your childhood fears to rest and stop worrying about keeping this from Ian. Once you see for yourself it is simply a vacant lot, with no ghost or goblins lurking around, you can do your job without feeling guilty."

FIVE

P ier Café had a new cook, and word around Frederickport, his clam chowder rivaled Pearl Cove's. Eager to take the taste test and too lazy to cook dinner, Danielle and Walt walked to Pier Café early Monday evening. When they arrived, they found the diner crowded, with not an empty table, booth, or place at the counter. Walt put their name on the waiting list as he and Danielle sat in the lobby, waiting patiently for an opening.

"I wonder if they're short on staff tonight," Danielle whispered to Walt. She watched as Carla the server dashed from table to table, her pink and purple hair looking as frazzled as the rest of her.

Leaning back on the small wooden bench, his arm casually draped around Danielle's shoulders, Walt looked briefly to Carla. "I don't see another server. Of course, one might be in the back." Walt glanced around the diner. When doing so, he spied their neighbor Pearl Huckabee sitting alone in a booth, reading the menu.

Walt gently nudged Danielle and said, "Pearl's over there, all alone in a booth. Should we ask if we can join her?"

"Yeah, right," Danielle said with a snort. Turning her attention back to Carla, she cringed as Carla attempted to juggle over six dinner plates. "Oh, Carla, be careful," Danielle muttered.

ACROSS THE CAFÉ, Pearl Huckabee closed her menu and set it on the table. Glancing around, looking for a server, she spied her neighbors, Walt and Danielle Marlow, sitting together on a bench in the front lobby. The pair stared across the room in the other direction, and by Danielle's expression—the way she cringed and brought her hand to her mouth as if gasping in surprise while grabbing ahold of her husband's wrist—piqued Pearl's curiosity.

She looked to see what had captured the Marlows' attention. It was Carla, awkwardly making her way across the dining room while trying to balance multiple plates of food along her arms. As a frequent customer of Pier Café—and of Carla's—Pearl had never seen Carla attempt to carry so many dishes at once. The way the server wobbled uneasily from side to side, along with her expression, Pearl suspected Carla regretted the decision to take on so many dinner plates at one time.

Fascinated at the sight, Pearl found herself unable to look away, while holding her breath, waiting for Carla to reach her destination. Just as Carla was about two feet from a table of eight, all of whom were busily chatting, waiting for their food and not noticing the approaching server, one plate slipped from Carla's grasp. Carla froze and watched in horror as the plate of food began falling to the floor. Yet to her surprise, instead of falling, the plate froze for a moment in midair, losing not a single french fry, while it righted itself and then gently floated over to the table, landing as easily as if Carla had set it there. Those sitting at the table assumed the server had placed the plate on the table.

Pearl's eyes widened in surprise. Not only had the customers at the table not been paying attention, none of the customers at the nearby tables seemed to have seen what had just happened. Looking back to Walt and Danielle, curious to see their reaction, Pearl found it odd that the pair, who continued to stare in Carla's direction, did not wear expressions of surprise. Instead, they leaned back on the bench and looked relieved. Danielle laughed and leaned over and gave her husband a quick kiss on the cheek.

Pearl furrowed her brow, still staring at the Marlows.

"I STILL THINK we should wait until it's dark," Melony told Adam. The two sat in Melony's car, parked in front of the For Sale sign at the Marymoor property. She glanced at her watch. It was almost six thirty. It wouldn't be dark for over an hour.

"It's dinnertime, that's night to me," Adam grumbled.

"But the point in doing this is to prove to you there is nothing to any of those stories," Melony insisted. "Nothing but urban legend. Then you can stop stressing over this offer."

Adam looked to Melony and asked, "So the toilet paper flying out of your hands over at the Barr property was nothing but urban legend, too?"

Melony frowned at Adam. The last time she had thought about that was when Danielle had asked her what had happened at the Barr house, those many years ago, when Melony was still in high school.

"It's not the same thing," Melony said. "I'm sure it was the wind that knocked those toilet paper rolls from our hands and blew them to the barn. I was young back then, an overactive imagination. Just like the stories about Marymoor. Young people have overactive imaginations, and stories get told and retold over the years until they take on a life of their own. Our memories are not always reliable. That's something I've learned as a defense attorney. We look back at things that happened when we were kids, but did they really happen just as we remember? Or has our imagination reshaped reality?"

Adam let out a sigh and looked over at the property. "Fine, let's get this over with."

"We should get something to eat first, and then come back later, when it's dark," Melony suggested.

"No. Let's just do this. Think about the old stories. Those things rarely took place at night. They supposedly happened in the middle of the day, like when Bill's dad broke his leg," Adam reminded her.

"Okay." Melony unbuckled her seatbelt.

Adam groaned and reluctantly unbuckled his seatbelt. "I don't know why I always let you talk me into doing stuff I don't want to do. You realize, you have been doing this since we were kids."

Melony laughed. "And you want to marry me."

Adam shrugged. "Hey, I'm a sucker for punishment. Let's get this over with." As Adam opened the car door, he grumbled under his breath, "I sure as hell hope you're right."

A moment later, Adam stood by the front of the car, Melony by his side, while he silently glanced around. If the place wasn't haunted, there were some definite positives. Every time he had driven through this neighborhood—which admittedly was not often —traffic seemed nonexistent. The homes were all well maintained, and from what he knew, none were in any of the rental programs. While that was not a plus for Adam, who profited from the rental program, it was a plus for the neighborhood, as rowdy weekenders weren't coming and going, disrupting the neighbors more than a full-time resident might.

"Are you just going to stand there?" Melony prodded.

"Hold on. I'm trying to get the general feel of the area. This seems to be a nice, quiet neighborhood. Well maintained. The only blight is the fenced-up piece of property," Adam noted.

"And when Ian's father takes the fence down and builds a new custom house it will improve the entire neighborhood."

"Let's get this over with. What do you want us to do?" Adam asked.

"Let's walk over to the gate. That's a start," Melony suggested.

Reluctantly, Adam started toward the fence surrounding the property. When they got there, Melony pointed to where the padlock had been on its gate, and said, "It's unlocked."

"Yeah, Ray sent out an email saying he was unlocking the gate. He told the agents to go in, check out the property, walk around."

Melony reached for the gate. "Let's go in." Adam waited as Melony opened the gate and walked into the fenced area. He reluctantly followed her in. The moment they stepped on the property, the air temperature dropped a good twenty degrees. They both noticed.

"I'd ask where that chilly breeze came from, but the air's still," Adam noted.

"That was weird," Melony muttered.

"Maybe this place comes with its own air-conditioning," Adam quipped.

Melony chuckled. "Must have been a pocket of cold air that came in from the ocean, got stuck somehow," Melony suggested.

"Yeah, right," Adam muttered under his breath.

No longer concerned over the change in air temperature, Melony walked farther onto the property, her back to Adam as she checked out the surroundings. "You know, I've never been back here before," Melony called to Adam. "It's been locked up for as long as I can remember. It would be a beautiful site to build a house."

Adam watched as Melony looked around while he remained standing just a few feet inside the gate.

"Come on, Adam, stop acting like a baby," Adam muttered to himself. "Look at Mel, she's not a big chicken like you."

Adam was just about to call out to Melony to wait up when motion to her right caught his attention. At first, he thought she'd disturbed a bird hiding in the bushes. But whatever flew out of the bushes was no bird, nor an animal. Unable to fathom what he saw, Adam's eyes widened as he focused on the object. It now hovered just behind Melony, out of her sight.

The instant he identified the object, he called out her name and rushed toward her. When she turned to his voice, Adam's body hit her full force, sending her to the ground. He held onto her, and together they rolled to the right. Melony's eyes looked up in time to see a piece of rusted pipe falling at high speed toward her head. Adam rolled her body away just before the pipe crashed down, barely missing her forehead. They continued to roll away, and each time the pipe rose back up in the air before crashing down again, barely missing Melony's head.

Together they scrambled to their feet, making a dash toward the open gate, while the pipe continued to take swings like a baseball bat. Yet fortunately for Melony and Adam, whoever swung the bat had poor aim.

The moment they exited the gate, the pipe stopped swinging and fell to the ground. Melony and Adam did not wait around to see what was going to happen next. Instead, they flew into the car and raced off without either one fastening their seatbelts.

CARLA HAD JUST CLEARED AWAY the dirty dishes from their table and left for the kitchen without saying a word.

Danielle watched Carla walk away. "Poor thing. I think when you saved that plate from falling, you stole her voice."

"She seems in shock. But I have to give her credit, she's doing her job, but without talking to the customers. Which for Carla might be an improvement." Walt chuckled.

"I hope she snaps out of it," Danielle said.

"I just hope she remembers to bring us the dessert we ordered."

Danielle laughed at Walt's comment.

"Hey, look who's here," Danielle said, pointing to the door.

Walt glanced toward the door and saw Adam and Melony.

"Wow, I think they're wearing Carla's expression," Danielle said. "Wonder what's wrong."

"I imagine they just noticed all the tables are full and realize they have a long wait," Walt said.

"They can sit with us," Danielle said, now waving her hand to catch Adam and Melony's attention.

When the pair noticed Danielle's wave, they walked to her table. As they did, Danielle moved to the chair next to Walt, freeing the two chairs across from them.

"You guys can join us," Danielle said when Adam and Melony got to their table. "The place has been crazy all night. We've already eaten, but we're getting dessert."

The moment Adam and Melony sat down, Adam blurted, "Do you believe in ghosts?"

SIX

"Ghosts?" Danielle squeaked. She and Walt exchanged quick glances.

"Remember my toilet paper story?" Melony asked Danielle.

"You mean when you were a teenager and went to toilet paper the Barr house?" Danielle asked.

"And the toilet paper rolls flew from all of our hands at the same time, ending up in the barn, and they hadn't even unwound," Mel finished for her.

"Yeah." Danielle frowned.

"This was a hundred times worse!" Melony exclaimed.

Before Danielle could respond, Carla walked up to the table, carrying two plates of pie and ice cream. The server didn't seem to notice the two new arrivals until she reached the table. When she did, she froze a moment, plates of pie in her hands, and scowled down at Adam and Melony.

"Did you want to eat something?" Carla snapped.

Startled at Carla's unfriendly question, Adam asked, "Wow, having a bad night, Carla?"

Carla slapped the two plates of pie on the table, setting one in front of Walt and the other in front of Melony, which was where Danielle had been sitting before Adam and Melony had arrived.

"Well, do you want to eat?" Carla demanded.

Adam arched his brows and said, "Sure, as long as you promise not to put arsenic in our food."

"Fine. I need to get you menus," Carla grumbled, turning abruptly from the table.

"Wow, what's with Carla tonight?" Adam asked, watching her walk away.

Melony glanced down at the pie in front of her, smiled, picked up the plate, and handed it to Danielle.

"Thanks," Danielle said, accepting the plate.

"She's had a rough evening," Walt explained. "It's been slammed all night, and she almost dropped all the plates she was carrying to a table. She needs a vacation."

"I guess," Adam muttered.

Before they could get back to their discussion on ghosts, Carla stomped back to their table and slapped two menus down in front of Adam. She abruptly turned and marched to the kitchen.

"So, what is this about ghosts?" Danielle asked before taking her first taste of pie.

"You know the Marymoor site?" Adam asked.

"Sure. Heather told me it's for sale," Danielle said.

Adam paused a moment and looked at Melony, as if wondering how to proceed. She reached over, patted his hand, and then looked at Walt and Danielle.

"Adam has a buyer for the property," Melony began. "And the buyer wants confidentiality. So he can't tell anyone who he is."

Danielle shrugged. "I imagine a lot of buyers want confidentiality when purchasing real estate."

"The thing is, I'm not comfortable with the sale," Adam said.

"Can't you tell the guy you don't want to represent him?" Danielle asked.

"It's not that. I would be happy to help him buy real estate in town. Just not that property."

"I assume it's because of the ghost stories. But if you don't feel good about selling it to him, perhaps you should just walk away. Tell him you can't help him," Danielle suggested.

Adam groaned. "If it were just that simple."

"It's about the confidentiality issue. Adam is friends with one of the buyer's family members. Adam believes the friend would not be thrilled with him if he sells the property to the family member without giving him a chance to discuss it, considering the property's background. And if Adam just walks away from the sale and says nothing, and he buys it from someone else, the friend would probably still be annoyed at Adam for not giving him the heads-up," Melony explained.

"Mel had this brilliant idea to go over to the Marymoor site, look around, you know, put all those old stories from my childhood to rest, so I wouldn't feel uncomfortable representing my client—and I wouldn't feel compelled to violate my client's confidentiality. After all, the buyer is an adult, free to buy whatever property he or she wants."

"Did you go over there?" Danielle asked.

"Didn't you hear what Mel said? It was worse than what happened to her at the Barr place!" Adam snapped. He took a deep breath, told himself to calm down, and then told Walt and Danielle what had happened to them minutes earlier.

When Adam finished the telling, the four sat in silence for a few minutes, the plates of apple pie forgotten. Finally, Adam said, "You think we're nuts, don't you?"

"No, I don't," Danielle said.

Walt looked at Adam and smiled. "Adam, this is not the first time something like this has happened to you."

Adam frowned at Walt. "What do you mean?"

"I heard a story about a croquet set attacking you in the attic of Marlow House," Walt teased.

"That didn't really happen," Mel said. "That was too much beer."

Adam stared at Walt a minute and then said dully, "Yes, it did, Mel. Just like that pipe attacked us." He slumped back in his chair and closed his eyes.

Furrowing her brows, Melony turned a questioning frown at Adam.

The four sat at the table, considering all that had just been said. Quietly, Walt and Danielle picked up their forks and began eating their pie and ice cream.

Danielle had just finished her pie and set the fork on the table when Melony said, "I don't understand. What happened tonight? Not to mention that time at the Barrs', or what Adam says happened to him."

"The way you say that, it's like you think I made it up," Adam grumbled.

"No, but…" Melony muttered.

"I think I can explain," Danielle offered.

The left corner of Walt's mouth twitched upward. He wondered what his wife was going to come up with, while Adam and Melony grew quiet and focused their attention on her.

"I think there is a lot in this world we don't understand." Danielle looked at Melony. "Mel, you are a very smart woman. You have an impressive career and have advanced in your profession, but you know there is much of this world you don't understand. I think that is true for all of us, even the most intelligent."

"I believe, the more intelligent someone is, the more they realize there is much about this world they don't understand," Walt added.

"Then I must be a freaking genus. Because I know I don't know crap," Adam grumbled.

Danielle chuckled and then said in a serious tone, "Let's look at what happened to you today—what happened to you both the other times. Science tells us we're made up of energy. And when we die, that energy doesn't die. There have been countless reports of paranormal activity around the world. Sure, a lot of those paranormal stories are made up. Fake stories, often perpetrated by con men. But I don't believe they are all fabricated. You have proof of that."

"You're saying that's what we experienced today?" Adam asked.

"If energy doesn't die, where does it go? And what happens to us after we die? If you believe spirits—or souls—live on, then perhaps they can harness some of that energy. Put energy in the hands of a conflicted soul, then who knows what might happen."

"Today it tried to play baseball with a pipe, and it wanted to use Mel's head as the ball," Adam said.

"I almost got myself killed trying to convince Adam he had nothing to worry about," Melony said with a groan.

"The good news, it didn't hit you," Danielle said. "I suspect a spirit who manipulates energy is limited in what they can do. After all, when was the last time you heard about someone getting killed by an inanimate object that suddenly came to life on its own?"

"If there was ever a place for bad energy from spirits to gather, it would probably be Marymoor," Melony said. She looked at Adam. "I'm sorry."

He shrugged. "You were just trying to help. And frankly, I thought all my childhood fears were silly. I just couldn't shake them. And now… not sure what to do. If I tell the buyer what happened, he'll think I'm nuts. And as much as I want to tell my friend so he can try to persuade his family member not to buy, I can't do it."

"So, which of the old residents of Marymoor swung that pipe, do you think?" Walt asked.

Adam looked at Walt and grinned. "For some reason, I'm not really surprised you and Danielle are taking this all in stride. Hey, if it were reversed, I would have fun teasing your wife."

Walt returned Adam's grin. "It's probably living in a haunted house that changes one's perspective."

"Not sure who was swinging that pipe, but I'm fairly certain if a spirit pitched that croquet set at me, it was probably the original Walt Marlow's spirit. So, I have to wonder, you and Danielle have your bedroom up there in that attic. Have you noticed anything flying around the room?" Adam asked.

Walt chuckled. "I suspect the ghost of Walt Marlow has moved on."

"If it was a spirit—or a ghost—swinging that pipe at me, it was probably the same one who killed the nurse," Melony said. "After he killed her, they shut the place down."

"First, we're talking about energy from lingering spirits, now ghosts," Adam scoffed.

Ignoring Adam's comment, Walt asked, "What ever happened to him?"

"I remember the story," Melony said. "The nurse's name was Molly."

Danielle looked to Melony. Molly was the name of the ghost she had once met at the Marymoor site. A ghost dressed in a blood-stained nurse's uniform.

"I don't recall her last name," Melony said. "Dad told me the story. She was stabbed. The head of the sanatorium walked in right after it happened, and her attacker fled. The killer's name was Waylon. I remember his name because when my father told me the story, I asked, *Like Waylon Jennings?* And Dad said, *Not sure, never heard if he could sing or not.*" Melony rolled her eyes and chuckled at her father's attempt at humor.

"What happened to this Waylon?" Danielle asked.

"He ran off. But they eventually found him. Not sure what happened to the guy, or where he was found. But they closed the sanatorium not long after that, and I suspect they just transferred Waylon to an institution for the criminally insane."

"If that was the case, I doubt Waylon was your batter," Walt said.

Melony looked at Walt. "Why do you say that?"

"If they transported Waylon to another institution, once he died, I doubt he'd return to Marymoor. I'd expect a confused spirit, bent on haunting, to stay where he was," Walt suggested.

"You know how these things work, do you?" Adam asked dryly.

"WAYLON, you shouldn't have done that," Molly chastised. Waylon sat dejected under the large oak tree, his chin resting on his bent knees.

"I'm sorry, Molly. But she was talking about building a house here."

Molly sat down next to Waylon. "You can't go around hurting people."

"I didn't even touch her," Waylon reminded her.

"True. But you could have hit her. That would get you in more trouble when Randal returns. You don't want to be in trouble again, do you?"

Waylon shook his head.

"You need to calm down. Everyone is waiting," Molly said.

"You go without me. I don't want to see them," Waylon said with a pout.

"It's important we stick together. We need to come up with a plan before Randal returns. That's why you must come with me."

"They'll just go away like Sean Sullivan did and leave me here."

"It was time for Sean to go. Now please, get up and stop sulking. Everyone is waiting." Molly stood up. She reached her hand out to Waylon. Reluctantly, he took it, stood up, and they both disappeared.

SEVEN

They sat together in the car parked near Pier Café, Melony on the driver's side and Adam in the passenger seat. Instead of starting the engine immediately, Melony contemplated all that had happened to them that day.

"I suppose I'm not surprised at Danielle's reaction," Adam finally said. "She's always had that goofy feng shui attitude about life."

Melony turned to Adam and asked with a laugh, "You do know what feng shui means, right?"

Adam shrugged. "It's some hippy dippy notion that how you decorate your home sends off positive or negative vibes. Or something like that."

"Not exactly sure how that pertains to what happened in this situation." Melony leaned back in the driver's seat again, looking out the front windshield, her hands now resting on the steering wheel.

"Just that if you buy into all that feng shui vibes thing, it's easier to accept lingering spirits and their energy. I remember how she didn't like to discuss the original Walt Marlow's death in the house. She didn't want to offend him."

"Now what?" Melony asked.

"Now we go get something to eat. I'm starved," Adam said. "I can't believe Carla walked out on her shift tonight."

While talking to Walt and Danielle in the diner, Adam and Melony wondered what was taking Carla so long to return to take their order. They eventually discovered she had walked off in the middle of her shift, leaving the diner more shorthanded than it had already been that night.

Melony put her key into the ignition. But before she turned on the engine, she looked at Adam and said, "We didn't get around to telling Danielle and Walt that we're engaged."

Adam chuckled. "I know. I thought about it when we were talking to them. But blurting out that we're engaged right after talking about a ghost trying to kill you, it didn't seem like the right time."

Melony laughed, leaned over and kissed Adam—who met her halfway since they both had their seatbelts on. When the kiss ended, Melony started the car's engine.

"I THINK I LEARNED A LESSON TONIGHT," Walt told Danielle after they walked home from Pier Café.

"What was that?" Danielle followed Walt into the living room. He flipped on the overhead light. They heard a meow and found Max lounging on the back of the sofa. The cat jumped down to the floor and walked to Danielle, weaving around her ankles until she stopped and picked him up. He snuggled into her arms and purred. Danielle absently stroked Max's head while waiting for Walt's answer.

"Sometimes we shouldn't help people. We need to let them make their own mistakes and learn from them. Helping can cause more problems." Walt walked to the sofa and sat down.

"You're talking about Carla?" Danielle sat down next to Walt, still holding Max.

"I am." Walt reached over and gave Max a scratch under his ear while silently conveying a greeting to the cat.

"Yeah, I think that freaked her out," Danielle agreed. "And I wonder if anyone else in the diner saw what happened. There might be some really confused person out there who thinks they're going crazy."

"I should've let her drop the plates. She'd learn the lesson not to

39

carry so many at one time. But now, no clue what she's thinking. I just hope she doesn't lose her job over this."

Danielle leaned back on the sofa. When she did, Max stood up on her lap, jumped to the floor, and then strolled from the room. Danielle flashed the cat a smile and said, "Carla is a fixture down there. I don't imagine this will get her fired. But it might get them to hire a couple more servers. And now that I think about it, had Carla dropped those plates, she may have still stormed out tonight. So maybe you did the right thing. At least the customer, whose plate you saved, got his dinner on time."

"Perhaps…"

They sat in silence for a few minutes, Walt sitting next to Danielle, his right arm draped over her shoulders, and both of their stockinged feet propped up on the coffee table. Finally, Danielle said, "I hope Eva knows what she is talking about."

Walt frowned at Danielle. "What do you mean?"

"I was thinking about what happened to Adam and Mel tonight. They were over there alone. If that pipe had hit Mel—killed her—Adam would probably be charged with her murder. I imagine he would grab the pipe, trying to stop it, get his fingerprints all over it. And who is going to believe a story that it started swinging at her itself?"

"The chief might, but that probably wouldn't help Adam. But I suspect Eva knows what she is talking about," Walt said.

"I hope you're right."

"Who do you think Adam was talking about tonight? Which friend?" Walt asked.

"No one in our circle. The way he was talking it was a family member of the friend." Danielle turned to Walt and said, "Do you realize most of our close friends have no family?"

"We have each other." Walt kissed her nose and then smiled at her.

"Heather doesn't, and Chris didn't until he met his brother. His uncle doesn't count. But it wouldn't be Chris, because if Adam told Noah about a haunted property, he would take it seriously. And while Mel has no family, it wouldn't be her anyway since she obviously knows who it is."

"True, but Lily and Ian have lots of family," Walt reminded her. "Most of whom will descend on us in a few days."

Danielle laughed. "Maybe it's Joe and Kelly. You know, now that they're getting married, maybe they're buying property to build a house."

Walt snickered. "And you find that possibility amusing?"

"Admit it; it would be kinda funny."

"I imagine Lily has her fill of hauntings with her association with us," Walt said. "I don't think she needs more from her family."

THE ONLY LIGHT came from the small window overhead. But the sun had set, and once again the attic room plunged into darkness. The small boy sat in a dusty corner, his arms wrapped around his bent legs, and his chin propped on a knee.

He couldn't recall when they had first locked him up. They wanted to keep him away from her. Once he escaped, but when he found her, she had refused to talk to him. Heartbroken, he had retreated to the attic room, resigned to his fate. Yet he never forgot her and the wonderful times they shared. He closed his eyes.

"DID you ever change the lightbulb in the attic?" Tammy Miller asked her husband when she walked into the den late Monday evening. He sat on his recliner, remote in hand, channel surfing. Upon hearing his wife, he muted the television, looked up at her, and asked her to repeat the question.

"I need to go up to the attic, and the last time we were up there, the bulb went out, remember? You were going to put in a new one. Did you ever?" She stood akimbo at the doorway leading to the hall, waiting for his answer.

"What do you need to go to the attic for?" he asked.

Letting out a sigh, she dropped her balled fists from her waist and walked to the empty recliner next to her husband's. She sat down.

"There's a box of toys I want to take to Lily," Tammy explained.

"Don't you think Connor will get his own toys at his birthday party?" he asked.

"These belonged to Lily, and I've been saving them for years. I want to give them to her while Connor is young, and he can enjoy them. She can decide what she wants to do with them. But I figured this would be a great time to get them out of the attic. And since we're driving up to Oregon this time, we have plenty of room to take them. So did you put a new light bulb in?"

"There's something wrong with the light socket up there. I need to call the electrician. Every time I put a bulb in it, the darn thing goes out after a couple of weeks. Tired of replacing them."

"Have you called an electrician?" she asked.

He let out a sigh. "No. But I will."

"If it's a short, couldn't that cause a fire or something?"

He shrugged. "It hasn't burned down the house yet. Just keep the switch off."

"I don't want to worry about that when we're up in Oregon."

He rolled his eyes. "It's been like that for years."

"Why didn't I know about it?"

He shrugged. "Probably because you only go into the attic every ten years."

"Well, I need to go up now."

"You'll have to take a flashlight."

Tammy considered the suggestion. "No, I'll go up in the morning. But I wish you'd call an electrician."

SUN STREAMED INTO THE WINDOW, brightening the attic room. He was just standing up when he heard footsteps coming up the stairs. Panicked, he ran to the stack of boxes along the far wall and hid behind them. Peeking out from the boxes, he stared at the door leading to the staircase, waiting for it to open.

When the door opened a few moments later, a woman walked in and paused at the opening. She reached for the light switch and gave it a flick. Nothing happened. She flicked it off and on again, and then sighed.

"It would be nice if it worked," she grumbled, and then looked around. "I just hope there aren't any spiders up here."

The boy hiding behind the stack of boxes watched as the woman walked to a shelf on the adjacent wall. She reached up to one box, lifted it from the shelf, and placed it on the attic floor.

"No!" the boy wailed silently. "That is my box! Stay out of there!"

The woman opened the box, looked in, and then, as if satisfied with what she saw, she picked the box up and carried it with her from the attic.

Shaken by what he had just witnessed, the boy stood up and walked from his place behind the boxes to where the woman had just stood.

"She took it. How can she do that? Isn't it enough they locked me up here?"

He looked to the door and wondered if she had remembered to lock it. Perhaps she hadn't, and then he could finally escape. Taking a deep breath and telling himself to be brave, he headed for the door.

When was the last time he had been on these stairs? He tiptoed down the steps leading from the attic room to the floor below, not making a sound. When he got to the main floor, he took care not to be seen or heard. He found her with the box and a man in the den. Without being seen, he slipped into the room, hiding behind the sofa while watching the pair.

The woman had the box open and pulled items from it, showing each priceless object to the man. She had no right.

"Since we're taking the truck, why don't you just leave them in that box. There's plenty of room. No reason to repack them," the man suggested.

"Lily doesn't know I kept all this. She's going to be tickled to see all her old toys!"

The man arched his brow, as if he did not agree with the woman's assessment.

"Lily?" the boy silently repeated. "They're taking those to Lily?"

The woman dropped the last toy she had shown him back into the box.

"Let's go have breakfast. I'll tape this up later." The woman closed the box and shoved it to the wall. Leaving it there, she and the man left the room.

When the boy was finally alone, he walked to the large box. With a smile, he climbed in. The woman returned an hour later and taped up the box.

EIGHT

Carla wasn't sure what she was walking into on Tuesday morning. Did she still have a job? Earl hadn't been working on Monday. It had been that new cook, Stan. While Stan didn't have the authority to fire her, as did Earl, she wasn't sure what he had told the head cook.

She stepped into the back door of Pier Café and almost walked into Andy, the busboy. Carla thought Andy was a nice kid. He'd graduated from high school that summer, and as far as she knew, he had no plans for college. Before she said hello or "excuse me for almost running into you," Andy grabbed hold of her wrist and quickly pulled her back outside while glancing over his shoulder to see if anyone was looking.

"Does this mean I'm fired?" Carla asked after she let Andy jerk her from the building.

"No. But if you don't want to be fired, you need to listen to me," Andy said in a whisper, glancing nervously back to the closed door as he released hold of her wrist.

"I'm listening," Carla told him.

"Not sure what set you off last night, but I told Stan you got sick, and that's why you ran out of the building. He thinks I saw you barf in the trash can. I told him I promised you I'd let him know you were sick so you wouldn't have to come back in to tell him."

Carla smiled. "You did?"

44

Andy nodded. "Yeah. I was dumping the trash when I saw you run outside and leave in your car. I figured I needed to make up something or Earl would fire you when you came in today. But Earl thinks you got sick last night too. Stan left him a note telling him, and about how I helped with your remaining tables, and how we got someone to come in and cover for you. So basically everyone except me thinks you got sick last night. I wanted to give you the heads-up before you walked in and said something else. Then we'd both be screwed."

"You lied for me?"

He shrugged. "Hey, you've covered for me a few times, figured I owed you. And it was nuts last night."

"I'm sorry I put you in that position. I should probably tell Earl it was food poisoning. Or he'll wonder why I didn't call in to take another day off."

"Or he might wonder if you're pregnant." Andy snickered.

Carla rolled her eyes. "Funny. But thanks. I owe you."

When Carla walked back into the café a few minutes later, Earl was just coming out of the nearby employees' restroom.

"How you feeling? You sure you should work today?" Earl greeted her. Andy, who followed Carla back into the restaurant, flashed her a smile and then left her alone with Earl.

"Yeah. It was something I ate," Carla lied. "I feel better today."

Earl scowled. "I hope it wasn't something Stan made."

"No. It… I ate a leftover breakfast burrito before I came into work yesterday," Carla lied. "It must have been that."

WHEN CARLA WALKED out onto the dining room floor on Tuesday morning to wait on her first customer, it relieved her to see it was regulars—Joe Morelli and his fiancée, Kelly Bartley. After Danielle Marlow had dumped Joe, and before he started dating Kelly, Carla had tried to get the handsome officer's attention. Yet Joe had obviously not been interested in taking Carla out before he started seeing Danielle, nor after. While she had never gotten Joe to look at her "that way," she felt he had become a good friend. After all, he ate in Pier Café several times a week, and she normally waited on him. Carla considered that a steady relationship—at least a steady relationship in Carla's world.

She picked up a pot of coffee before reaching Joe and Kelly's table. When she did, they both greeted her and then watched as she filled their cups. After Carla finished pouring the coffee, she glanced over to the table where the *"thing"* had occurred. Since it had happened, she thought of it as the *"thing."* The memory of what happened overwhelmed her.

"Are you okay, Carla?" Joe asked after noting Carla's change of expression and how she just stood there, saying nothing and staring across the room.

Giving her head a little shake, as if trying to come back to earth, Carla looked from where she had been staring and then back to Joe and frowned. "Not really," she muttered. Without asking permission, Carla sat down on one of the two empty chairs at the table, sitting next to Kelly. Still holding the coffeepot, she set it on the table.

"What's wrong?" Kelly asked, noting the color had drained from Carla's face.

Carla glanced to Joe and then to Kelly. "Last night, when I was working, something really freaky happened here. And... well... I just can't get it out of my head."

"What happened?" Kelly asked.

Carla considered the question for a minute and then said, "You'll think I'm crazy. But I'm sure someone else had to have seen it. Walt and Danielle were here, and so was Pearl Huckabee. Most everyone else were tourists. Maybe some were locals; I didn't recognize them." Carla paused and then frowned and said, "Adam Nichols and Melony Carmichael were here too, but I think they came in after... yes... they came in after it happened."

"What happened?" Joe asked. Both he and Kelly waited for Carla to finish her story.

Carla took a deep breath and said, "We were slammed last night. I had this big table, and I tried to carry more plates to the table than I should. One plate fell. But it didn't fall. Not really."

"What do you mean it didn't fall?" Kelly asked.

"It fell. But then it just stopped. Floated there a moment. And then it landed on the table, like some invisible hand placed it there."

Both Joe and Kelly stared at Carla, neither one commenting.

Carla noted their reaction and then shrugged. She stood and picked up the pot of coffee. "Yeah, I know it sounds nuts. Which is why it's so freaky. You guys ready to order?"

After Carla took their order and left the table, Joe chuckled. "I think that hair dye Carla uses is finally getting to her. It's causing some serious brain damage."

Kelly glanced over to where Carla now stood at the window leading into the kitchen. "What was that all about?"

Joe shrugged. "Who knows? Carla has always been out there."

"She sounds like Heather," Kelly said with a snort.

"True. While she didn't mention ghosts, she said something about an invisible hand," Joe snarked.

Kelly shook her head at the idea and picked up her cup of coffee.

"I wanted to tell you," Joe began, changing the conversation while Kelly sipped her coffee. "My sister wants to give you a bridal shower while your parents are here for Connor's birthday."

"That means we need to set the wedding date," Kelly reminded him.

"I know. I figure when your parents are here, we can set the date. We can't really set it if we don't know when they can make it."

Kelly placed her cup on the table, reached out, and patted Joe's hand. "I think they are pretty flexible. After all, now that Dad's retired, I kinda figure their schedule is open to walk his only daughter down the aisle." After the words left Kelly's mouth, she remembered how critical she had been of Danielle asking the chief to walk her down the aisle, since she had no father. Kelly had said something snarky about why did she need a man to give her away. Now, when considering her own wedding and wanting her own father to walk her down the aisle, Kelly felt a wave of guilt. She realized in that moment, her father walking her down the aisle had nothing to do with him giving her away—despite the fact that phrase was often attached to the tradition.

"Kelly?" Joe said for the second time. He had just asked her a question, yet she had not responded.

"Oh, I'm sorry," Kelly said with a blush.

"You zoned out for a minute there," Joe teased. "I was saying, not only do we need to set the date, I have to decide who I want to ask to be my best man. Have you decided who you want to ask to be your maid of honor?"

Kelly let out a sigh and sat back in her chair, looking across the table to Joe. "I wish I had a sister; it would make it so much easier."

"You have a sister, sort of," Joe reminded her.

"I know. You're thinking of Lily."

"You were in her wedding," Joe said. "And now that she's married to your brother, she's the closest thing you have to a sister."

"You know what really bothers me?" Kelly asked.

"What?"

"I don't really have a close girlfriend to ask. Heck, I imagine Lily would have asked Danielle to be her maid of honor if it wouldn't have hurt Laura's feelings. But I don't even have a best friend here to ask."

Joe studied Kelly a moment before asking, "Do you regret not having the wedding in your hometown?"

Kelly shrugged. "No. Not really. Fact is, I haven't lived there for years. And there's no one I knew in Portland I feel especially close to. Not close enough to ask to be in my wedding. So, tell me, have you decided on a best man?"

"I'm leaning more and more to Brian."

Kelly's eyes widened. "Really? I thought you'd ask your brother-in-law."

"I'm fond of Craig. I consider him a good friend. And I plan to ask him to be one of my groomsmen, especially since you're asking my sister to be a bridesmaid." Joe paused a moment and then asked, "Or are you still planning to ask her?"

Kelly nodded. "Of course, I am. So why Brian?"

Joe shrugged. "I guess when I think about it, we work together every day, have each other's backs. I figure Brian is one of my closest guy friends."

"I wonder if he'll bring someone to the wedding," Kelly asked.

"Hey, I know that look," Joe teased.

"What look?" Kelly asked with faux innocence.

"No more playing matchmaker with Brian, remember?"

Kelly shrugged. "Maybe the last one didn't work out. But matchmaking at weddings always has a high success rate."

Joe laughed. "You mean in the movies. I don't think that happens in real life."

Kelly flashed Joe a smile. "We could test the theory."

"No. Promise me, no orchestrating wedding matchups. If Brian wants to bring a date, he can. If he wants to go solo, then he can do that too."

"Good morning," a female voice interrupted the conversation.

Joe and Kelly looked up to see Pearl Huckabee walking by, en route to an empty table.

"Good morning, Mrs. Huckabee," Joe greeted her.

Kelly offered a greeting, but right as Pearl Huckabee continued to the table, Kelly called out to her.

"Yes?" Pearl asked.

"Mrs. Huckabee, can I ask you a question?" Kelly asked.

Pearl returned to the table and looked at Kelly. "What is that?"

"We were talking to Carla, the waitress here," Kelly began.

"Yes, I know who Carla is," Pearl said.

"Carla told us about something strange that happened here last night. She said you might have seen it," Kelly said.

Pearl stared at Kelly and then asked, "Are you talking about the floating plate?"

NINE

"They accepted your offer," Ray told Adam on the phone Tuesday morning. "I'll send over the signed contract, and we can open escrow."

Adam and Ray exchanged a few more words, said goodbye, and Adam hung up the phone. With a sigh, Adam leaned back in his office chair and stared at the phone. He sat alone in silence for a few minutes before a familiar voice called out from the doorway, "What happened, did you lose your best friend?"

Adam glanced up and watched as his handyman and longtime friend, Bill Jones, walked into the office. While they were the same age, Bill always looked older because of his years of smoking and careless eating habits. He wore denims, a faded blue work shirt, and work boots.

What Adam and Bill didn't see, a second presence entered the room at the same time—Marie Nichols, the spirit of Adam's deceased grandmother.

"I have to agree with Bill." Marie flashed the handyman a look of disdain. "As much as it pains me—but you do look depressed. And you should be looking happy. You and Melony are getting married. I hope nothing is wrong between you two."

"I wouldn't call him my best friend," Adam muttered under his breath, thinking of how Ian might react when hearing the news.

"I have something that might cheer you up. A new listing." Bill took a seat in front of Adam's desk.

"Oh yeah? Whose?" Adam asked.

"My nephew, Cory. He's selling his house."

Adam arched his brow. "Really?" By Bill's smile, Adam wondered briefly if the nephew intended to share some proceeds with his uncle, considering the house had originally belonged to Bill's parents, and the bulk of his parents' estate had gone to Bill's troubled sister and then to her only son.

"Yeah. I convinced him he needs to get away from here. Get some help. Living in that house is not healthy for him, and the money from the sale will support him while he gets things worked out."

I guess that means he isn't sharing, Adam said to himself. Aloud he asked, "Is he waiting for the house to sell before leaving?"

"He's already gone. I have a cousin in California who agreed to take him in for a while and get him hooked up with a job and some counseling. He's told some pretty far-out stories about what happened up on that mountain when he followed Marlow and the others up there."

"Does much need to be done to the house?" Adam asked.

"Not really. I'm having someone give it a good cleaning, and then you can go over there, take pictures, and get it on the market. So, tell me, why do you look so bummed?" Bill asked.

"I had an accepted offer."

"Well, damn, if an accepted offer puts that expression on your face, maybe I'll take Cory's listing somewhere else, to cheer you up," Bill teased. He absently fished a cigarette from his shirt pocket yet returned it a moment later when Adam flashed him a disapproving scowl.

"It was the Marymoor property," Adam explained.

Bill's eyes widened. "You found a buyer for Marymoor?"

"Yep." Adam leaned back in his desk chair.

"Oh dear. Does this mean Ian's father bought it?" Marie muttered before vanishing.

"Damn, who did you get to buy that place? Do they know its history?" Bill asked.

"They're from out of town. I told them everything about it. But they weren't too concerned."

Bill shrugged. "Well, if it wasn't for how that place creeps me out, I'd say it's a nice piece of real estate. Level, good neighborhood, nice views. But there's something about it that makes my skin crawl. After Dad's experience working over there, he wouldn't even drive down that street again."

DRAWING the curtain to one side, Pearl Huckabee peered out her upstairs bedroom window, looking down at the sidewalk below. Walking past her house was her neighbor to the south, Heather Donovan. The young woman dressed peculiar, she thought, today wearing a long black skirt with a dark blouse, and her jet-black hair pulled up in a messy knot atop her head. It certainly was not a summery dress, Pearl thought. Heather carried something in her hands—a small package. Pearl continued to watch as Heather entered the side yard of her neighbor to the north, the Marlows.

"BREAD DELIVERY!" Heather announced when she walked into the Marlows' kitchen. Walt and Danielle sat at the kitchen table, eating breakfast. Already dressed for the day, Walt in slacks and a button-up linen shirt, while Danielle wore jeans and a summery blouse.

"Morning, Heather," Walt said, giving her a brief salute with his cup of coffee before taking a sip.

"Is that your sourdough bread?" Danielle asked with a smile.

"Yes. I finally have this thing down. I make four loaves at a time. It's easier to manage Harvey." Heather set the loaf of bread on the table next to Danielle.

"Harvey?" Walt frowned.

"That's what she named her sourdough starter," Danielle said with a giggle.

"Of course, it takes all evening, since I can only bake one loaf at a time," Heather explained as she walked to the counter to pour herself a cup of coffee.

"What are you going to do with four loaves of bread?" Danielle picked up the loaf of bread. Heather had wrapped it in beeswax paper instead of plastic wrap. She gave it a sniff.

"Giving some away." Heather brought her cup of coffee to the table and sat down.

"I love homemade sourdough. Thanks." Danielle set the loaf of bread back on the table.

"Why aren't you at work?" Walt asked.

"Chris gave me the morning off since I worked a few hours Sunday. I'm going in the office after I have lunch with Brian."

Danielle grinned. "Aww... where is he taking you?"

"My house. I really can't be seen with him." Heather sipped her coffee.

The next moment, Marie Nichols appeared in the empty seat at the table. Her abrupt appearance startled Heather, making her spill some of her coffee. Heather grumbled, but silently wiped up her spill with a nearby napkin.

"Good morning, everyone!" Marie chirped.

"Hey, Marie, where have you been?" Danielle asked.

"I just came from Adam's office," Marie explained.

"We saw Adam and Melony last night at Pier Café," Walt told her.

"He said he had a buyer for the Marymoor property, but he wouldn't tell us who it was," Danielle said.

"Who would buy that place?" Heather asked with a shudder.

They all looked at Marie for an answer.

Marie considered the question for a moment. If she were to tell what she knew, there was no doubt Danielle would tell Lily. And once Lily knew, she would tell Ian, who would feel compelled to talk to his father about the property, and his father would believe Adam had told him.

Marie smiled weakly and said, "I have no idea. But what do you think of their engagement?"

Danielle frowned. "Whose engagement?"

"Why, Adam and Melony's, of course. Didn't they tell you?" Marie asked.

AFTER THEY FINISHED breakfast at Pier Café, Kelly dropped Joe off at work. At the station, he found Brian sitting in the chief's office, chatting.

"Morning," the chief greeted when Joe entered the office.

"How's it going today?" Joe asked.

The chief motioned to the empty chair for Joe to sit down. "Kind of slow."

"Slow is good." Joe sat down in the chair.

They chatted about work for a few minutes before the conversation drifted to a discussion of Joe's breakfast with Kelly and what Carla and then Pearl had told them. When Joe finished his story, the chief and Brian exchanged quick glances, each thinking the same thing—Walt had saved the plate from crashing to the floor.

"Pearl seems to feel it was some sort of magic trick," Joe continued. "But from what Carla told us, the entire thing freaked her out. I keep trying to figure out what really happened, because we all know a plate doesn't float and move around on its own. And when you drop something, it falls unless something stops it."

"Maybe it was a magic trick," Brian suggested. The corner of the chief's mouth twitched upwards in response as he glanced from Brian to Joe.

"A magic trick?" Joe frowned.

Brian shrugged. "Had to be. Unless plates really fly. You say Marlow was there, and we all know he dabbles in magic. Well, sleight of hand. Not real magic. No such thing as magic." The chief rolled his eyes at Brian's comment.

"You're suggesting what Carla and Pearl claim happened was really some sleight-of-hand trick by Marlow?" Joe asked.

"Do you have any other plausible explanation for what they saw?" Brian asked.

"If both Pearl and Carla hadn't told us the same story, I would assume they simply imagined the whole thing. But I don't see Pearl and Carla as being two friends who made up a story to punk Kelly and me. That would be more implausible than a floating plate. I didn't ask where Marlow was sitting when all this happened. I suppose it's possible." Joe shrugged and stood up.

When Joe left the office a few minutes later, the chief looked at Brian and chuckled. "Never a dull day."

"I know Walt was just trying to help, but sometimes he just needs to let the dishes fall," Brian said.

BRIAN PARKED his car behind Heather's house and entered through the back gate. He found her in the kitchen, cutting slices of homemade sourdough bread.

"Why don't you let me take you out for lunch?" Brian asked as he walked into the kitchen. He stood behind Heather as she sliced bread. Wrapping his arms around her, he gave her a quick hug and kiss on her cheek.

"Careful, I have a knife," she teased before turning her face to him and placing a quick kiss on his lips.

"Seriously, I could take you somewhere nice." Brian released her and stood by the counter, watching her prepare lunch.

"You don't like my cooking?"

"I think I'm addicted to your damn bread, and if I'm not careful, I won't be able to fit in my uniform. But seriously, Heather, we need to step out of the closet."

"Come on, isn't it fun sneaking around?" Heather teased.

Ten minutes later, they sat on her back patio, each with a plate of food and a glass of iced tea. Brian told her Joe's story about falling plates at the diner, and Heather told Brian about Adam making an offer on the Marymoor property.

"I heard this morning at the office that there was an accepted offer on that property," Brian told her.

"I wonder if it was Adam's buyer."

"So that place is really haunted?" Brian asked.

"Oh yeah, in a creepy Friday the Thirteenth, Stephen King sort of way." She then told Brian what Adam and Melony had experienced at the property, from what Danielle had told her.

"Wow."

Heather frowned. "I wonder who the buyer is."

"I have no idea. One of the guys who works over at the city office stopped in to talk to the chief about something and mentioned it went under contract," Brian said.

"We asked Marie if she knew who Adam's client was. She claims she doesn't know, but I think she does." Heather took a sip of her iced tea.

About to take a bite of his sandwich, Brian paused and looked up at Heather. "Why would Marie know that?"

Heather shrugged. "Marie is always hanging out at Adam's office—or at his house—or wherever he is."

"That's rather creepy," Brian said. "Not sure how I'd like my grandma stalking me from the grave."

Heather grinned. "Fortunately for you, if your grandma decided to stalk you, I would probably see her and could give you the heads-up."

Brian frowned and shook his head before taking another bite of his sandwich.

"What?" Heather asked.

"I don't know, I just wonder what Adam would think if he knew his grandma was always hanging around—eavesdropping."

Heather shrugged. "They were close."

"I know but…"

Heather laughed. "I don't imagine Marie hangs around when he and Mel are getting busy."

Brian scowled. "Damn, I didn't even consider that."

"Oh, and you know what else Marie said? Adam and Mel got engaged. I knew it all along! I told Danielle and Lily I thought Adam was going to ask Mel to get married when I saw him take the Winterborne ring out of the bank. But they thought Adam and Mel were just taking the ring to a buyer. Looks like I was right all along. I guess they didn't say anything to Danielle and Walt about their engagement when they saw them last night at Pier Café. So you probably shouldn't say anything about the engagement until they announce it. The only reason we know about it is because Marie overheard Adam proposing."

TEN

Four days later, on Saturday, Danielle and Walt decided to host a potluck barbecue at Marlow House. According to the weather reporter, afternoon temperatures in Frederickport would be just under seventy degrees, with clear skies, which Danielle deemed ideal weather for a September outdoor gathering. Since Lily's and Ian's families would arrive the next Friday and planned to stay for two weeks, Danielle figured this might be one of the last times of the season they could invite their friends over to Marlow House for outdoor entertaining.

Chris arrived first, a little before three p.m., to pick up Walt. Together, the two men drove to the meat market to buy steaks and seafood to cook on the grill. While they were at the store, Heather arrived with four loaves of sourdough bread she had baked the day before. After setting the bread on the kitchen counter, she pitched in to help Danielle prepare for the guests. Lily arrived a few minutes later with a large bowl of macaroni salad. Ian, Connor, and Sadie were still across the street and would arrive later, after Connor woke up from his nap.

The three neighbors chatted in the kitchen while Danielle made a pitcher of iced tea, Lily made lemonade, and Heather cut up lemons to garnish the drinks.

"You still drinking lemonade?" Lily teased Danielle.

"Um… yes…" Danielle flashed Lily a grin.

"But you could drink tea if you wanted?" Lily prodded. Lily had been so busy the last few days, she and Danielle hadn't had a chance to talk.

Danielle shrugged. "Not sure."

Heather stopped slicing lemons and looked from Lily to Danielle, a frown furrowing her brow. "What are you two talking about?"

"Iced tea and lemonade, of course." Lily flashed Heather an innocent smile.

Heather narrowed her eyes and stared at Lily. "What did you mean, she could if she wanted?" Before Lily responded, Heather let out a gasp and said, "Oh my gawd, you think you might be pregnant!"

Danielle flashed Lily a scowl and said, "You never could keep a secret."

Lily shrugged, and Heather squealed. "Oh, my gawd, when is it due?" Heather looked Danielle up and down. "You aren't showing."

"I don't know if I am," Danielle said. "So please don't say anything. But I'm late, and I went off birth control."

"Why don't you take a home pregnancy test?" Heather asked.

"I will."

"Oh, how fun, another baby!" Heather grinned.

"I might just be late," Danielle said.

"Oh, come on, Dani. Walt's mother practically told Walt you were pregnant," Lily said.

Heather arched her brow. She looked from Lily to Danielle. "Excuse me?"

Danielle let out a sigh and rolled her eyes at Lily. She turned to Heather and said, "It was in a dream hop. Walt saw his parents, and his mother sort of implied we would be having a baby soon. But until I get a positive pregnancy test, I don't want to tell anyone."

"I bet Marie is over the moon," Heather said.

"I have said nothing to Marie yet. So please, keep this between us," Danielle urged.

WHILE ADAM and Melony had failed to tell Walt and Danielle about their engagement when they ran into them at Pier Café earlier that week, Melony finally told Danielle about the engagement on Friday when Danielle called to invite her to the barbecue.

"We haven't told anyone yet," Melony said during the phone call. "But I have an appointment to have the Winterborne ring sized tomorrow morning, so I'll be wearing it, and I suppose your gathering would be a good time to announce our engagement."

Keeping secrets on Beach Drive wasn't easy with ghosts passing on bits of news they overheard to the mediums. When Melony told Danielle about the engagement, she did not know many of those coming to the barbecue already knew, thanks to Marie.

"I'm dying to see the Winterborne ring again," Heather told Danielle before the others arrived.

"Remember, you don't know," Danielle reminded her.

"Didn't I tell you and Lily even before Marie spilled the news?" Danielle chuckled. "True."

WALT AND CHRIS returned to Marlow House just minutes before Ian arrived with Connor and Sadie. The chief showed up a few minutes later with his sons, Evan and Eddy Jr. Both boys immediately ran to the side yard to throw the ball for Hunny and Sadie.

By the time Kelly and Joe arrived, Melony and Adam were already there, standing on the back porch talking to everyone— except the MacDonald boys, who continued to toss the ball for the dogs. Adam had announced their engagement while Melony showed off her ring. It now fit perfectly.

Melony was just presenting her left hand to Lily for closer inspection when Joe and Kelly joined the group.

"What's going on?" Kelly asked, looking curiously at the way her sister-in-law, Lily, held Melony's hand.

"Adam and Mel are engaged," Chris announced brightly.

"I confess, I can't quite get over the fact Adam got over his aversion to matrimony," Danielle whispered to Walt.

"It is amazing how that particular aversion can disappear when the right person shows up," Walt whispered back.

"Congratulations," Joe said, extending a hand to Adam. "Have you set a date?"

"Not yet," Adam said. "Mel's still getting used to the idea. I don't want to scare her off." He laughed.

Joe wrapped his arm around Kelly's shoulder and pulled her close. "We plan to set the date when Kelly's parents are here."

"That's the ring Danielle gave Adam," Kelly said impulsively.

"It is," Melony said with a smile, now looking at the ring on her hand.

"The Winterborne engagement ring..." Kelly murmured, still staring at Melony's ring.

"Yes." Melony looked up to Kelly. "Your ring, it was Joe's grandmother's, wasn't it?" Melony reached out, and before Kelly could pull away, Melony took hold of her left hand, bringing Kelly's ring closer for inspection.

From the sidelines, Danielle cringed. Kelly's ring was truly horrendous, Danielle thought. Comparing the two rings almost seemed cruel from Danielle's perspective. By the expression on Kelly's face and the way she snatched back her hand, Danielle wondered if Kelly regretted drawing attention to her own ring.

"It's a family heirloom," Joe said, oblivious to Kelly's reluctance to show off her ring.

Melony smiled sincerely at Joe. "I think that's really sweet. Especially when there is family to pass the ring down to. In some ways, I feel the Winterborne ring is perfect for me."

"It is gorgeous," Heather said.

"Yes, it is. But I was thinking, Eloise Winterborne didn't have any children to pass it on to, so it couldn't remain an heirloom in her family," Melony explained.

"It can become one in yours," Joe suggested.

Melony turned her smile to Joe. "No. Adam and I don't plan on having any kids. So, like Eloise, when that time comes, maybe I'll pass it down like she did, to some unsuspecting stranger."

"Hey, we aren't even married yet, and you're already killing me off and getting rid of the ring," Adam teased.

Melony laughed and kissed Adam. They continued to chat for a few minutes longer; then Brian Henderson showed up for the party. After entering through the side gate, he walked toward the group.

"They invited Brian?" Kelly whispered to Joe.

"You know how Walt and Brian bonded after their little misadventure in the mountains," Joe whispered back.

"I WONDER WHO'S NEXT," Chris asked. He looked at Edward MacDonald. "What about it, Chief?"

The chief chuckled and shook his head. "Don't look at me."

"What about you?" Chris asked Brian while handing him a beer.

"Before he gets married, he needs to start dating someone first," Kelly said. "But how about you, Chris?"

Heather laughed. "Chris is having way too much fun playing the field these days."

Chris frowned at Heather. "What do you know about it?"

"More than you think, Romeo." Heather grinned.

"Maybe you'll be next," Chris teased Heather.

"I don't think my current guy is the marriage type," Heather said, sipping her beer.

"You're dating someone?" Kelly asked.

Heather smiled at Kelly. "Yes. We've been seeing each other for a while now."

"Will he be here tonight?" Kelly asked.

Heather shrugged. "I'm afraid not. He's a little shy."

"So you are seeing someone?" Chris muttered. "I thought so."

"Do we know him?" Kelly asked.

Heather looked at Kelly and shrugged again. "I'm not sure. I haven't asked him if he knows you or not."

"So, what is this guy like?" Brian asked. He sipped his beer and watched Heather.

Heather turned to Brian and smiled. "He's a little younger than me. I think that's why he's so shy. A little intimidated."

Brian grinned. "Interesting."

"That's a change for you," Chris told Heather.

"What do you mean?" Heather frowned.

"You always seem to date older guys," Chris said.

Heather shrugged. "Older guys are too set in their ways. I think I'm over it."

"YOU'RE OVER IT?" Brian asked Heather when he found her alone in the kitchen twenty minutes later, refilling the iced tea pitcher.

"I lied."

"You are a brat," he told her.

"I think you've told me that before," Heather said.

Brian laughed and stole a kiss before they returned outside with the others. They found their friends engaged in a new topic of conversation, the Marymoor property.

"Come on, Adam, who is the buyer?" Joe asked.

Adam frowned. "How did you even know I was the buyer's agent?"

"Word gets around in Frederickport," Joe said. "At least tell us, is it a local?"

"I can't see a local buying that property," Ian said.

"What's really wrong with it?" Kelly asked. "I don't get what the big deal is. I've driven by, and it's a nice neighborhood. Great views. I'm surprised no one has built on it before now."

"The city has owned it for years. At one time they planned to build a park on it. That was when they cleaned up the site after the fire. But one accident after another waylaid those plans. Over the years they tried to sell it. A few times it went in escrow, but the buyers always backed out during inspection," MacDonald explained.

"Why?" Kelly asked. "What came up in the inspection?"

"It's those pesky ghosts," Joe said with a laugh.

"Seriously?" Kelly frowned.

Joe shrugged and rolled his eyes. "Ghosts sound more interesting than the truth."

"What is the truth?" Kelly asked.

"Back when they were clearing the site, there were some accidents. That's when the stories of the place being haunted or cursed began," Joe explained. "And then later, when it went under contract a few times, the buyers always backed out after the inspection. Rumors started circulating that something happened during the inspection to make them back out of the deal."

"What happened?" Kelly asked.

"I doubt anything happened other than the buyers deciding they didn't want the property for some reason. But rumors over the years claim the prospective buyers saw paranormal activity on the property that scared them off. Nothing but overactive imaginations. It's silly, really. After all, I've never heard any of the residents in that neighborhood complaining about unexplained occurrences." Joe turned to Adam and added, "But just in case the place is haunted, maybe you'll be lucky, and your buyer won't be afraid of ghosts."

LATER THAT EVENING, after they had all finished dinner and sat by the fire talking, Adam received a call on his cellphone. He excused himself and went into the house to answer the call. When he hadn't returned fifteen minutes later, Melony went inside, looking for him. She found Adam sitting at the kitchen table, slumped over with his forehead propped in the palms of his hands.

"Adam, is something wrong?" Melony asked, taking a seat at the table.

"That call, it was from Ian's dad," Adam explained.

"And?"

"He ordered his inspections. They can do them Monday. He told me if everything is okay, then he wants to close early—before he gets here. His house there is closing escrow next week, and he wants a simultaneous close so the proceeds from his house pay for the lot. I just hope he isn't using all his equity to buy the property."

Melony's eyes widened. "Oh…"

They sat in silence for a few minutes. Finally, she said, "Remember what Eddy told us, that's when the other buyers backed out, after their inspection."

"That's only because the buyers attended theirs and probably experienced something like we did the other night."

ELEVEN

On Monday morning, the inspector pulled up in front of the Marymoor property. He sat in his car for a moment, reviewing the paperwork on his clipboard. After a few minutes, he got out of the vehicle, carrying a small briefcase in one hand and the clipboard in the other. He approached the front gate.

"THERE'S ANOTHER ONE," Waylon told Molly as they watched the man approach. The two stood some distance from the front gate leading onto the property.

"I remember when this was a nice quiet street," Molly grumbled.

"I did what you said. I haven't done anything since that last couple was here. But they keep coming."

Molly let out a deep sigh. "Perhaps you're right."

Waylon perked up. "Then I can do something?"

"Just don't hurt him. You could have done real damage with that pipe, and I fear that would just get us in more trouble. I don't want to give Randal any reason to come back."

"Randal won't find out. Anyway, it's been a long time since he's been here," Waylon reminded her.

"Perhaps. But you hurt that man with a pipe, and Randal could show up early, and that could interfere with our plans," Molly warned.

"Okay. I'll just scare him off. I promise I won't hurt him."

THE INSPECTOR APPROACHED the chain-link fence surrounding the property. Before entering the unlocked gate, he paused and glanced around. He had heard the bizarre stories, yet he told himself they were nothing but urban legend, the product of overactive imaginations. With a smile he entered the gate yet paused when he noticed a drop in temperature. After a moment, he headed toward the area where the buildings had once stood.

Intending to take soil samples, he noted the site looked undisturbed. Before coming over today, he had reviewed the photographs and other documents the city had on file for the property. Reaching the perimeter of the original foundation, he set the briefcase on the dirt by his shoes and looked for a moment at the clipboard. When doing so, he heard rustling on the ground and looked down.

At first, he thought he had set the briefcase on an unlevel spot and now it was about to fall over. But the briefcase wasn't falling to the ground, it moved while remaining upright. He watched in stunned fascination as the briefcase moved away from him, heading back to the gate he had just entered.

Without thinking, he chased the briefcase, believing for a moment it must be the wind. But there was no wind, and when the briefcase reached the gate, it stopped moving, sitting on the edge of the property line.

With a frown, the inspector reached for the briefcase and picked it up. While trying to understand what had just happened, he convinced himself wind must have taken hold of the case. But when he tried walking back to the foundation site, something ripped the briefcase from his grip and hurled it from him, through the open gate and onto the dirt just outside the fence enclosure.

Stunned, he stared at the briefcase now sitting motionless on the dirt. He looked around. Anxiously licking his lips, his eyes darting from side to side, he exited the fenced area and picked up the briefcase.

"It had to be the wind," he muttered to himself. But when he reentered the area, the briefcase again jerked from his grip. But this time, instead of flying through the open gate, it flew over the top of the fence, as if someone had just pitched it. Once again, the briefcase landed in the dirt.

Without another thought, he ran through the open gate, picked up the briefcase, and raced to his car.

"LOOKS like we're going to save some money," John Bartley told his wife when he walked into the kitchen late Monday afternoon.

"That would be nice, considering what we're paying for the movers. I'm still having sticker shock," she grumbled as she stood at the kitchen counter, sorting through her dry goods.

"We're too old to pack up this house ourselves and move everything to Oregon. And we have the money," he reminded her.

She glanced up and asked, "When did you say the movers will be here in the morning?"

"They're supposed to be here by eight."

"I hope I'm ready," she muttered before asking, "What is this about us saving money?"

"I just got off the phone with the inspector I hired." John took a seat at the breakfast bar, facing his wife.

June stopped what she was doing and looked at her husband. "When is he going to be done with the inspection?"

"It's already done, although technically he didn't do one."

June frowned. "I don't understand."

"The inspector called, said before he went over there, he reviewed all the paperwork the city had on the property—such as reports on the cleanup after the fire, and soil tests taken over the years. When he started the inspection on the site, he said he could tell nothing had changed. The place has been locked up for years, no way for anyone to get on the property. Free from any illegal dumping."

"I don't understand. Are you saying he isn't going to do an inspection himself?"

John shook his head. "He said I could hire someone else if I wanted. But that he felt he would be taking advantage of me if he accepted money for an inspection when all the information is already on file with the city. In fact, he emailed copies of all the documents the city had on file. No charge."

"He didn't charge you anything?" June frowned at the idea.

"Nope. Craziest thing." John shrugged.

"What about a perc test?" she asked.

"I was wrong earlier. We can hook up to the sewer, so we don't need a perc test. Not having to put in a septic system will also save us some money." John smiled.

"What now?"

"Now, I'm going to call Adam and tell him to wrap this thing up."

June grinned. "I can't wait to see our son's and daughter's expressions when we tell them we are Frederickport property owners!"

THE GHOST of Marie Nichols found Eva Thorndike sitting atop the theater's roof, watching the sunset. Eva's bare feet dangled below her long skirt. While she normally wore her hair up, this evening she wore it down, freely flowing past her shoulders. People normally compared Eva's appearance to Charles Dana Gibson's drawing of the Gibson Girl, yet now she looked more uniquely herself instead of a likeness to a pen and ink drawing. She also looked more like a girl, as opposed to a worldly woman and onetime silent screen star.

"I have been looking everywhere for you!" Marie said when she sat next to her fellow spirit.

Eva glanced over to Marie and smiled and then looked back to the sunset. "It is so beautiful, don't you think?"

"Yes, it is lovely," Marie agreed half-heartedly.

"Is there something wrong?" Eva asked after a few moments of silence.

"I have a problem, and I'm not sure how to handle it," Marie explained.

"What sort of problem?" Eva asked.

"I was over at Adam's, and he's so upset." She then told Eva about Ian's father buying the Marymoor property.

"Oh my. And if you tell Danielle or any of the mediums, they might feel compelled to tell Ian."

"Yes, and even though Ian will know Adam didn't violate his father's request not to say anything…"

"Ian may not be able to help himself, and he would say something to his father," Eva finished for Marie.

"Exactly, and then Ian's father will assume Adam behaved unprofessionally. I can't do that to Adam." Marie let out a weary sigh.

"Perhaps his father won't buy the property once he sees it. I certainly hope not."

"Who exactly is haunting that place?" Marie asked. "Can't you ask them to leave?"

"I honestly don't know who haunts it. It's one place I've avoided for years. The negative energy is too overwhelming." Eva shivered at the thought.

"Which is why we need to stop Ian's father from buying the property. If he builds his home there, they will expect Connor to visit his grandparents' house. I'm sure they will want him to spend the night sometime. Children always spend the night at their grandparents' house. We can't expose Connor to that type of evil energy."

Eva looked at Marie, a concerned frown on her face. "Oh dear, I hadn't even considered that."

"I have. While spirits may not be able to physically harm an innocent like Connor, it doesn't mean they can't scare the poor child. It would be a nightmare for him."

"I'm afraid you're right," Eva agreed.

"What can we do?" Marie asked.

"I suppose one option, let Ian know what his father is up to. He certainly won't want his parents living there if he knows about the place. I'm sure with Danielle's help you might come up with a story that someone other than Adam told Ian. Wouldn't the other real estate agent know the buyer's name?"

Marie considered the suggestion and frowned. "I do wish I had thought of that earlier, but I was so frazzled. I'm afraid it might be too late now. From what I heard from Adam when I was over there, they might close escrow anytime now, before we can do anything."

"Why didn't you come to me earlier?" Eva asked.

"I told you, I have been looking all over for you!" Marie reminded her.

The two spirits sat in silence, considering what to do while watching the sun slip into the ocean. Finally, Marie asked, "Perhaps we can convince the ghosts it's time to move on? What do you know about them? I've always heard a patient killed a nurse over there, which is why they closed Marymoor. Is the killer sticking around because he doesn't want to deal with the consequences?"

"I'm not sure. I suppose it's possible. Back when the murder happened, I was spending a great deal of time at the Salem cemetery. Was such a nice little group there. But they all have since moved on," Eva explained. "I wasn't around when all that happened at Marymoor."

"So you don't know much about the murder?" Marie asked.

"What I know is what I heard from fellow spirits around at the time. I know a young nurse was stabbed—murdered. Everyone was out looking for the killer. I was told they found him hiding in an abandoned building. After his capture, they took him back to the sanatorium. They didn't take him to the police station. Caused quite a ruckus, because once he was returned to Marymoor, he killed himself."

"I wonder if he's the one haunting Marymoor."

"Considering the amount of negative energy, that would be my guess," Eva said.

"According to Danielle, she once saw the spirit of a nurse at the Marymoor site. She wore a bloodstained uniform," Marie said. "Her name was Molly."

Eva nodded. "I believe that was the name of the murdered nurse."

"That's what I understood, too. Is it possible the killer and victim are both haunting the site?" Marie couldn't imagine being trapped for eternity with the woman who had smothered her.

"If so, that might explain the negative energy emanating from the area," Eva said. "The killer and his victim, forever trapped together to replay the gruesome act."

"Do you think that's what's happening?"

Eva shrugged. "Or perhaps other inmates are haunting the place along with Molly. Marymoor was an institution for the mentally insane. Some patients, like the killer of the nurse, were criminally insane. Insanity is not a defect of the spirit—but the body. Yet, as long as the spirit is tethered to earth—trapped between life and death—they are in a sense tethered to the damaged body. Once they can free themself of those tethers, move on to the next plane, the spirit becomes whole again. No longer confused," Eva explained. "No longer insane."

Marie frowned. "I don't understand."

"Our physical form has limitations. When we move on, we are no longer limited by those imperfections of our bodies. Over at the Marymoor site, those spirits have not moved on and are not aware of their true state. Unfortunately, there are probably a number of insane spirits, dangerous in the fear they can evoke, haunting the property. Yet, fortunately, not capable of physically harming anyone. At least, not fatally... I think."

TWELVE

N o one could see them aside from any spirit that might linger nearby at the Marymoor property. They stood on the opposite side of the street, Marie Nichols and Eva Thorndike. Marie, the image of an elderly woman wearing a floral-print housedress and straw hat, chose to present herself how she looked in her early eighties, as opposed to when she died in her nineties. She would have gone younger, yet those living—who could still see her—would not recognize a much younger version.

Eva didn't have that issue, considering she had died at such a young age. No longer wearing her hair down, she now had it pulled atop her head in a knot, with wisps of hair artfully escaping. She wore an outfit more the style of the early 1900s, with a long skirt, and a fitted, tucked-in blouse, prim with a button-up collar.

Both ghosts studied the property, and neither noticed any lingering spirits nearby—other than themselves.

"You know what I find odd?" Marie asked, her gaze fixed on the property.

"What is that?" Eva asked, glancing at Marie and then back to the Marymoor site.

"Over the years I rarely came down this street," Marie began. "Before the fire, I remember driving by and thinking the old abandoned buildings looked out of place with all the residential houses springing up around it. For a time, there was talk of building a park. And then someone wanted to buy the property to build condominiums. But the residents here pitched quite a fit with the city. They didn't want multifamily housing on their street. There were a couple of bigwigs who lived here; they prevented that from happening by passing several zoning laws. And they never could divide the property into more single residential lots, even though it's large enough."

"Why is that?" Eva asked.

"According to my father, when Marymoor donated the land, one stipulation was that they could never subdivide the property. Something about his legacy. Of course, I have no idea if any of that would hold up in court today if someone wanted to divide it. But considering the spirit activity, I don't imagine that would be such a good idea."

"What was it that you thought odd, exactly?"

"I do tend to wander." Marie chuckled and then continued. "After the Marymoor Sanatorium burned down, I came by a few times to see the damage—and later to see what it looked like when they cleared the property. There were stories when they were clearing the site. I thought it bunk. I remember Adam avoided coming down this street; it gave him the willies. But it never bothered me—at least, not until I died."

Eva nodded knowingly. "It's because you're now on this side, more sensitive to the energy of other spirits. When spirits emit negative energy, not everyone can feel it. Someone like Danielle can, but typically not a non-medium. Yet, once you move over to our side, just as you can now see and hear other spirits, you can also feel their negative energy—and with it, their pain."

Marie wrinkled her nose and cocked her head slightly. "Yes, there is an element of pain to it, isn't there?"

Eva nodded. "It's one reason I tend to avoid these types of hauntings. Unless I feel I can help the spirits move on, I would rather not get involved. I suppose that's selfish of me. Yet I also know the Universe will give me a nudge if I need to intervene." Eva paused for a moment and glanced up at the sky. "I do believe you're nudging me now."

Marie looked around the neighborhood. "It certainly hasn't stopped people from building on this street. Aside from stories specific to the property, I've never heard about the residents claiming to experience ghostly activity."

"Living next to a haunted house can have an element of charm, and I don't believe it hurts the property values in a neighborhood. Look at Marlow House," Eva reminded her.

Marie smiled. "Yes, over the years, I heard stories of Marlow House being haunted—the same way I heard about the Marymoor site. And the same for Presley House—although over there, I recall Millie being quite annoyed each Halloween because of the attention it drew."

"From what I understand, it seems any ghostly activity tends to take place within the fenced area, and only those sensitive to spirits —like us or one of the mediums—would sense anything from this distance, as we do."

"Which is why I'm so troubled with the thought of Connor's grandparents building here and then bringing the child to this site. I don't want him subjected to any of that," Marie said.

"Then let's see if we can do anything about it." Eva took one step off the sidewalk and headed across the street. Marie let out a sigh and followed her.

MOLLY NOTICED the two approaching women. She wasn't sure if she had ever seen them before, but there was something familiar about the younger one. When they reached the gate, she looked into the eyes of the younger woman, trying to place her, when the woman gave her a smile.

"You can see me," Molly said in surprise.

"Yes, we can," Eva said.

"What do you want?" Molly asked.

"My name is Eva, and this is my friend Marie. May we come in a moment to talk?"

Molly frowned at Eva. "Talk about what? If you're one of those people who want to buy this property, it isn't for sale."

Eva flashed Molly another smile. "No. We're not interested in buying the property, we just want to talk."

Molly let out a sigh. "I suppose I can spare you a minute. But I'm busy today. So just a minute." If Molly thought it odd Marie and Eva moved through the gate without opening it, she said nothing.

Eva and Marie stood just inside the fence, some six feet from Molly. "We told you our names. What is yours?" Eva asked.

"I'm Molly."

"You were a nurse here?" Marie asked, now staring at the blood-stain on Molly's nurse's uniform.

"I still am," Molly said primly.

"Do you have a lot of patients?" Eva asked.

"Yes, that's why I said I'm busy," Molly snapped. "Now what is it you wanted to talk to me about?"

"Where are they? Your patients?" Eva glanced around, as if a patient might suddenly appear.

"Did Randal send you?" Molly demanded.

"Randal?" Eva frowned. "I don't know a Randal."

"Then why are you here? Why are you asking about my patients?"

"Eva, dear, can't you just cut to the chase?" Marie pleaded.

Eva looked at Marie and said, "These matters require diplo-macy—discretion. One can't blurt out certain things."

"Are you here to make me leave?" Molly asked. "Am I being fired? Randal did send you!"

"I told you, I don't know any Randal," Eva insisted. "I am here to help you… to help you understand."

"Understand what?" Molly demanded.

Eva considered the question a moment and then said, "To help you understand your reality."

"You aren't making any sense," Molly snapped.

"I have to agree with Molly," Marie muttered under her breath.

"Do you ever feel as if you no longer belong here?" Eva asked, ignoring Marie's grumblings.

"You are trying to get me to leave!" Molly accused.

"I can't make you leave. Only you can do that. I am simply trying to show you the way," Eva said.

Marie rolled her eyes and impatiently folded her arms across her chest.

"Show me the way where?" Molly asked.

"It's important for you to remember. To think back and remem-ber, put things in perspective," Eva said.

"I don't know what you're trying to say," Molly snapped.

"Perhaps we start with the fire and work back. Do you remember the fire?" Eva asked.

Molly frowned. "What fire?"

"The fire that burned down the buildings." Eva nodded toward the old building site.

Molly glanced to where the buildings had once stood and then looked back to Eva. "What are you talking about?"

"The buildings that used to stand there. Where you worked. Do you remember when they burned down?" Eva asked.

"You're talking nonsense. The buildings are still there." Molly vanished.

"Molly! Come back!" Eva called out.

Marie and Eva stood for a few moments in silence, looking to where Molly had been standing.

Finally, Marie asked, "Do you think she really believes the buildings are still there?"

"I suppose it's possible," Eva said.

"What are you doing here!" a male voice called out.

Marie and Eva turned to the right just in time to see a young man pick up a rock and hurl it in their direction. It flew through Marie and landed on the ground. Upon seeing the rock move effortlessly through Marie, the man let out a scream and disappeared.

"Another ghost?" Marie said.

"Obviously."

"I wonder how many of them are here," Marie said.

"I was hoping to get Molly to come to terms with her reality, and once her perception cleared, she would be more willing to identify the other spirits haunting this site, and help us get them to move on," Eva said with a sigh.

"If they refuse to listen to us, how can we convince them to move on?" Marie asked.

"I suppose we will just need to be persistent and make them listen!"

MARIE AND EVA remained on the property for several more hours. Unfortunately, they didn't see another ghost, yet they could feel them. The unsettling sensation they first experienced when arriving not only continued, it intensified.

"Why is it I keep expecting Freddy to come out of the bushes, brandishing a chain saw?" Marie asked.

Eva chuckled. "It is fascinating how people pay to watch movies that give them the same sensation we're feeling now."

"What should we do?" Marie asked.

"I suppose leave and come back later. We're obviously being ignored," Eva said.

MARIE DIDN'T RETURN to Adam's on Tuesday, so she didn't know if the property would close escrow before Ian's parents arrived in Frederickport. She also avoided Danielle and the other mediums, not wanting to see them until she could assure them the troubled spirits at Marymoor had moved on.

She and Eva returned to the Marymoor site the next day. Not long after stepping onto the property, a tree limb fell from a tree, falling through Eva and landing on the ground.

"That would have hurt," Eva muttered, looking down at the fallen branch.

"Good thing you don't have a head," Marie snarked.

"That was rude," Eva said.

"The branch falling on you, or my comment about your head?" Marie asked.

"Both."

They remained for several more hours, yet not a single spirit showed him or herself.

On Thursday they arrived at nightfall, wondering if the evening might be a better time for the spirits to show themselves. Again, the uneasy and unpleasant energy engulfed the property. They didn't see Molly or the young man who had thrown a rock at Marie during their first visit. Yet another man showed himself. He wore what looked like an orderly uniform. Marie and Eva surmised this man had worked at Marymoor, while the other man had been a patient. This new ghost started screaming at the pair, threatening to get Randal if they didn't leave. When Eva asked him to get Molly, the man screamed an obscenity, threw a large rock at her, and vanished.

Eva turned around and looked down at the rock that had flown through her body. "This does not look good."

"I suppose we can look at the bright side," Marie chirped.

"Bright side?" Eva asked.

"Even if Ian's father arrives tomorrow and escrow has already closed, once he steps on this property, he may not see ghosts, but I imagine he'll notice the rocks flying about and tree limbs falling. That will prevent him from building here."

THIRTEEN

Danielle's cat, Max, looked up from where he napped under the kitchen table in time to see Marie's spirit materialize by the door to the side yard. He glanced over to Danielle, who stood at the counter, her back to Marie. Looking to Marie, Max yawned. Their eyes met briefly, and they exchanged a silent hello. Closing his eyes, Max yawned again and resumed his afternoon nap.

"Hello, Danielle," Marie greeted her hesitantly.

Stopping what she was doing, Danielle turned from the counter and faced Marie. "Well, hello. Where have you been the last few days?"

Marie shrugged. "Here and there. When are Ian's and Lily's families arriving?"

"Sometime this afternoon."

"I was just across the street. I stopped in to see Connor. He was waking up from his nap. We played a few minutes before Lily came in to change his diaper and get him up. I'm going to miss that little guy the next two weeks."

Danielle frowned. "Why are you going to miss him?"

"It's probably best if I stay away while the grandparents are here. It might cause some problems," Marie explained. "Especially now that he's starting to say a few words."

Danielle smiled. "Yeah, they might wonder who Connor is

waving or smiling at. But I don't think it's necessary to stay away when they're over here and Connor is home."

"Perhaps." Marie let out a sigh.

"Does that mean you aren't coming to his birthday party?" Danielle asked.

"I don't think so. Eva and I discussed it, and we decided it is best for Connor to spend the day with the living."

Danielle started to respond, but Marie cut her off with a hasty goodbye and disappeared.

"Well, goodbye to you too," Danielle grumbled. She started to turn back to the kitchen counter when Lily burst excitedly through the door.

"Hey, Dani!" Lily greeted her.

"You just missed Marie," Danielle told her.

"I wouldn't have seen her anyway," Lily said with a laugh as she closed the door behind her. She walked into the kitchen and said, "Mom just called. They're about twenty minutes from Frederickport. Wanted to let you know."

Danielle grinned at Lily. "You excited to have all the families together again?"

"Excited and nervous." Lily took a seat at the kitchen table. "Before they get here, I wanted to know, have you bought that pregnancy test yet?"

"No, not yet. I'll tell you when I do," Danielle promised.

"I don't know why you're waiting. I'd think you'd want to know. It doesn't mean you have to tell anyone yet. Just me."

Abandoning what she had been doing at the counter, Danielle poured her and Lily each a glass of lemonade and walked to the table. She handed one glass to Lily and then took a seat across from her.

"Don't worry, when I take it, you'll be one of the first to know."

"I'd better."

Danielle grinned and then said, "Marie told me she's going to avoid being around Connor while the grandparents are here." Danielle took a sip of her drink.

"I think that might be a good idea. I keep wondering what I'm going to do when Connor gets a little older and starts saying more than ma and dadda. And frankly, when he says ma, I'm not sure if Connor is trying to say Marie or mama. I'm just grateful none of them live in Frederickport. It's enough having Kelly live here."

"When are Ian's parents arriving?" Danielle asked.

"Ian says they should get here later tonight. I still don't get why they're driving. Of course, my parents are driving too." Lily shrugged and sipped her lemonade.

"Some people just don't like to fly."

"Nah, his parents don't have an aversion to flying. They've done a lot of traveling. They've been to Europe a few times. But now that John's retired, maybe they just wanted to take a road trip."

"They're both retired now, right?"

"Yep. He officially retired a couple of months ago. Ian keeps saying he hopes his mom doesn't kill him." Lily laughed.

"Why does he say that?"

"I like Ian's parents, but they're both kinda hyper. I don't think either of them can just kick back and relax, do nothing. And they're kind of bossy; they like to tell everyone how to do things. I imagine it'll be hard for June with John underfoot. I have this vision of him deciding to rearrange her kitchen and putting labels on everything like he has in his shop." Lily laughed at the thought.

"Ahh… didn't June rearrange Ian's kitchen when they were here for your wedding?"

"Yep. And when they were here later, she seemed rather annoyed that I had moved things around," Lily said.

"But why would John rearrange her kitchen?" Danielle asked with a frown.

"Because it's something I can see him doing, too. And while June had no problem changing someone else's kitchen around without asking, she would not appreciate the same favor."

"What does he have planned for his retirement?"

"Ian thinks they might get a motorhome and do some traveling."

"That way they can come see you more," Danielle teased.

Lily grinned sheepishly. "You make me feel so guilty."

"How so?" Danielle frowned.

"Ideally, I think it would be wonderful for Connor to grow up living close to his grandparents, both of them. But I am also a realist, and frankly, life is easier without those complications."

"I've always heard marriage problems typically stem from money problems, sex problems or in-law problems," Danielle said.

"Ian and I definitely don't have the first two—and I'm working to avoid those in-law problems." Lily paused a moment and asked,

"How did you get along with Lucas's parents?" Lucas was Danielle's first husband.

Danielle considered the question for a moment. "Lucas's dad wasn't in the picture much. They divorced when he was a toddler. I only saw him a couple of times in all the years during our marriage. His mother was always very sweet to me and not the type to butt in. I feel a little guilty not keeping in touch with her. She absolutely doted on Lucas. And I suppose considering some mothers like that can be a nightmare mother-in-law, she never was. Everything felt so awkward after he died, and I think she felt as awkward as I did. But it thrilled her when I gave her the portrait. I also think she was a little sad when I gave her the wedding rings back. But they had been her mother's, and I figured she might want to give them to one of her sister's kids."

HE HAD CLIMBED out of the box after they put it in the back of the truck. From what he overheard; they were off to see Lily. His Lily. There was lots of room in the back of the truck, and he rather enjoyed the drive and seeing all the sights along the way. They had stopped once at a motel, and she had insisted he carry the box into the motel with them so no one would steal it. The man had removed it from the truck before he had time to climb back in, so he ended up spending the night alone in the truck's bed. But he was able to watch the stars overhead, which he rather enjoyed.

In the morning he watched the sun come up, and the couple came out of the motel room, the man carrying the large box, and the woman with a couple of suitcases. They had locked some other boxes in the truck's cab, but when they returned in the morning, they moved the boxes to the truck bed again.

He wasn't sure how long they had been driving when he caught the salty scent of the ocean. He closed his eyes, vaguely remembering the smell. It conjured up long-ago memories of his parents and a trip to the beach. He remembered building sandcastles, something he later taught Lily to do. He wondered if they might build sandcastles again.

Momentarily lost in memories, he opened his eyes when he heard the truck stop. Hurriedly, he climbed back into the box of toys and waited. He wondered, had they arrived?

CONNOR SAT on the living room floor, playing with building blocks, while his family's golden retriever napped nearby, and his father sat on the sofa, reading the newspaper. Noise from the front door broke the silence and caught Connor's attention. Sadie jumped up and dashed to the door. Connor heard voices. Adult voices.

His father tossed the paper he had been reading to the floor, stood up from the couch, and followed Sadie. More voices and commotion came from the entry hall. Connor watched curiously, waiting for the people attached to the voices to walk into the living room.

"Connor, look who's here!" his mother's voice called out as she walked into the room, followed by two older people, his father, and the dog. The man carried a large box. Connor frowned and studied the new arrivals. They looked vaguely familiar. He had seen them before.

"There is my baby!" the woman squealed before hurrying toward him. Connor opened his eyes wide in surprise as the woman swooped him up from the floor and squeezed him tightly. His first inclination was to cry. But she was soft, and her familiar scent evoked a faint memory of cookies. This woman had given him cookies before, and he wondered... did she have cookies with her?

"Oh, he's gotten so big!" the woman said as she sat down on the sofa with Connor on her lap.

"I think he remembers you," the man said, setting the box on the floor near the sofa.

"Of course he does," the woman cooed while peppering kisses over Connor's face.

Connor looked at his parents. Both smiled in his direction. He glanced over to Sadie, who sat next to the man, her tail wagging. Feeling safe, Connor looked back at the woman. She stared in his face, jabbering words he did not understand. But one thing he knew, he wanted a cookie. Connor reached out, grabbed her right cheek with one chubby fist, and used his other hand to gently pat her left cheek. *I want cookie*, he thought.

The woman laughed and kissed his hands. Connor frowned. *Where is cookie?*

"What's in the box?" Connor heard his mother say. He looked to the large cardboard box sitting on the floor.

"Your mother insisted we bring it," the man said.

"What is it?" Lily asked.

The woman nodded toward the box. "Go ahead, open it."

Connor wondered if that was where she hid the cookies. He watched as the man opened the box for his mother.

Lily looked inside the now open cardboard container. "Are you serious? You still have these?" She laughed.

To Connor's surprise, a little boy climbed out of the box.

"Where is Lily?" the little boy asked, now standing in front of the sofa, looking around. All the adults ignored Connor and the boy. Instead, they focused on the objects Lily pulled from the box.

The boy looked at Connor and asked, "Who are you?"

Connor smiled at the boy. The boy smiled back.

"You look like Lily. But you aren't Lily, are you?" the boy asked.

Connor gurgled.

Spying the blocks on the floor, the little boy asked, "You want to play blocks?"

Connor watched as the boy sat by his blocks. Wiggling, Connor tried to get off the woman's lap. She held on tighter.

SEEING her mother struggle with Connor, Lily said, "Mom, why don't you put him down. Unless he's sleepy, he's not much of a lap sitter. And he just woke up from a nap not long ago."

Doing as her daughter suggested, Tammy gently helped Connor off her lap and onto the floor. The adults watched as Connor crawled to the pile of blocks and sat down. He picked up one block and then held out his hand, as if offering it to someone. But no one was there.

"I just had a flash of déjà vu," Tammy said.

"What do you mean?" Lily asked.

"Not only does he look just like you at that age, you used to do that with your toys too."

"Do what?" Ian asked.

"She always looked like she was playing with someone," Lily's father said.

"Yes, Lily's imaginary friend." Tammy laughed.

FOURTEEN

L ily and Ian visited with Lily's parents for another hour while Connor played contently with blocks on the floor nearby.

Looking down at her grandson, Tammy smiled and said, "He certainly entertains himself."

"Yes, he does..." Lily murmured. She narrowed her eyes and studied her son. *Is Marie here?* Lily wondered. Connor normally played contently when being entertained by someone. When left to his own devices, he often got fussy or into mischief. She remembered what Marie had told Danielle about not coming around while the grandparents were there—*Did she change her mind?*

"I suppose we should take our suitcases over to our room and say hi to Dani and Walt," Tammy said, interrupting Lily's train of thought.

"Oh, sure," Lily said, standing up. "I'll take you over there."

"Shouldn't you call her first, let them know we're on our way?" Tammy asked.

"I just texted them," Ian said.

"You young people and your texting," Lily's father, Gene, said. He stood up. "Are we all going over?"

"Lily can take you," Ian said. "I'll stay here with Connor. I need to finish making dinner."

Now standing, Tammy looked at Ian and said, "I do love a man who cooks."

84

"Me too." Lily grinned. She reached up and kissed Ian's cheek.

"Hey, I barbecue!" Gene reminded her.

"Did I say I didn't love you?" Tammy chuckled. She walked over to Connor, leaned down, and dropped a kiss on his head.

TWENTY MINUTES LATER, Lily left her parents at Marlow House to settle in while she returned home to help Ian with dinner and to feed Connor. Walt had helped her father carry the suitcases to their room on the second floor.

"Lily said you wouldn't mind being upstairs," Danielle told Tammy after Lily left, and Gene was in the bathroom. The two women stood in the hallway on the second floor. Walt had returned to the first floor.

"We don't mind," Tammy said. "I know June has that knee issue, so the first-floor bedroom is better for her. This is very kind of you to let us stay here. I wish you would let us pay you something."

"Don't be silly," Danielle said. "Anyway, if you paid and our neighbor Pearl found out, she would throw a fit."

Tammy chuckled. "Yes, Lily told me about that neighbor of yours. I'm sorry she forced you to close your B and B."

Danielle shrugged. "Actually, it all worked out. When Walt and I came back from our honeymoon, we considered closing it anyway. I still enjoy having guests—like with you and Ian's parents—but we decided we no longer wanted to be tied down with strangers coming and going."

"Yes, I've heard about some things that have happened," Tammy said with a shiver.

Danielle grinned. "Well, it makes things exciting."

"I suppose."

"I'm sorry Lily's brother and sister weren't able to come. I know she was hoping they could make it."

"Glad you mentioned that—I almost forgot!" Tammy glanced at her watch. "I need to call the Seahorse Motel."

"The Seahorse?" Danielle frowned.

"Yes. Laura called us right before we got to Frederickport. She was able to work out something with her boss, so she's coming. She'll be flying in tomorrow morning. Her father is picking her up at the airport. Don't tell Lily, it's a surprise. I wish Cory could have made it, but he couldn't get off work."

"That's great. But why do you have to call the Seahorse Motel?" Danielle asked.

"I need to get her a room."

"She can stay here; we have plenty of room."

"But it's such short notice. I didn't want to be an imposition."

"Don't be silly. Anyway, Joanne put clean sheets on all the beds yesterday, so we have a room all ready for her," Danielle insisted.

HIS CAR'S GPS took him right to the property. He parked along the sidewalk in front of the chain-link fence.

"There it is," John announced, turning off the engine.

"Oh, I love it!" June gazed at their future home's building site.

"And it is officially ours," he said proudly.

June noticed the For Sale sign, no longer standing but lying on the ground. "It doesn't look like they bothered to put up a Sold sign. They just pushed the For Sale sign over."

"I imagine the listing agent will come by and pick it up later," John said while taking off his seatbelt. "You want to walk around before we head over to Ian's?"

June glanced at the late afternoon sky. "Sure." She unbuckled her seatbelt.

"THEY JUST KEEP COMING," Waylon told Molly. They stood at the fence, watching the man and woman approach. When the man looked in Molly's direction, she waved.

"Why did you do that?" Waylon asked.

"I wanted to know if they can see us. I don't think they can," Molly said. "Either that, or he's ignoring us."

"I don't understand. Why do some people see us, and others don't?" Waylon asked.

Molly shrugged. "I don't know."

Waylon nodded toward the couple. "They're coming in."

They watched the man open the gate for the woman. She walked onto the property first. The man followed her inside. Waylon picked up a rock and threw it at the man before Molly could stop him. To Waylon's annoyance, the rock behaved like a boomerang, and before reaching its target, it changed course and flew back to Waylon, without either the man or woman noticing the incoming—and outgoing—missile.

"I hate when they do that," Waylon grumbled.

"THIS IS BEAUTIFUL." June stood at the building site and looked around. "I can't believe how much land there is. And you can't subdivide it?"

"Apparently not. Which I'm sure makes you happy."

"When are we going to tell the kids?" June asked.

"We should do it tomorrow. We can tell them we want to take them for a little ride, bring them over here. Show them the property and then tell them."

HE SAT in the bathtub with Connor, a pile of bath toys bobbing in the water between them. Connor laughed, picked up a rubber truck, and handed it to him. When he tried to take hold of the truck, it fell through his hands and back into the water, making a splash. Connor giggled, and he smiled.

"You're as much fun as Lily," he said. "You look a lot like her."

TAMMY STOOD in the bathroom doorway with her daughter, watching her grandson play in the bath.

"Connor is a good-natured little guy," Tammy said. "He reminds me so much of you at that age."

"How so?" Lily leaned against the doorjamb, her eyes still focused on her son.

"You were like that, always happy. Always entertaining yourself. Now, your sister, she got bored easily, always wanted to be entertained. As for your brother, he was too busy getting into mischief." Tammy laughed at the memory.

"I have to say, Connor isn't always like this. He has his moments."

New voices came from down the hallway. Lily paused and looked that way. She glanced back to Connor and said, "Sounds like Kelly is here."

"She's having dinner with us?" Tammy asked.

"Yes."

"When are Ian's parents going to be here?" Tammy asked.

"They should be here soon. His father called him about an hour ago, said they should be here before it gets dark. I hope you don't mind eating so late."

"No, it's fine. Your father and I always end up eating later this time of year."

"We just thought it would be nice if we could all eat together when everyone gets here." Still leaning on the doorjamb, Lily continued to watch Connor while she talked to her mother.

"Dani and Walt aren't coming?" Tammy asked.

"Not tonight."

FRESHLY BATHED and dressed in his flannel pajamas, Connor found himself being passed around the room like a football. His new friend sat in the corner of the living room, watching the commotion. New people kept coming into the house. There was the cookie lady and the man who had brought the box with his new friend. His aunt Kelly was here, along with another older couple. He had seen them before. The woman, like the cookie lady, kept giving him kisses, tweaking his cheek, and kept telling him to, "Say grandma."

This new lady snatched him from the cookie lady and plopped him on her lap as she sat on the sofa. She kept jabbering unrecognizable words in his ear when Sadie came up to him. Connor smiled at the dog, waved his hand in her direction, and was awarded with a slobbery, wet kiss across his open mouth.

"Ian!" the woman gasped, pushing the dog away. "You need to put Sadie somewhere."

Ian, who stood by the bookshelf and had been talking to his father and father-in-law, stopped talking and turned to face his mother, who sat on the sofa with Tammy, Connor on her lap.

"What's wrong?" Ian asked.

"Sadie just licked Connor's mouth!" June took a tissue from her nearby purse and wiped her grandson's mouth. He resisted the assault and tried squirming away.

"Sadie always does that, Mom," Kelly said.

"It's not sanitary. You really need to restrict the dog's access to the baby. It isn't safe," June said.

With a sigh, Ian walked to his mother and picked up Connor. "He's fine, Mom. But it's past his bedtime. I need to put him down."

June watched as Ian took Connor from her. He let everyone kiss his son goodnight before carrying him to the nursery, Lily trailing behind him.

Tammy stood and picked up the dirty dessert dishes left on the coffee table and carried them to the kitchen. Gene went to the restroom, leaving Kelly alone in the living room with her parents.

"It's too bad Joe couldn't have come tonight," her father said.

"Like I told you, he had to work tonight," Kelly reminded him.

———————

ALONE IN THE nursery with her husband and son, Lily changed Connor's diaper while Ian found the Pooh bear to put in the crib. After finishing the diapering, Lily glanced over to where the dry-erase board had been hanging. They used it to communicate with Marie, but they had decided at the last minute to remove it before the parents arrived.

"This is going to be a fun week," Ian said dryly as he handed his son the stuffed animal.

Lily chuckled. "Poor Sadie. Maybe Walt can talk to her about not licking Connor when your mom is around."

"That might be a good idea."

"You had dogs when you were a kid. Did your mom get that upset when they licked you?" Lily asked.

"I don't remember. But when I was a kid, they kept our dogs in the yard."

"Dogs belong in the house," Lily said.

"I agree. But at least my parents didn't keep our dogs on a chain or rope, like some people. We always had a fenced yard and a nice doghouse. Dad saw to that." Ian leaned over the crib and gave his son a quick kiss. "Night, buddy."

"I'll be out in a minute," Lily said as Ian headed toward the door.

"You just want some quiet time," Ian teased.

Lily giggled and watched as Ian left the nursery. She turned back to Connor and smiled softly.

"You were sure a good boy tonight. Impressed the grandparents." She leaned over and kissed Connor's brow. Instead of leaving, she continued to watch her son. Lily frowned when Connor picked up his Pooh bear and seemed to offer it to someone.

"Marie?" Lily said aloud. With a frown, Lily stared at the foot of the crib where her son focused his attention. "Marie, are you here? If you are, make Winnie fly."

"Lily, who are you talking to?" June asked from the open doorway.

FIFTEEN

Turning quickly from the crib, Lily faced her mother-in-law. Momentarily speechless, Lily wondered what exactly June had overheard.

"Lily? Are you okay?" June asked, her voice softening.

"Um... you just startled me," Lily said, laughing nervously.

"Who were you talking to?"

Behind Lily, Connor jabbered, "Bah bah..."

Glancing to her son and back to June, Lily said, "I was talking to Connor, of course."

With a frown, June walked all the way into the room. "I heard you say, 'Marie, are you here? If you are, make Winnie fly.'"

Lily stared at June for a moment and then blurted, "I was telling Connor a story. Yes, I was telling Connor a story. A bedtime story. I like to tell him a story at bedtime." Lily turned back to Connor and looked into the crib. He smiled up at her and yawned.

"Sounded like an interesting story," June said, now standing next to Connor by the crib. "What book is it from?"

"Um... it's not from a book. I just like to make up stories for Connor," Lily lied.

"I used to read to Ian and Kelly when they were little," June said, now looking into the crib. She reached out and gently brushed her fingertips over Connor's brow, studying the child. "I like to think that's why both of them love to read now."

"I read books to him too."

"I'm trying to figure out who Connor looks like. When he was younger, I thought I saw Ian in him, but now, not so much. Who does he look like?" June frowned down at her grandson.

"I suppose he looks like me at that age. That's if I can believe my baby pictures and what Mom tells me." Lily grinned.

Withdrawing her hand from the crib, June looked at Lily and frowned. "I suppose that's possible; he might look like you," June muttered.

"We should probably leave so Connor can get to sleep," Lily suggested.

LILY SAT ALONE in the corner of her living room, talking on the phone to Danielle. The grandparents had all gone across the street to retire for the night, and Ian was in the shower.

"Yes, they're all in their rooms, and their lights are out," Danielle told Lily. "I imagine they're exhausted from the long trip. How has it gone so far?"

"Aside from Sadie licking Connor's mouth and me talking to Marie, everything's peachy."

"What?"

Lily told Danielle what had occurred in Connor's bedroom.

"I'd be surprised if Marie changed her mind," Danielle said. "But I suppose it's possible."

"If she did, she obviously left before I asked her to give me a sign."

"At least you came up with a plausible explanation," Danielle said.

"I picked that up from hanging around you all the time."

Danielle chuckled.

"But you know what really annoys me?" Lily asked.

"What?"

"June seemed to not quite understand why Connor looks like me."

"You are his mother," Danielle reminded her.

"Exactly!" Lily said.

"I'm sure she didn't mean anything. You're just feeling overwhelmed having all the family here. It's only two weeks, Lily. Try to enjoy the visit and let the other stuff slide," Danielle suggested.

"I know, you're right. Anyway, having them all come for Connor's birthday was my idea. I don't know why I'm complaining," Lily grumbled.

"THIS IS SO nice of you, making us breakfast," Tammy told Danielle the next morning as the grandparents gathered in the Marlow House dining room with Walt and Danielle. She snatched a cinnamon roll from the basket on the table. Tammy sat next to her husband at the table, with June and John across from them, and Walt and Danielle at the ends of the table.

"Ian and Lily aren't coming over?" June asked after taking a sip of her coffee.

"No. This morning Lily wanted to run down to Old Salts to order Connor's birthday cake, and Ian had some work he had to get off to his editor," Danielle explained.

"Did Lily take Connor with her?" June asked.

"No. He's at home with Ian," Danielle said.

"Someone has to watch Connor while Ian works. Perhaps I should go over there?" June suggested.

"Ian watches Connor all the time while he works," Danielle said.

June arched her brows. "Really? And what is Lily doing?"

"Probably watching soap operas and eating bonbons," Tammy snarked.

June frowned at Tammy.

Gene chuckled. He reached over, patted his wife's hand, and told June, "You'll have to get used to my wife's odd sense of humor."

Tammy chuckled and took a bite of her cinnamon roll.

"I just assumed, since Lily is no longer teaching, she spends most of her time taking care of Connor. After all, Ian has a job," June said.

"We need to leave soon," Gene piped up, hoping to divert the conversation, for fear his wife might pick up her fork and use it to harpoon June.

"Where are you going?" John asked.

"We're driving to Portland," Gene explained.

Tammy looked at Danielle and said, "I decided I would go with him. I told Lily we wanted to go shopping in Portland for Connor's present."

"You're going shopping?" June asked.

"Actually, we're going to the airport to pick up our other daughter," Gene said.

"But it's a surprise. So please don't tell Lily or Ian," Tammy said quickly, flashing her husband a reprimanding scowl.

"That will be nice. Lily mentioned last night she was sorry her sister and brother wouldn't be here," June said.

"I guess there will be lots of surprises for Lily and Ian today, and it isn't even their birthday," John said with a chuckle.

"What do you mean?" Tammy asked.

"We have a surprise for them, too," John said with a grin.

"What kind of surprise?" Gene asked.

It was June's turn to flash a reprimanding frown to her husband before saying, "We really need to tell Ian and Kelly first."

"THIS WORKS OUT PERFECTLY," John told his wife when they returned to their room after breakfast.

"I agree. When Tammy and Gene drive to Portland, it will give us a chance to be alone with Ian and Kelly and show them the property. I can't wait to see their expressions when they realize we're moving to Frederickport!"

"You're leaving out someone," John scolded.

June frowned. "Who?"

"Lily. Of course we'll ask her to come with us," John said, now sitting on the side of the bed, changing his shoes.

"I've been thinking about that," June began, sitting next to her husband. "Someone has to watch Connor anyway. It would be nice if we could have some time alone with our son and daughter. I know Joe is working today, so he wouldn't be able to come with us anyway. And if Joe won't be with us when we tell the kids, I think it's okay if Lily doesn't go."

"Lily is our daughter-in-law," John reminded her.

"And Joe will be our son-in-law," June countered.

"He isn't yet. Anyway, there's no reason Lily can't come with us and bring Connor along."

"Why don't we ask Lily if she would like to take a drive with us —or if she would rather stay home with Connor. Let her decide," June asked sweetly.

"For one thing, it's not just a drive. And she won't know that."

"It's going to be crowded in our car, with the four of them in the back seat, especially with the car seat. I suppose we could go in their car, but that would ruin the surprise if Ian drives."

"Fine." John stood. "Ask her if she wants to go, or would she rather stay home with Connor."

LILY WALKED out of the nursery with Connor after changing his diaper, to find her in-laws had come over from Marlow House.

"Did you get the birthday cake ordered?" John asked cheerfully. He stood by the breakfast bar with Ian and his wife. They all turned to look at Lily as she entered the room. Just as she set Connor on the floor, June picked him up and gave the squirming boy a hug, refusing to let go.

"I did. They make awesome birthday cakes," Lily said. "Actually, they make awesome everything."

"I always made Ian and Kelly their birthday cakes," June said, giving Connor a little jiggle to get him to stop wiggling. "Kelly always wanted German chocolate."

"My dad wants to take us for a drive; he wants to show us something," Ian said.

"What?" Lily asked.

Ian shrugged. "They won't say. We're picking up Kelly."

"Would you like to go with us?" June asked. "Of course, we'll need to get the car seat."

Lily glanced from June to Ian and considered the offer for a moment.

"I THINK they wanted some alone time with their kids," Lily told Danielle on the phone fifteen minutes later. Her in-laws had just left with Ian to pick up Kelly. Lily leaned back on the sofa in the living room while Connor sat on the floor, playing with his toys. "I don't think they really wanted me to go. I get it. And frankly, moving the car seat from our car to theirs would be a pain. Ian tried to talk them into taking our car, but they insisted they had to drive. That's when I realized they really didn't want me to go."

Lily talked to Danielle a few minutes longer. When she ended the phone call, she looked down at Connor and noticed he continued to entertain himself in the same way he had last night. She watched as he offered a toy to someone who was not there—*or is she?*

"Marie?" Lily blurted. "Ian's parents left, so you can give me a sign. If you are here, please give me a sign."

Nothing happened.

Lily continued to stare at her son. Finally, she shrugged and said, "Cool, the kid can entertain himself."

"WHERE ARE WE GOING?" Kelly asked as her father drove away from her house. She sat in the back seat with her brother.

"We have a little surprise for you both," June said.

"What kind of surprise?" Kelly asked anxiously. She looked at her brother. "Do you know what it is?"

Ian shrugged. "I have no clue."

A few moments later, they turned down the street leading to the Marymoor property.

"Did you take a wrong turn?" Ian called out.

"Why do you say that?" June asked with a giggle. The next moment, John pulled his car up in front of the Marymoor property and parked.

"What are we doing here?" Kelly asked, looking warily to the fenced property and back to her brother.

John turned off the ignition, and he and his wife each unbuckled their seatbelts. Wearing silly grins, they turned in their seats to face their son and daughter in the back seat.

"What are we doing here?" Ian asked.

"You both know I retired," John said.

"Yeah. Why did you park here?" Kelly asked.

"With both of you living in Frederickport—our only children, and now our grandson. And with Kelly marrying Joe, I don't imagine they'll be leaving the area, considering his job…" June rambled.

"What are you trying to say, Mom?" Ian asked.

"What your mother is trying to say is," John said, "we sold our house and are planning to move to Frederickport."

"You're selling your house?" Ian asked incredulously.

"No. We sold our house. In fact, before we left yesterday, the movers had already been to the house and packed up our belongings, everything we own—aside from what we brought with us," John explained.

"You sold your house?" Kelly gasped. "Where is your stuff?"

"It's in storage for now until we get settled," June told her.

"Where are you going to live?" Kelly asked.

"We obviously can't live at Marlow House indefinitely," John said with a laugh. "We plan to find a rental to move into while I build our forever home."

"Where are you building?" Kelly asked.

"Haven't you figured that out yet?" With a flourish, June used one hand to point at the Marymoor property. "Guess what your father and I bought."

SIXTEEN

The weather forecaster claimed the morning clouds would move aside for a clear and sunny afternoon. The clouds had another idea. Not only did they stick around, but they grew darker, more ominous, and within minutes of June announcing they had purchased the Marymoor property, rain began to fall.

"Oh, drat, I wanted us all to get out and walk around," June moaned. The rain pelting the car's roof intensified.

"Did you really buy this?" Kelly asked. "Or are you just thinking of making an offer?"

Ian remained silent in the back seat, listening.

"It closed escrow yesterday," John told her.

"Why didn't you say something?" Ian asked, looking warily at the property through the car window.

"We wanted to surprise you, of course," June said. She frowned at her son. "You don't seem very excited we're moving to Frederickport."

Ian looked at his mother and smiled weakly. "Mom, it isn't that. It's simply a lot to process. You tell us you already sold your house, the house we grew up in. You already moved out and bought property here without saying anything to us."

"We wanted to surprise you," John said.

"Well, you did that," Ian said dryly.

"But did you really buy this property? How did you even find it?" Kelly asked.

"I've been checking out the real estate websites, and when the listing popped up, I called that real estate friend of yours."

Kelly frowned. "What real estate friend?"

"Adam Nichols," John told her.

"Adam sold you this?" Ian asked.

"I figured we should work with someone you trust," John said.

"And he actually sold you this?" Ian asked again.

"Is there a problem?" June asked.

"Aside from everyone saying this place is cursed or haunted?" Kelly asked.

John laughed. "Yes, Adam told us about that. Since we don't believe in ghosts or curses, it's not really a problem." John laughed again.

"I wish we could get out, and you could see it," June said. "We stopped by last night, after we got here, and looked around. But we wanted to get over to your house, so we really haven't had a chance to walk it completely. I can't believe we could find a lot this size so close to the beach. Of course, it's not on the water like yours. But frankly, I wouldn't want to be right on the beach, pestered by tourists walking up to your house. Not enough privacy."

Ian silently listened to his parents as he gazed out the window, staring at the property.

***

ON THE OTHER side of the fence, Molly and Waylon stood in the rain and watched the people sitting in the car.

"They're the ones who were here yesterday," Molly said.

"I tried to throw a rock at them, and it just came back at me. I should try again," he said.

"Go ahead. But I bet it'll come back like the other one."

"Maybe not," Waylon said, looking around for a rock, oblivious to the rain falling through him. Instead of a rock, he focused on a boulder—something larger and more substantial. He assumed Molly would not approve, but he didn't intend to tell her. She would see it herself, but by then there would be nothing she could do. This size could not come back to him, Waylon told himself. He would like to see it smash the hood of the car. That would keep the people from coming back and bothering them.

IAN LISTENED to his sister and parents discuss the land's history while his gaze remained focused on the property in question. Movement by the fence caught his attention. Narrowing his eyes, he studied an object. It lifted from the ground and over the top of the fence. At first, Ian thought it was a large paper sack, taking flight from the early afternoon breeze.

The next moment he realized it was not a large sack, but a small boulder, now hurling in the car's direction. The other people in the car with him failed to notice the incoming missile.

Ian almost called out but froze when the boulder stopped in midair and hovered there a moment before changing course, landing a few feet from its original location.

"Ian, you really don't seem happy we're moving here," Ian heard his mother say.

Ian looked to his mother and swallowed nervously. "Why don't we head home, and we can discuss it there. This rain doesn't look like it's going to stop, so we won't be able to get out."

A few minutes later, after John started up the engine and pulled out into the street, Ian noticed his mother, now turned around in her seat, her back to him. She looked out the windshield, her arms folded across her chest in a pout.

As they drove back to his house, Ian removed his seatbelt and leaned forward, closer to his parents in the front seat.

"Of course we're thrilled you'll be living here," Ian told his mother. "It's not that. But it is a lot for us to take in at once. I just think it would be better for you to buy an existing house instead of Dad spending the next year building something. You could use it as your home base."

June turned to her son and frowned. "What do you mean our home base?"

Ian shrugged. "I assumed you'd both want to do more traveling when you retired. Dad always talked about buying a motorhome, seeing more of the country. Why spend the next year in a rental while Dad is busy building a house? And it would probably take longer than two years to build. You should travel and enjoy your-selves while you still can."

June flashed Ian a smile. "There is time for that. We aren't that old. Anyway, I'm going to be busy planning your sister's wedding. There is so much to do."

"Planning my wedding?" Kelly muttered under her breath, her forehead drawing into a frown.

"And this way Lily can go back to teaching in the fall," June added.

"Mom, kids are already back to school here," Kelly told her.

June shrugged. "Well, she can substitute, then. I'm sure they need substitutes, and that will probably make it easier to get her own class again when school starts next year."

"Why would you moving to Frederickport mean Lily would go back to teaching?" Ian asked.

Still turned in her seat so she could see her son and daughter, June's smile broadened. "Because I'm here, of course. I can babysit Connor. And help take care of you."

"Um… take care of me?" Ian asked.

"Certainly. You can't be watching an active little boy while trying to work. And you need to eat proper meals. When I come over to take care of Connor, I could make you lunch so you can keep work-ing. And before I leave, I could get dinner started for Lily. I'm sure she would love that. Who wouldn't? Of course, I really need to do something about that kitchen of yours. I had it all organized when we stayed with you during your wedding. But I could see last night poor Lily has it all disorganized. She can use my help. I don't think her mother taught her much about properly organizing her home. I suspect Tammy might have been a hippy when she was younger."

Speechless, Ian stared numbly at his mother. June flashed him a smile and then turned back in her seat while saying, "Ian, dear, put your seatbelt back on."

Ian flopped back in the seat in time to hear his sister let out a snort. He turned to Kelly, who leaned back in the seat, her arms crossed over her chest. Kelly arched her brows at her brother and whispered in a snarky tone, "Listen to Mommy and put your seat-belt on."

Absently Ian did as Kelly suggested.

Kelly let out another snort and whispered, "I was freaking when she said she was planning my wedding. But then I heard what she has in store for poor Lily."

"She can't be serious," Ian whispered back.

Kelly arched her brows again. "She is our mother. What do you think?"

Ian groaned and slumped back in the seat.

They were silent for the rest of the ride back to Ian's house. Just before John pulled into the driveway, the rain stopped.

"That was good timing," John said. A moment later, he parked and turned off the engine.

June unfastened her seatbelt first and turned around to face Ian and Kelly. Hesitantly she asked, "You are happy we're moving to Frederickport?"

"Of course, Mom, but you hit us with a lot at once," Ian said.

"I don't understand." June frowned.

"I sort of agree with Ian," Kelly said. "I don't know why you want to build a house there. And seriously, that property has a horrible reputation." Kelly paused a moment and looked at her father, who turned in his seat, looking back at them, his seatbelt off. "Dad, haven't you always told us that when building a house, you need to consider resale? From what I understand, that property was off and on the market for years. And no one wanted it. After a house gets built on it, it could have the same problem."

"Resale is not an issue," John said. "We plan to make it our forever home. I don't see you two ever leaving Frederickport, considering Joe and Lily. If you're here, this is where we want to be."

"And we plan to live a long life," June said. "So when you inherit the house, I'm sure whatever stigma the property had will be long forgotten by then. Now, let's go tell Lily. I hope she's a little more excited about all this and not such a naysayer like you two."

"I have one favor to ask you," Ian told his mother.

"What's that?" June asked.

"When you give Lily your news, please don't say anything about her going back to teaching," Ian asked.

June frowned. "Why not?"

"Like Ian said, this is a lot to take in," Kelly said, opening her car door.

SADIE HEARD THEM FIRST. She waited patiently by the front door for it to open, while Lily stood by the breakfast bar, going over a to-do list for Connor's birthday party.

The moment the four walked into the kitchen, Sadie trailing behind them, her tail wagging, Lily announced in a soft voice, "Connor is napping."

John looked down at Sadie and asked, "How did you train Sadie not to bark when we come in? I remember how she used to always bark when anyone came to the door."

"I don't know how they did it," Kelly said, setting her purse on the breakfast bar. "But since Connor was born, she only seems to bark at people when he's awake. It's like she knows she can't bark when he's napping."

"Now, if you could just teach the dog not to lick Connor," June said, setting her purse next to her daughter's.

"What was it your parents wanted to show you?" Lily asked Ian.

"Our parents are moving to Frederickport," Kelly blurted.

Lily's eyes widened. "Really? When?"

"Technically, we are homeless now," June said with a laugh.

Lily looked questioningly to Ian.

"Our parents have sold their house, and the new owners have already moved in," Ian said.

Lily looked at her mother-in-law and asked, "Where is all your stuff?"

"It's in storage," June explained.

"My father plans to build a house and, in the meantime, find something here to rent," Ian explained.

"Wow," Lily muttered. "Um… that's great. But I imagine it'll be hard to find a lot for sale. Not many vacant lots in Frederickport."

"Our parents already bought a lot," Kelly said.

Lily looked to Kelly.

"They bought the Marymoor property," Kelly told her.

SEVENTEEN

"You're joking?" Lily looked from Kelly to her husband.
Ian shook his head in a silent, *no, she is not joking.*

Lily turned to her mother-in-law, who stood frowning from Lily to her two adult children.

"I certainly did not expect this reaction," June blurted. Turning from the group, she marched to the living room, leaving the rest of the family standing by the breakfast bar in the kitchen.

"I'm sorry. I didn't mean to hurt her feelings," Lily said in a rush, glancing nervously to the living room, where her mother-in-law had fled.

"We were so excited to give you this surprise." John looked to Ian and Kelly and said, "Your mother especially. She's the one who wanted to keep it a secret. We never expected this reaction."

"John, it's not about you moving here. It's awesome you're going to be living in Frederickport. It will be wonderful for Connor to grow up with his grandparents nearby," Lily insisted. "The reaction is about the property you bought. It's just that it really has a reputation in Frederickport. That's what threw me."

"She's right, Dad. I really wish you would have discussed this with me first," Ian said.

"Discussed it with you? I didn't realize I needed to ask your permission." John turned and joined his wife in the living room.

Kelly groaned. "I can't believe this is happening." With dramatic

104

flair, Kelly rested her folded arms on the breakfast bar and buried her face in them.

Lily stared at her sister-in-law a moment and then asked, "This isn't just about them buying that lot, is it?"

Kelly peeked up at Lily, her elbows still resting on the breakfast bar. She arched her brows. "Are you seriously okay with them moving here?"

Lily blinked several times, glancing from Kelly to Ian and back to Kelly. "You don't want your parents to move to Frederickport?"

Kelly groaned again and threw her face back in the nest of her arms for a moment before looking back up. After another groan, she said, "Oh, part of me would love my parents living in Frederickport. I miss them, and it really would be nice not to feel guilty when we don't spend Christmas with them."

"And part of you doesn't want them to move up here?" Lily asked.

"Yes, that part of me that doesn't want Mom taking over my wedding or generally trying to manage my life," Kelly explained. "But you still didn't answer my question. Are you seriously okay with them moving to Frederickport?"

Ian wrapped his arm around Lily's shoulders and said, "Lily is exempt from answering those types of questions."

Kelly scowled at her brother. "Why?"

"It's in our contract," Ian teased.

CONNOR WOKE up not long after Ian, Kelly, and their parents arrived back from their drive. Lily changed his diaper and brought him and his stuffed Winnie the Pooh out to the living room. She set them both on the floor. A moment later, June snatched the boy up and onto her lap. He didn't seem to mind, yet a moment later he began shouting, "No, no, no!"

They all looked at June and Connor. Startled, June stared down at her grandson, who continued to yell, "No, no!" while pointing to his Pooh bear on the floor. Connor didn't seem to be upset with his grandmother—he seemed angry with his stuffed animal.

Sadie started barking, yet not at the belligerent child, who continued to shout while waving one chubby hand toward the stuffed animal. The dog stood in the middle of the living room, focused on the space behind Winnie, and kept barking.

"Quiet, Sadie," Ian ordered. Reluctantly the dog sat down, stopped barking, yet continued to stare at the floor behind the stuffed animal.

Lily walked over to June, took Connor from her, and set him on the floor. He stopped screaming and immediately crawled to his stuffed animal. The adults watched as he grabbed Winnie, hugged him to his chest, and looked to the spot where Sadie focused her attention. Waving his hand at the spot, he shouted once more before giving his stuffed animal a tight hug.

"What was that all about?" John stammered.

"I don't understand," June said, shaking her head in confusion. "He seemed fine with me picking him up, honest. He was sitting on my lap all happy, and then it was like he saw something that upset him."

Kelly, who stood silently behind her brother and Lily, watched her nephew a moment and said under her breath, "Sometimes I feel like this house is the one with the issues, not the Marymoor property."

While she didn't intend to be heard, everyone in the room had. They all turned to her.

"What is that supposed to mean?" June asked.

Unprepared for the question, Kelly looked from Connor to her mother and the others. She shrugged.

"June, I'm sorry if you misunderstood me," Lily said, refusing to respond to Kelly's comment. "We're thrilled you're moving to Frederickport. But you have to understand, it just threw us when we heard you bought the Marymoor property. But that's only because it's sort of infamous here in Frederickport."

"I LIED TO MY MOTHER-IN-LAW," Lily told Danielle and Walt thirty minutes later. The three sat in the parlor, with Connor on Lily's lap.

"Lied about what?" Danielle asked.

Lily recounted the events of that morning.

"Well, we heard Adam had sold the property. But none of us imagined it was to Ian's parents," Danielle said.

"I could clobber Adam for not giving Ian the heads-up," Lily grumbled.

"That's not really fair," Danielle reminded her. "From what I understand, John expressly told Adam not to tell anyone about the purchase. Adam had to follow his client's instructions. And if he had told Ian—or you—Ian would have said something to his father, and that would come back and bite Adam."

Lily let out a sigh and sat back on the sofa. "I suppose."

Connor wiggled restlessly on Lily's lap. Silently, Walt stood up, retrieved a bucket of toy blocks from the desk, and dumped them on the floor by the sofa. He took Connor from Lily and set him by the blocks. The small boy happily accepted the offering.

Lily flashed Walt a smile. "Thanks."

Walt smiled at Lily and sat back down.

"You said the sale is final?" Danielle asked.

Lily nodded. "That's what John said."

"What was it you lied to them about?" Danielle asked.

Lily cringed. "About me being all happy about them moving here."

Walt smiled at Lily. "It might be nice to have Connor's grand-parents nearby."

Lily glared at Walt. "Now you're making me feel horrible, like your wife does."

Walt chuckled.

"Ian's parents seem pretty nice," Danielle said.

"You know what I find interesting," Lily said.

"What?" Danielle asked.

"I always assumed Kelly was super close to her mother. Heck, they are so much alike. But from what Kelly was saying, she doesn't seem to be thrilled her parents are moving here. That sorta surprised me."

"Are you close to your mom?" Danielle asked.

"You know I am. Of course, why?" Lily frowned.

"Would you be thrilled if your parents moved to Frederickport?" Danielle asked.

"Happier than Ian's parents moving here." Lily paused a moment and then frowned.

"What?" Danielle asked.

"This is going to drive my mom nuts. The *other* grandma living near Connor, seeing him all the time." Lily groaned.

"Does that mean you would want your parents to move to Frederickport or not?" Walt asked.

Lily considered the question for a moment. Finally, she smiled softly, looking from Walt to Connor, back to Walt. "Honestly? I would probably love it. But the fact is, Mom and Dad would never move here. Laura and Cory both live near them. I have the only grandchild, but someday, I imagine Laura and Cory will give them grandkids. And I understand why June and John want to move here. I totally get it. In fact, I once mentioned to Ian that I bet his parents would be moving up here if Kelly married Joe. He insisted his parents would never move. He was pretty emphatic."

The sound of the front door opening, followed by dog paws racing over the wood floor, and then the sound of the front door closing, interrupted the conversation. They all looked to the open doorway and watched as Sadie raced into the room, followed by Ian a few moments later.

"Figured Sadie would lead me to you," Ian said with a chuckle as he entered the parlor.

"Hi, Ian," Walt and Danielle chorused.

"I assume she told you what is going on," Ian said.

Danielle nodded. "She did."

Ian sat on the sofa next to his wife. Connor looked up at his father and smiled. Ian returned Connor's smile. With a block in one hand, Connor crawled to Ian.

"Where are your parents? Are they coming over here?" Lily asked.

"No. Dad went to the store to pick up something, and I left Kelly with Mom. I can't believe this is happening." Ian reached down to Connor and accepted the block he offered.

"You're that against your parents moving here?" Danielle asked.

"No. In fact, I think it's a good idea for them. I never imagined they would consider moving. But the Marymoor property, that's another thing. I wish Adam had told me before this deal closed." Ian handed the block back to his son. Connor happily accepted it and crawled back to the rest of the blocks.

They discussed Adam for a few minutes, including how reluctant he had been to sell the lot. After Danielle told them what Adam and Mel had experienced at the property, Ian groaned and looked at Lily. "I didn't tell you what I saw over there." Ian then told them how he had witnessed a boulder heading toward their car, only to react like a boomerang and return to where it had come from.

"That's not good," Danielle muttered. "Yet, one thing to remember, no one was hurt. Perhaps Eva is right about spirits being unable to hurt us."

"But I still saw it. And I'm concerned about what this little guy might see over there." Ian nodded to Connor.

"We can't have Connor exposed to such negative energy. Maybe the ghosts can't physically hurt him, but do we really want our son exposed to the spirits of the criminally insane?" Lily asked.

"It's possible my parents will experience something like I did today, and that will prevent them from moving forward with their plans," Ian suggested.

"What if it doesn't? What if your parents never see what's going on? They will want us to come over to their house. They will want to babysit Connor or have him stay overnight. I can't allow that." Lily shook her head emphatically.

While they discussed the negative impact the spirits of Marymoor might have on an innocent child, Sadie walked over to Walt and rested her chin on his knee. Walt looked down at Sadie. Sadie looked up at Walt. Their eyes locked. After a moment Walt broke into the conversation by saying, "Um, we have a more pressing issue than the Marymoor spirits."

"What could be more pressing than that?" Lily asked.

"The ghost currently hanging out at your house and playing with Connor," Walt said.

"What ghost?" Lily squeaked.

"I don't know," Walt said. "But according to Sadie, he wanted to get scissors and remove Winnie the Pooh's stuffing. Connor was not amused."

EIGHTEEN

"A ghost is haunting our child?" Lily gasped.

"Sadie didn't say he was a ghost, but considering she understood what he was thinking, and no one else seemed to see him, that's my guess," Walt said.

"Who is this guy? It is a guy? You said it is a he?" Lily asked.

"Sadie was fairly certain of that," Walt said.

"Who is he?" Ian demanded. "Or more accurately, who was he?"

"No one Sadie recognized," Walt said.

"What does he look like?" Lily asked.

"Unfortunately, dogs aren't very good at giving descriptions," Walt said. "She's fairly certain it is a he, judging by the people she knows. But dogs often rely on smells more—and a ghost does not have a smell."

"That's not entirely accurate," Danielle reminded them.

They all turned to her. Walt asked, "What do you mean?"

Danielle arched a brow at Walt. "When you were a ghost, even the non-mediums picked up the cigar smell."

Walt frowned. "The smell did not come from me. I didn't smell like cigars. And when I wasn't smoking and in a room, no one smelled anything."

Danielle shrugged. "I'm just saying a ghost can be associated with a smell."

"Well, this ghost isn't," Walt said.

"How old is he?" Lily asked. "Is some creepy old man hanging out with our son?"

"Even if it is the ghost of an older man, it wouldn't necessarily mean he's creepy. It could be some kindly old guy who misses his grandchildren," Danielle suggested.

"Really? One who wants to take the stuffing out of Winnie? Sounds like a serial killer to me," Lily snapped.

"I'm just saying—" Danielle began, only to be cut off by Lily.

"Oh no!" Lily looked at Ian. "Did one of those insane ghosts follow your parents to our house? To our son?"

"You haven't seen any objects flying around your house, have you?" Danielle asked.

Lily frowned at Danielle. "What kind of question is that? Obviously if things were flying around, I would have said something."

"I'm just saying, whatever spirit or spirits are causing havoc at the Marymoor site, they obviously have levitation powers, considering what Ian, Adam, and Mel saw over there," Danielle said.

"Perhaps Sadie can give us a clue where he came from," Walt suggested.

They all turned to Walt and silently watched as he and Sadie stared into each other's eyes. After a few minutes, Walt said, "According to Sadie, the ghost arrived at your house around the same time as Ian's parents. She can't remember if he showed up before your parents arrived—or after."

"Why didn't Sadie let us know when she first noticed him?" Lily demanded.

Walt flashed Lily a smile. "And you would have understood her?"

"She could have barked, something. We would have brought her over to talk to you."

"In fairness to Sadie," Ian interrupted, "she did try to tell us. Remember, she was barking at something—and now we know what that something was."

"From what Sadie saw, he and Connor were getting along. Until they had a disagreement about what to do with Connor's stuffed animal," Walt said.

Lily groaned. "Oh no… I saw Connor playing with the ghost."

"What do you mean?" Danielle asked.

"The way Connor was playing, it was like someone was there.

At first, I assumed it was Marie. I figured she changed her mind about staying away. I asked her to give me a sign—like lift something. Nothing. I just figured Connor was entertaining himself."

"It definitely was not Marie," Walt said. "And Connor wasn't entertaining himself."

"We need to find this ghost and make him leave my son alone!" Lily looked around as if expecting to find the ghost hiding in a corner.

"I don't think this ghost followed you guys over here," Danielle said. "I haven't seen anything. He either stayed back at your house or has left already."

"Then you guys need to come back to our house with us, now, and make him leave!" Lily insisted.

"You are forgetting, my mother and sister are over there," Ian said. "And Dad won't be gone that long. Walt and Danielle can't deal with this spirit while my parents are around."

"Then I guess we stay here." Lily stubbornly crossed her arms across her chest and leaned back. "I will not take my son home, where he's exposed to some pervy ghost!"

"We don't know if he's pervy," Danielle reminded her.

"This is why you can't let your parents build on that property," Lily told Ian. "It's bad enough we have stray ghosts wandering through our house from time to time. But Connor visiting a home where the residents of an insane asylum haunt? No way!"

"Let's take care of the ghost currently haunting our son," Ian suggested. "And then we can deal with my parents."

"I wish Marie were here. If Marie were here, she could handle him even if your parents were in the house," Lily said.

"For whatever reason, Marie has decided to make herself scarce while your family is here. But Walt and I can walk over there with you. And even if we can't talk to him while June and Kelly are there, we might see him. That will at least tell us something," Danielle suggested.

"I SUPPOSE Ian and Lily heard about the property by now," Marie said with a sigh. She and Eva sat atop one of the older standing headstones at the Frederickport cemetery.

"You haven't looked in?" Eva asked.

"Not since I went over there to see Connor before his grandparents arrived yesterday. I was hoping we might fix this thing. But those Marymoor spirits refuse to listen."

"I've been giving that serious consideration. They obviously don't intend to tell us anything about themselves or why they continue to haunt the site. I understand one or two confused spirits lingering, but I get the impression there are more over there. It makes me wonder, why? Finding out who they are and why they haunt Marymoor should help us find a way to encourage them to finally move on. And when they do, there will be no reason Ian's parents can't build on the property."

"How do we do that?" Marie asked.

"We start at the museum. See if they have anything on the Marymoor Sanatorium," Eva suggested.

WHEN MARIE and Eva arrived at the museum, they found Millie Samson in the museum gift shop, talking to several visitors.

"Good, Millie's up front," Marie said. "Hopefully, no one's in the office." The next moment, Marie and Eva moved to the office in the back of the museum.

"Where should we begin?" Eva asked.

"The files. Let's see what they have." Marie opened one of the file drawers. She began pulling one drawer out after another, quickly flipping through the files while Eva peered over her shoulder.

"It would be much faster if you could move things," Marie grumbled as she opened another file drawer.

"We all have our special gifts." A flurry of glitter puffed up around Eva and then disappeared.

Marie paused a moment, catching sight of the appearing and disappearing glitter. Marie rolled her eyes and continued searching through the files.

THE MORNING DOCENT could not come into the museum that day because of a family emergency. Fortunately, Millie was already at the museum, catching up on paperwork in the office.

"You're here early," Millie said when the afternoon docent arrived.

"I heard your morning person wasn't coming in, and you had to cover for her. I wasn't doing anything, thought I'd come in early," the docent explained. "Let you get back to your own work."

"Thank you. I do have some paperwork I need to finish," Millie said.

"Have we been very busy?"

"Steady. A couple just left a few minutes ago," Millie explained.

They exchanged a few more words before Millie left the docent alone in the museum store. When Millie reached the office, she opened the door and walked in. To her surprise, she found a file drawer wide open.

Millie frowned. "I wasn't in those files. Who's been in here?" She walked to the drawer and slammed it shut.

"Hey! I wasn't finished looking through that!" Marie snapped.

Millie turned from the file drawers and grumbled, "Do I need to start locking the office?"

"I just want one more peek," Marie said, carefully sliding the file drawer open. Yet she wasn't careful enough. It made a squeaking sound. Just as Marie reached a hand all the way into the drawer, Millie turned around abruptly and let out a gasp. The next moment, Millie slammed the drawer shut—with Marie's hand still inside.

Marie looked down at her hand. It hung in front of the now closed file drawer. She looked at Millie and frowned. "You could have chopped off my hand!"

Eva chuckled. "I seriously doubt that."

"Well, if I were alive, she could have."

"If you were alive, she would have seen you standing there with your hand in the file cabinet, and then she would not have slammed the drawer shut," Eva reminded her.

"You don't know Millie," Marie said with a huff. "I bet she would have still slammed it shut on me."

"And if it had been possible to injure your hand as you are in this state, it would have been your own fault since you really don't need your hand to move those files. It's all show," Eva reminded her.

Like your glitter? Marie thought to herself.

Marie remained standing next to the file cabinet while she talked to Eva, her hand still where it had been when Millie slammed the drawer shut. Hesitantly, Millie walked back to the file drawer and pulled it open. While open, Marie looked back inside at the files. Millie closed the drawer again. She then reopened it. Once again, Marie looked back inside. This continued for several minutes; each time Marie snuck a peek at its contents. Finally, Millie shook her head, shut the file drawer, and walked to the desk and sat down.

"There was nothing useful in that drawer," Marie said.

Eva let out a sigh. "What now? We've gone through all the files."

Marie considered the question a moment and then blurted, "Of course, why didn't I remember? What was I thinking?"

"What are you talking about?" Eva frowned.

"After they closed the sanatorium, the city stored some of their files. A couple of years ago they moved those files here. I heard Danielle and Lily looked through them when they were trying to learn more about Sean Sullivan. He was the friend of Danielle's great-aunt's mother. He had been committed to Marymoor."

"Yes, I remember now!" Eva said. "They're in the storage room. I doubt they've moved them."

Eva and Marie disappeared from the office, leaving Millie alone and unaware of the ghosts.

When the pair entered the storage room, Marie flipped on the overhead light.

Eva glanced up at the fixture. "I hope no one notices the light."

Marie shrugged and started looking around. "Since neither of us can see in the dark, we don't really have a choice. I suppose if Millie comes in and turns off the light, we can come back tonight."

They looked around for a few minutes, each reading box labels. Finally, Eva called out, "Here are some boxes marked Marymoor!"

Marie focused on the box and willed its lid to lift. The two ghosts spent the next fifteen minutes sorting and reading through files—with Marie doing all the sorting.

"I remember her," Eva said with a sigh.

"Who?" Marie asked.

"Viola Hawkes." Eva pointed to a photograph on the table. "I'm sure it's her. She was a patron of the theater. Very wealthy. But why is her photograph in that box? She was from Portland, I believe."

"Her picture was with these." Marie picked up an envelope she had set on the table a minute ago. Viola's photograph had slipped out. The envelope held seven other pictures, all of women. Marie showed Eva the envelope's contents without removing the remaining photographs.

Marie set the envelope back on the table and looked at Viola's picture. "I don't recognize her face, but I do the name. My father told me about her. She was from a very wealthy family. But she had a breakdown. Her husband had her committed to Marymoor."

NINETEEN

June sat with Kelly on the sofa in Lily and Ian's living room. She held her daughter's left hand in hers, inspecting the engagement ring. It was the first time she had an opportunity to get a close look at it.

"It's ugly, isn't it?" Kelly whispered.

June cringed. "Well, it has a nice diamond. It's quite large."

"But the setting. It's horrid!" Kelly whined, looking down at the ring.

June sighed and released Kelly's hand. "That picture you texted me did not do it justice."

"How do you mean?" Kelly frowned and studied the ring on her left hand.

"I'm afraid it looks worse in person."

Kelly groaned. She leaned against June, who wrapped an arm around her shoulder.

"You haven't told Joe how you feel?" June asked softly.

"I can't tell him how I really feel about the ring. It would hurt his feelings. And it belonged to his grandmother. You're the only one I've said anything to. I didn't even say anything to Ian. Promise not to tell anyone!"

June let out another sigh, her arm still around her daughter as she gave it a little pat. "Don't worry, dear. I don't have to say anything. Anyone who sees it will know how ugly it is."

Kelly laughed. "Mom, you're awful. You could lie to me and tell me it's really beautiful."

"No, dear, when I say crazy things like that, I risk being committed."

Kelly chuckled. Still leaning against her mother, she said, "Mom, I'm glad you're moving to Frederickport. But you have to make me a promise."

"What?" June asked.

"This is my wedding, and while I would love you to help, I want to plan my own wedding."

"Are you going to pay for this wedding too?" June asked.

Kelly pulled away from her mother and looked her in the eyes. "Are you blackmailing me?"

June studied her daughter for a moment and then smiled. "Oh, maybe a little. But mostly I'm being mean. Your initial response to us moving here and how you obviously don't like the property we bought, that stung."

"I'm sorry. You have to understand, my reaction, well, that was mostly because the sale of that land has been something of a discussion around here. It just seemed so bizarre that it turned out my parents were the buyers."

"Discussion, how?" June frowned.

"Joe heard through work it sold. But he had no idea who bought it. And we were discussing its history and how it had been an albatross around the city's neck for years."

"What does Joe think about the property?"

"He doesn't take the ghost stories seriously. Joe thinks there is a logical explanation for everything."

"Joe seems like such a levelheaded young man. I don't understand why he can't see his grandmother's engagement ring's setting is not attractive. The diamond is nice; he should simply let you pick out a setting and use his grandmother's diamond."

"His grandmother is still alive. He doesn't want to hurt her feelings."

"Is that what Joe told you?" June asked.

"No. We never discussed it."

"And she no longer wanted to wear the ring?"

"She's a widow; her husband died years ago. And she can't wear the ring anymore because of arthritis in her hands, so she gave it to Joe."

"Yeah, right. That's what she says. She was probably eager to get rid of it," June snarked.

Kelly giggled. "We're horrible."

"Yes, we are." June gave Kelly's arm another pat.

Kelly sat up straighter on the sofa, held her left hand up, and examined the ring. "Perhaps I'll come to love the ring. After all, I love Joe. And whenever I look at it, it will remind me how love is blind."

"How so?"

"Joe loves his grandmother, and he can't see how ugly this ring is."

"I suppose you could come to love it."

"Careful, Mom, suggesting that might get you committed."

"You said it first," June reminded her.

Kelly let out a sigh. "You're right."

IAN'S FATHER hadn't returned from the store yet. But Kelly and June were still sitting in Ian and Lily's living room when Danielle and the others arrived. Instead of taking Connor directly to his bedroom, Ian sat down on his chair, holding his now sleeping son. Lily stood with Walt and Danielle and watched as the two quickly surveyed the room.

"Don't tell me he's sleeping again?" June asked, looking at her grandson.

"He's had a big morning," Ian said, glancing down to his son.

When June and Kelly were looking the other way, Danielle mouthed a quick, "Nothing," to Lily and then turned a bright smile on June and said, "I heard we're going to be neighbors. That's wonderful."

June's smile brightened. "At last, someone seems excited to hear our news."

"Mom, I told you, it's not that we don't want you to move to Frederickport. We love the idea. We only have an issue with the property," Kelly reminded her.

Lily glanced at Kelly and remembered her comments in the kitchen after her parents had gone to the living room.

June frowned at her daughter. "You just told me five minutes ago you thought our property would be a beautiful site for our new home."

Ian looked at his sister. "You told her that?"

Kelly shrugged. "Sure, it would. It is a freaking enormous piece of property, and Mom told me what they paid. They got a great deal on it. Yeah, when they first told us what they bought, it shocked me, considering its reputation."

"But you're okay with it now?" Ian asked.

"Of course. Why not? It's not that I actually believe any of those stories. Heck, people are always saying Marlow House is haunted and telling stories about that place." She paused a moment and looked at Walt and Danielle, who stared silently at her.

Kelly shrugged again and said to Walt and Danielle, "It's no secret, all the stories about Marlow House." She looked back at her brother. "But it didn't stop Lily from living there before she married you. And Mom and Dad are staying there now. You don't have a problem with that. Yeah, at first, it threw me, knowing what they bought, considering its reputation. But now that I've thought about it, I don't see what the big deal is."

Connor squirmed and woke up.

Lily reached down to pick Connor up from Ian. "Let me take him. I imagine he needs a diaper change." She glanced at Danielle.

Together, Danielle and Lily walked into Connor's bedroom.

"Is anyone here?" Lily asked as they entered the room.

"I don't see anyone yet," Danielle said, closing the door behind her.

"What a bunch of BS," Lily said as she laid Connor in the crib. He looked up at her and kicked his feet.

"What do you mean?" Danielle asked, handing Lily a diaper from the changing table.

"Kelly acting like she's thrilled about her parents moving here."

"Well, you don't really expect her to be truthful, do you? You aren't being truthful with June," Danielle reminded her.

"Shut up, Dani," Lily grumbled as she began changing Connor's diaper.

Danielle shrugged and said, "Just sayin'..." She began walking around the room, looking for any ghostly hiding places. When she came to the closet, she opened it. After she did, she let out a gasp and stepped back.

"Um… well… hello…" Danielle stammered, still looking into the closet.

Lily turned quickly from the crib and looked at Danielle. Danielle's back was to her as she stared into the now open closet.

"Someone is here?" Lily asked.

"You can see me?" the ghost hiding in the closet asked.

"Yes. I can hear you too," Danielle said.

"You're talking to the ghost, not me, aren't you?" Lily asked.

The ghost frowned. "Did she just call me a ghost?"

"Lily, please say nothing," Danielle said, still looking at the ghost.

Lily didn't ask why. Instead, she silently watched Danielle.

"Why does everyone call her Lily? She isn't."

"That's her name," Danielle said.

The ghost shrugged. "I guess there can be more than one person named Lily. But you didn't answer my other question."

"Why don't you tell me your name?" she asked.

"I'm not supposed to talk to strangers. So I shouldn't be talking to you," he said.

"But you talk to Connor," Danielle reminded him.

"That's different. Connor is a kid. Kids are safe," he said. "But he got mad at me."

"Why did he get mad at you?" Danielle asked.

"Because I wanted to take the stuffing out of his stupid stuffed animal. But he didn't want to, and he got all mad when I said I was going to do it if he wouldn't."

"And he understood all that?" Danielle frowned.

"Why wouldn't he understand?" he asked.

"He's only a year old. Technically, he won't be a year until next week," Danielle said.

"So? Kids, we understand more than you give us credit for."

"Why did you want to take apart his stuffed animal?" Danielle asked.

"Because Connor likes it better than me. I can tell. Why would he like something that's not even alive better than me? That isn't right. I'm alive. That stupid stuffed animal isn't."

"Tell me where you were before you came here?" Danielle asked.

Over in the crib, Connor stood up and held onto the rails. He looked past his mother to the closet and saw who Danielle was talking to. He began jumping on his mattress while jabbering nonsensically.

The ghost ignored Danielle's question and smiled at Connor. "He's not mad at me anymore. He wants to play. Can we play?"

"At least tell me how you happened to come here. How did you find Connor?" Danielle asked.

Before he answered, the door swung open, and June walked into the nursery. "Your husband is so silly," she told Lily while walking to the crib.

"What do you mean?" Lily asked, glancing nervously to Danielle and back to June.

June picked up Connor and gave him a quick kiss. "He told me Connor was probably sleeping, not to come in. But I couldn't imagine he was sleeping if you both were in here with him." She looked over to Danielle, who stood at the open closet, looking her way.

"We were just talking about Connor's birthday party," Danielle lied.

Connor began squirming in June's arms.

"Um, he is pretty heavy," Lily said. "You can set him down on the floor."

June cringed. "The floor is dirty!"

"I vacuum every day," Lily lied. "And Connor likes playing on the floor with his toys, like he does in the living room."

"If you kept that dog out of here, it would stay cleaner," June said as she begrudgingly set Connor down with his pile of toys.

While June focused on Connor, Danielle turned back to the closet and whispered, "Please, tell me, why did you come here?"

The ghost looked at Danielle for a moment and then said, "I came looking for Lily. They said she was here. She wasn't. But I found Connor and decided to stay."

TWENTY

"Lily, can you come here for a moment?" Ian asked from the open doorway.

Lily glanced briefly to her mother-in-law and Connor and over to Danielle. When she looked back to Ian, she nodded and told Danielle and June, "I'll be right back."

"Couldn't you keep your mother from barging in?" Lily asked in a whisper when they were out in the hallway.

"Is that a serious question?" Ian asked.

"I suppose not," Lily conceded.

"Was the ghost there?" Ian glanced down the hallway to the open doorway leading to Connor's room.

"Yes, he's in the closet. I assume he's still there. But your mom walked in when Danielle was talking to him. You need to get her out of there."

"I have an idea."

Lily arched her brows. "I'm listening."

"Let's go in the living room to talk. I don't want Mom to overhear. And Dad will be back anytime."

"What about your sister?" Lily asked.

"She left to have lunch with Joe."

Together, Lily and Ian walked into the living room. Walt sat quietly on the sofa. He looked up when they walked into the room and asked, "Anything?"

"He was in there a moment ago," Ian said. "Hopefully he'll stick around."

"So what's your plan?" Lily asked.

"When Dad gets back, I'm going to ask him to take us to see the property. It's not raining now. Walt and Danielle will stay here, under the pretense of watching Connor. Our cars are in the garage, Dad's car will already be in the driveway, and without a car seat, we can't take Connor anyway. While we're gone, Walt and Danielle can deal with our ghost."

Lily considered the suggestion for a moment and then frowned. "Will we have to get out of the car over there?"

"I assume so. It's not raining," Ian said.

"But what if they start throwing boulders again? Or something worse?" Lily asked.

"Then that solves another one of your problems," Walt said from the sofa.

Lily turned to Walt. "How so?"

"I don't imagine Ian's parents will want to build on property where boulders are flying around," Walt reminded her.

"What if one of the flying boulders kills us?" Lily asked.

"Ahh, Lily, have faith in what Eva says about the limits of a spirit's powers," Walt said.

"Could it hit the car?" Lily asked. "Not kill anyone, but smash up the car?"

Walt shrugged. "It's not your car. Why do you care?"

Lily giggled. "You're bad, Walt."

JUNE SAT on the rocking chair near Connor and looked down at the child as he played with his toys. Danielle glanced at the ghost still standing in the closet and whispered, "Please wait so we can talk."

June looked up at Danielle and frowned. "Did you say something?"

Danielle flashed her a smile. "I have a habit of talking to myself."

"Kelly mentioned that," June said.

She did? Danielle thought.

Danielle glanced back to the closet.

"Okay, I'll wait. I'm curious. I have a couple of questions for you. If you promise to answer my questions, I'll stick around," the ghost said.

Danielle nodded to the ghost, turned, and walked to June and Connor.

June's right hand rested on one arm of the rocking chair. She glanced down and rubbed her palm along its worn edge. "Did Lily pick this up at a yard sale? I remember Ian saying she likes yard sales."

"Um… no… it belonged to our friend Marie. You met her. She was Adam Nichols's grandmother."

"Oh, yes." June smiled up at Danielle. "Certainly, I remember Marie. She was quite the character. I believe Tammy, Marie, and I got a little snookered at Lily's bachelorette party." She giggled.

"Do you remember the article Ian wrote on Emma Jackson?" Danielle asked.

"Certainly. I read everything my son writes."

"The rocker belonged to Emma. After she died, she left it to Marie. They had become close friends," Danielle explained.

June smiled and again ran her hand over the chair arm, as if caressing it. "This rocker has its own story. Lovely."

Danielle moved from the closet and sat on the floor with Connor. He handed her a block. She absently accepted it while looking up at June, who remained in the rocker.

"I do hope Lily is happy about us moving here," June said.

"I'm sure she is," Danielle insisted.

"There are many advantages for her with us moving here. For example, she can go back to teaching. I can watch Connor when she works."

"Um… I'm pretty sure Lily wants to be a stay-at-home mom," Danielle said.

June chuckled. "Lily is a teacher. She will have summers off to be with Connor. This will be good for her."

Danielle didn't know how to respond, or if she should.

"Mom, Dad's back," Ian said from the doorway. "And he's going to take us all to look at the lot again. It's not raining now, so we can get out and walk around."

"That's nice. I'm glad to see you're all moving beyond all that haunting nonsense." June smiled at Ian and then looked back down at Connor.

Ian stood in the doorway a moment, waiting for his mother, but after a while he realized she had no intention of getting up.

"Mom, come on, we're all waiting," Ian said.

June looked up at her son. "I'll stay here with Connor. You all go and have fun."

"Walt and Danielle are staying with Connor," Ian told her. "Come on, everyone's waiting."

June frowned and glance briefly at Danielle. "They don't have to do that."

"Go, June," Danielle insisted. "Walt and I love staying with Connor."

With a sigh, June stood up. "Fine."

When June leaned down to kiss the top of Connor's head, Ian mouthed, *"Thank you,"* to Danielle.

KELLY THOUGHT she was meeting just her fiancé, Joe Morelli, for lunch at Lucy's Diner. But when she arrived, she found him sitting in a booth with fellow officer Brian Henderson. She liked Brian, but she wanted some time alone with Joe after her stressful morning with her parents.

"He's agreed to be my best man," Joe said when Kelly reached the table.

Kelly smiled dully and took a seat next to Joe.

"So I wasn't Kelly's first choice?" Brian teased.

Kelly let out a sigh. "Sorry, it's not you, Brian. It's my parents. I just spent the morning with them."

"Didn't they just get in last night?" Brian asked.

Joe frowned. "What's wrong?"

"To begin with, they're moving to Frederickport."

Joe's eyes widened. "Really? When?"

"Now," Kelly said.

Joe frowned. "What do you mean now?"

Before Kelly could answer, the server walked up to the table to take their order. While none of them had picked up a menu, they all knew what they wanted. After the server took the orders and left the table, Joe repeated his question.

"They've already sold their house—even moved out. I guess everything is in storage," Kelly explained.

"Did Ian know?" Joe asked.

"No. They wanted to surprise us. Boy, did they!"

"I guess you weren't too thrilled with their surprise?" Brian asked.

"Your parents are great," Joe said. "You aren't happy they're moving here?"

Kelly studied Joe a moment and asked, "You're okay with this?"

Joe shrugged. "It'll make holidays much easier. Both of our families will be here."

"If they already sold their house, does that mean they've already bought something in Frederickport?" Brian asked.

Before Kelly could answer the question, her cellphone rang. She looked to see who was calling. With a sigh she said, "It's Mom." She answered the call and after a few moments hung up. Kelly set her cellphone on the table. She looked at Joe and asked, "After lunch, can you go with me, and I'll drop you back at the station."

"Why?" Joe asked.

Kelly glanced briefly at Brian. "You asked if they already bought a house. No. But they bought a piece of property, and Dad intends to build on it. Mom told me they're going over to the lot and wondered if we could meet them there when we finish lunch."

"That's terrific," Brian said.

"I imagine many people would not agree with you," Kelly said with a snort.

"What do you mean?" Joe asked.

Kelly smiled at Joe. "My parents bought the Marymoor property."

"You aren't serious?" Joe asked.

"Oh, I am," Kelly said.

Brian reserved comment.

"I'd love to go with you, but we have to get back to the office by two. We have a meeting. I hate to make you leave your parents to take me back so soon," Joe told her.

"I have an idea," Brian suggested. Kelly and Joe looked at him. "I'll follow you guys over there, and Joe can go back to the office with me, so you don't have to leave right away."

"That would be wonderful," Kelly said.

BRIAN WATCHED Joe get in the car with Kelly while he sat in the police car. Instead of turning on the ignition, he picked up his cellphone and placed a call, his eyes still focused on Kelly's car.

"Hey, catch any bad guys?" Heather Donovan asked when she answered her phone.

"Not yet. Am I interrupting your work?" Brian asked. He watched as Kelly drove her car out into the street.

"Sorta, but that's okay. What's up?"

"I wanted to tell you something interesting," Brian began.

"Hey, I'm always up for interesting, what?"

"Guess who bought the Marymoor property."

"Not a clue? The way you say that, I assume it's someone I know?" Heather said.

"Oh yeah. It's Kelly and Ian's parents."

"Shut up! You aren't serious?" Heather blurted.

"Kelly's driving Joe over there right now to show them the property with her parents. I'm supposed to be following them over there so I can take Joe back to the office with me when they're done."

"Did she know they were going to buy it?" Heather asked. "No way would Ian have let his parents buy that. Oh crap, I bet Lily is having fits!"

"I don't imagine Lily or Ian are happy about it, knowing what they do. Of course, Kelly seems to find the entire haunting thing amusing."

"From what I understand, it's not a friendly haunting like Marlow House," Heather said.

"As I recall, Marlow House was not always so friendly. Walt slugged me once," Brian reminded her.

Heather laughed. "Yeah, and you deserved it. Well, you be careful over there. I doubt you're an innocent."

WHEN BRIAN ARRIVED at the Marymoor property, Joe and Kelly were already out of the car and talking to Kelly's parents, while Ian and Lily stood some distance away, talking amongst themselves. Brian could only imagine what they were thinking.

He was about to take off his seatbelt when movement near the fence caught his attention. Someone had pushed the For Sale sign down, and at first, he assumed the breeze now moved the edges of the sign. There was only one problem, none of the leaves in the nearby tree moved. Narrowing his eyes, he watched in fascination as the sign lifted from the ground and began flying toward Kelly's small group.

Without thinking, Brian shouted, "Watch out!" But with his window up, no one heard him. The next moment the sign stopped in midair and made a U-turn, returning to its original spot. The four unsuspecting targets continued to chat amongst themselves, unaware of what had just happened. Brian glanced over to Lily and Ian, and by their expressions, he assumed they had witnessed the sign's brief flight.

TWENTY-ONE

By the time Brian got out of his car, Ian and Lily stood just a few feet away.

"Did you see that?" Lily whispered, glancing over her shoulder at her in-laws, who remained oblivious to the recent attack and continued to chat with their daughter and soon-to-be son-in-law.

"Yes. But they obviously didn't." Brian nodded over to the four people.

"I was just about to yell out when it did a boomerang," Ian said. "Holy crap, is this how it's going to be?"

"You need to get your parents to get rid of this place," Lily said, taking hold of his hand.

Ian looked at Brian. "This is the second time I've seen something like this here. The first one was a boulder. Almost hit my dad's car. Then it just turned around, returned to where it had been."

"Nice," Brian said dryly.

"I assume you were at lunch when my sister told Joe about Mom and Dad buying the property. Is she really okay with it now? Did she say?" Ian asked.

Brian shrugged and glanced briefly to Joe and Kelly and back to Ian. "From what she said, I don't think she takes the haunting seriously."

"If they would just see something, maybe..." Lily didn't finish her sentence. In the next moment, her in-laws and Joe turned and walked up to them.

"Mom, Dad, do you remember Brian? He's going to be Joe's best man," Kelly announced.

"Really?" Lily said, flashing Brian a smile.

John shook Brian's hand, and the group exchanged small talk. Finally, June said, "Brian, come see the property with us."

"Unless he's afraid of ghosts," John said with a laugh.

A few minutes later, the group approached the open gate leading onto the property. Kelly and her parents didn't notice Lily, Ian, and Brian's reluctance, nor the way the three glanced around warily. Kelly was too busy grilling her father on what type of house he planned to build, and what he intended to do with so much land.

Ian's parents were the first to walk through the gate. But once they did, June stopped a moment and shivered. "Does the weather always change so abruptly here?"

"It's like someone just turned the thermostat down," Kelly said.

Ian, Lily, and Brian again exchanged glances, each remaining vigilant for incoming missiles.

NOT LONG AFTER Ian and Lily left with Ian's parents, Walt went to Connor's bedroom.

"They're finally gone," Walt said from the open door. "June insisted on waiting for Kelly to join them."

Danielle, who remained sitting on the floor with Connor, nodded at Walt and then looked to the open closet. The ghost remained standing just inside, his eyes on Danielle.

"You can come out now," Danielle told him. "We can talk."

When the ghost stepped out of the closet, Walt blurted in surprise, "You're just a boy."

The ghost stopped walking and frowned at Walt. "Who are you?"

"This is Walt, my husband. And my name is Danielle. You haven't told me your name yet."

The ghost frowned. "I'm not sure I should. But you promised to answer some questions for me."

"Okay, why don't you sit in the rocking chair, and you can ask your questions, and then I'll ask mine," Danielle suggested.

The ghost let out a sigh, walked to the rocking chair, and sat down. Walt took a seat on the floor with Danielle and Connor. He entertained Connor by helping him move toy trucks around while silently listening to what the ghost was about to tell them.

"I don't understand why everyone can't see me. But I sort of got used to it. At first, I thought they were just ignoring me. But why do you both see me?"

"Connor sees you too," Danielle reminded him.

"Lily did too. But then they got mad and separated us," he grumbled.

"Connor's mother is named Lily, but you said you didn't mean her," Danielle asked.

The ghost shook his head. "No. She's not my Lily. She's way older than my Lily."

Walt looked up at him and asked, "What did you mean they separated you?"

He shrugged. "Her parents never liked me. Neither did her sister. They liked me okay at first. But later, her mom locked me in a room and told Lily she had to stay away from me. I didn't think Lily would let them do it. Lock me in the room like that. But she did. And then she never came to see me."

"How did you get out of the room?" Danielle asked.

"They left it unlocked," he explained. "I snuck out, overheard them. They were going to see Lily. I figured if I could just see her again. Talk to her. Maybe she would be my friend again, and I wouldn't have to stay locked up."

"What happened?" Danielle asked gently.

He shrugged. "They came here. They didn't know I hid in the box. But Lily wasn't here. Connor was."

"What box did you hide in?" Danielle asked.

He pointed to a box in the corner. "That one."

Danielle stood up and walked to the corner. She looked in the box. "It has some old toys in it."

"They belonged to Lily," the ghost explained. "I thought they were bringing Lily her toys. But they gave them to Connor. Where do you think Lily is? Do you think they locked her up in a room too?"

WHEN LILY RETURNED HOME with Ian and his parents, Kelly was with them. Lily wanted to talk to Walt and Danielle and find out what they had learned, but they would get no privacy with Ian's family. Not long after Walt and Danielle returned to Marlow House, Lily made an excuse to run across the street.

"Stay here and keep an eye on Connor," Lily whispered to her husband. Already her mother-in-law had snatched up the boy and sat with him on the sofa, while Kelly and John sat nearby, discussing the building plans for their house. If Lily could pry her son away from his grandmother and take him with her, she would.

"THAT WAS QUICK," Walt said when Lily walked into the back door of Marlow House. He sat at the kitchen table while Danielle stood at the counter, removing slices of bread from its package.

"I'm making lunch. You want a sandwich?" Danielle asked.

"No, thanks. I just want to know what you found out." Lily took a seat at the table.

Walt told Lily what they had learned while Danielle made lunch. Just as Walt finished his telling, she brought the sandwiches to the table.

"Where did you get that box of toys?" Danielle asked. She handed Walt one of the plates and then sat down at the table across from him.

"Are you talking about the cardboard box sitting in the corner of Connor's room?" Lily asked.

"Yeah. It looked like it had some old toys in it. I saw a Cabbage Patch doll in there," Danielle said.

"Those were some of my old toys. Mom and Dad brought them," Lily explained.

"Well, according to your ghost, he came in that box," Danielle said.

Lily frowned. "That makes no sense. And you say it's a little boy?"

"Yes. My guess, if he were alive, he would be around seven or eight. Did you know a boy who died around that age?" Danielle asked.

"Do you think I know this ghost?" Lily asked.

"Like I told you, he said he came here looking for Lily. Duh… you are Lily," Danielle said before taking a bite of her sandwich.

"And he did say the toys in the box belonged to his Lily," Walt added.

"He also said the Lily he's looking for is a little girl," Lily reminded them.

Danielle shrugged. "It's possible he's someone you knew when you were a child."

"And he's just now trying to find me?" Lily frowned.

"Did you know of a boy who died around that age?" Danielle asked.

Lily considered the question for a moment and then shook her head. "No. Not when I was a child. In fact, when I was in college, one of my friends, her little sister died of leukemia. She was only six. I remember thinking back then that I had never known a child who had died before. There was something so much more—tragic —about it. It really hit me hard back then. So no, I don't believe I ever knew a little boy who died when I was a child. I'm sure I would remember that."

"If you're right, then this is some screwy coincidence," Walt said.

"We need to help him move on," Danielle said. "I doubt he understands he's dead, considering what he said. His comments and reactions are typical of a spirit in that confused phase. Where they think they are still alive yet accept the fact some people can't see or hear them, and they find nothing odd about moving through walls."

"I agree. I'm sure there is some family waiting for him. If not parents, grandparents," Walt said.

"Fortunately, I don't feel you need to worry about Connor while he's here," Danielle said.

"He wanted to disembowel Winnie," Lily reminded her.

"A little-boy stunt, not a serial killer in the making," Danielle said.

"But why is he here? How did he turn up with my toys?" Lily asked.

They considered the various possibilities. Finally, Walt said, "Perhaps his spirit was lingering by one of the stops where your parents got gas at on their way up here. Maybe he heard them talking about how they were going to see Lily, and he thought that was his Lily, so he hitched a ride."

"Did he tell you his name?" Lily asked. "It really bothers me what you said about someone locking him in a room. How did he die? Did he have any obvious wounds?"

Danielle shook her head. "He refused to tell us his name. Called us strangers. And there was nothing to indicate how he died. But if they locked him in a room, I suppose it's possible he died of starvation. He is kind of thin."

"Oh no," Lily groaned. "All I wanted was for this ghost to leave my little boy alone. But he's just a little boy too. One people abused!"

"He actually looked pretty healthy aside from being thin," Danielle noted.

Walt arched his brow. "Healthy for being dead?"

Danielle shrugged.

"You didn't tell him he's dead? It seems once you do, spirits typically adjust quickly and want to move on," Lily said.

"I was reluctant to tell him," Danielle said. "Sometimes a spirit will just disappear after you tell them. But does that mean they've accepted their reality and moved on? I don't know. Considering the age of this spirit, I don't want to scare him away and risk him wandering around confused. Like you said, he is just a little boy."

Lily groaned again. "I don't want that."

"If we can learn more about him, find out who he was, it'll be easier to help guide him to his reality and get him to move on," Danielle said.

"I don't think he's going to tell us much. And if some adult locked him in a room for a long time, that might explain his distrust," Walt said.

Danielle looked to Walt. "Unfortunately, I have to agree with you."

"Perhaps we can get another child to help him open up. He seems to be quite comfortable with Connor," Walt suggested. "I bet he's told Connor his name already."

"I doubt Connor will be much help," Lily said with a snort.

"I wasn't thinking of Connor," Walt said. "I was thinking Evan."

"Evan?" Lily and Danielle said at the same time. They looked at Walt.

"Isn't he the obvious choice? I'm sure we can come up with some excuse to bring Evan over to your house. He can talk to the spirit, play with him and Connor for a while. Gain his trust, get him to open up," Walt said.

"You think the chief will allow that?" Lily asked.

"I think so. It's too bad we can't do it over here. But it seems our young ghost is hanging tight at your house," Danielle said.

TWENTY-TWO

Glitter rained from the parlor's ceiling. Danielle stopped talking, and both she and Walt looked up.

Lily frowned. "What is it?"

"Eva's here," Danielle explained.

"Good, maybe she knows where Marie is," Lily said.

"I'm here!" Marie announced, a transparent vision of her former self appearing before them. It flickered for a moment before coming into focus, looking now like a living woman—at least, it did to Walt and Danielle. Lily still could not see or hear Marie. The next moment, Eva's vision appeared next to Marie.

"Marie is here, with Eva," Danielle said.

"Wonderful, you are all here. I wanted to talk to you about Marymoor," Marie said.

Danielle repeated what Marie said to Lily. Lily responded with a groan.

Marie looked down at Lily with concern. She attempted to pat Lily's back, yet only sent her hand through Lily's right shoulder. Marie gave it another try, this time willing her energy to replicate what a pat on the shoulder might feel like. It did not have the desired effect. Instead of comforting Lily, it sent her jerking back in startled surprise.

"Oh, I'm sorry, dear," Marie muttered, taking back her hand.

"What was that?" Lily asked.

"I believe it was Marie's misguided attempt at giving comfort," Danielle explained.

Lily looked to where she believed Marie stood and asked, "So you know about our ghost?"

Marie frowned. "Which ghost is she talking about?"

"The little boy over at her house," Danielle explained.

"There is a little-boy ghost at her house?" Eva asked in surprise.

Danielle went on to tell Eva and Marie about their mystery ghost.

After Danielle finished the telling, Lily buried her face in the palms of her hands and shook her head wearily while muttering, "I can't believe my house is haunted and my in-laws are going to be moving into a haunted house."

"Technically, your house has been haunted for some time." Walt looked over at Marie.

"Yeah, but Marie is a friendly ghost," Lily said.

"This boy ghost isn't friendly?" Eva asked.

"Does this mean Lily isn't mad at me?" Marie asked hopefully.

"Why would she be mad at you?" Walt asked.

Lily lifted her head and asked, "Who's mad?"

"Marie thought you might be mad at her," Danielle said.

Lily frowned. "Why?"

Marie smiled sheepishly. "I knew Ian's parents were buying the Marymoor property, and I didn't say anything."

"We sort of figured that," Danielle said.

"But we are trying to fix it," Marie explained.

"Fix it how?" Walt asked.

"Why am I mad at Marie?" Lily asked.

"We've been trying to contact the spirits haunting the area, to help them move on," Eva told them.

"But they are ignoring us. They refuse to show themselves," Marie added.

"You didn't see any of them?" Danielle asked.

"Three of them. One was Molly. I believe she's the murdered nurse," Marie explained.

"I've met her," Danielle said.

Lily groaned and leaned back in the chair. "Go ahead, just ignore my question, and carry on."

Danielle glanced at Lily and smiled. "Marie and Eva went over to Marymoor and tried to get the spirits to move on."

"They obviously weren't successful. Unless they went after we were there less than an hour ago," Lily said.

"I'm afraid not," Eva said. "Molly vanished and refused to come back. Two male ghosts appeared. One threw a rock at us, and the other screamed at us. Both disappeared, and we tried going back over there several times, but the spirits refuse to show themselves."

"They also mentioned someone named Randal," Marie said. "They seemed to be afraid of him. But I'm afraid Lily was right. We weren't successful."

Danielle turned to Lily. "You didn't tell us what happened over there."

"No, trying to learn more about Connor's ghost friend distracted me," Lily said.

"So what happened?" Walt asked.

Lily shrugged. "Oh, nothing out of the ordinary. One ghost tried to bash my in-laws with the For Sale sign, but the Universe must have intervened."

"What did Ian's parents' say?" Danielle asked.

"They didn't see it. Then the temperature dropped like twenty degrees the moment we stepped on the property," Lily explained.

Danielle frowned. "They must have noticed that."

"Yes. But they found nothing especially bizarre about it. They just sort of accepted it," Lily said.

"Anything else?" Walt asked.

"Yeah. Someone kept poking me. I think they poked Kelly first, but she made some crack to Joe about him bumping into her, and he just sort of blew it off. Oh, and Brian was there. Like us, he saw some of what was going on, but it was nuts. Ian's sister and parents were totally oblivious. Aside from Kelly thinking Joe bumped into her and the drop in temperature, they acted like it was a normal day. And I kept thinking, there is no way I can bring my son over here."

"I'm sorry, Lily," Marie said.

"You never answered my question," Lily told Danielle. "Why am I mad at Marie?"

"I assume she meant because she knew Ian's parents were buying the property and didn't tell you," Danielle said.

Lily shrugged. "Yeah, well, to be honest, I doubt Ian could have stopped his dad from buying it without it blowing up into a major family fight. Both his parents are pretty stubborn."

Marie looked visibly relieved Lily harbored no animosity.

"But," Lily added, "I know what Marie can do to make it up to me."

Walt chuckled. "I thought you just said she couldn't have done anything to prevent it."

"True. But I could still use her help," Lily said.

"What do you need?" Marie asked.

"Marie wants to know what you need," Danielle said.

"I would really appreciate it if she would stay with Connor until we figure out how to get this boy ghost to move on. Maybe he's harmless, but he wanted to chop up Winnie," Lily said.

"I assume you're trying to do what we did at Marymoor; help him move on?" Marie asked.

"Yes. But like the spirits wouldn't talk to you and Eva, he refused to tell me his name. Without that, it's difficult to figure out where he came from. Walt was hoping Evan might get him to open up," Danielle explained.

"In the meantime, I'll keep an eye on things. And perhaps I'll have better luck with your boy ghost than we did with the Marymoor spirits," Marie said.

"Marie said she'll keep an eye on the spirit," Danielle said.

Lily looked hopefully to Danielle. "Any chance she can go over now? I know Ian is with him, but Ian can't see what the ghost is doing to our son."

Without another word, Marie vanished.

"I think she just went over there," Danielle said.

"Good," Lily said in relief. "But we should have told her to find out who he is. Maybe she can get him to tell her his name, and we can figure out where he came from."

"Marie already thought of that," Walt said.

Eva turned to Walt and Danielle. "When Marie and I were unsuccessful with the Marymoor spirits, we couldn't help but wonder why they refused to leave. I feel there are more than just three spirits over there. So we went to the museum to see what we could find out."

Lily stood up. "I'd better head home and let Ian know Marie is there so he can relax a little."

WHEN MARIE ARRIVED in the Bartley living room, she found Ian sitting on the floor, playing with Connor and what appeared to be a little boy slightly younger than Evan. At least, he appeared to be a little boy. Marie knew differently, and she understood only Connor could see him.

Kelly sat on the sofa with her parents, discussing her upcoming wedding.

The little boy's eyes widened when he saw Marie appear before them.

Sadie looked up from where she lay, her tail now wagging. Marie looked to Sadie, silently giving the dog a greeting and telling her to stay put.

"Who are you, and how did you do that?" the boy ghost asked Marie.

"I'm Grandma Marie. And what is your name?"

Connor smiled and reached for Marie, saying, "Gama..."

June, who had been listening to her daughter while watching Connor, immediately put out her hand to stop Kelly from talking.

"Did you hear that!" June squealed, interrupting the boy ghost, who was about to say something to Marie. "Connor! He just reached for me and said grandma!"

"I didn't hear anything," Kelly said.

"Of course, because you were talking." June jumped from the sofa and swooped a laughing Connor from the floor and into her arms. He stopped laughing and cried while reaching for Marie—whom none of the non-mediums could see.

"Oh, dear, you're making him cry!" Marie fretted while taking hold of one of Connor's extended hands and giving it a little squeeze. "It's okay, Connor, Grandma Marie is here."

"Mom, please, Connor doesn't want to be picked up," Ian said.

"But he wanted me," June said with a pout, now putting Connor back on the floor. He immediately stopped crying and crawled to his toys.

"He said grandma, he did!" June insisted.

"Mom, Connor jabbers lots of words, but I don't think he knows what many of them mean," Ian said.

The next moment Sadie let out a bark and jumped up; she raced to the front door. A few moments later, Sadie returned to the living room, Lily by her side.

"Connor just called me grandma!" June said the moment Lily and Sadie walked into the room.

Lily arched her brows. "Really?"

"And Mom made him cry." Kelly snickered.

"That's not nice," John reprimanded. Kelly shrugged.

Connor smiled up at his mother and then looked away. He laughed and offered a toy to someone. Was he offering it to the boy ghost or to Marie? Lily wondered.

"Ian, can I see you in the kitchen for a moment?" Lily asked.

"Oh, secrets," Kelly teased as her brother went into the kitchen with Lily.

"Marie is here," Lily announced when they were out of earshot from Ian's family.

"I wondered about that." Ian glanced toward the living room and then back to Lily.

Lily frowned. "Why?"

"Connor did say something that sounded like grandma. But I suspect he meant Marie, not Mom."

Lily cringed. "Oh…"

Ian shrugged. "Mom doesn't know that."

Lily quickly told Ian all that she had learned while across the street.

"I've been giving the Marymoor property some thought," Ian began.

"And?"

"If those things keep happening over there, I can't believe my parents won't eventually see something."

"I wish they would have today; it might make convincing them to buy something else easier," Lily said.

"The only problem, they already closed escrow on this one. So even if they get buyer's remorse, they could get stuck with the property. I'd happily offer to buy something else for them, but there is no way my father would accept a loan or gift like that from his son. His pride wouldn't let him."

"Won't they have the money from the sale of their house?"

"Didn't you hear what my parents said, they had a simultaneous close for their house and the property. They paid for the property with the proceeds from their house," Ian explained.

"I know. But your parents owned that house forever, and they lived in a pretty nice area. I imagine houses go for a fortune in their old neighborhood."

"Unfortunately, my parents always used their house as a piggy bank."

Lily's eyes widened. "They borrowed on it?"

"Yes. It's how they paid for all their vehicles over the years. I suspect they have enough from the house sale to cover building expenses, but not enough to keep the lot and buy a house."

"What are you going to do?"

Ian glanced at his watch. "I'm going to talk to Adam. See how hard it's going to be to unload that nightmare."

TWENTY-THREE

W hen Lily and Ian walked back into the living room, Lily announced, "I'm going to make lunch. Would you like to join us, Kelly?"

Kelly stood up. "I already had lunch, with Joe. And I need to get home and finish up my blog. But thanks."

"Don't forget, Chris is taking us all to Pearl Cove tonight," Lily reminded her.

Kelly flashed her a grin. "Oh, I won't forget. Joe and I are looking forward to it."

June stood up. "Let me help you with lunch."

"Why don't you stay with Connor and watch him?" Lily suggested. "I'm just going to make something light, since we're going out tonight. And Ian has to run some errands."

June looked at her son. "Aren't you going to have lunch first?"

"I'm not hungry. I had a big breakfast," Ian lied. "And since we're going to Pearl Cove tonight, I'll save my appetite."

"You want me to go with you?" John offered.

"No, Dad. Stay here and have lunch with Mom and Lily. I shouldn't be long."

"CONNOR'S MOM said he's going to have to take a nap after lunch," the boy ghost grumbled to Marie as he watched them take Connor into the dining room.

"You like Connor, don't you?" Marie asked.

"Yeah. He's fun, like Lily was."

The two ghosts sat alone in the living room. They could hear the voices of the living people now sitting at the breakfast bar in the kitchen.

"Connor's mother's name is Lily," Marie noted.

"Yeah, but she's not my Lily. My Lily was a little girl."

"How old was your Lily?" Marie asked.

He shrugged. "About my age." He frowned for a minute. "Well, she wasn't always my age. I remember when she was about Connor's age. He even looks a little like she did back then. But I guess all babies look alike."

"And you stayed your age while Lily got older?" Marie asked gently.

He frowned at Marie. "So what?"

"Why don't you tell me your name?" Marie urged.

"I don't want to. I'm not supposed to talk to strangers, but since you're Connor's grandma, and he seems to like you, and you can see me, then I guess it's okay. But I still don't want to tell you my name. They knew my name, and they locked me in that room."

"Can you tell me how you met Lily? Not Connor's mom, but the Lily who was your friend," Marie asked.

The boy ghost considered the question for a minute and then smiled. "She was younger than Connor the first time I met her. I remember, now."

"Younger?" Marie asked.

"Yeah. Real little. They had her and the others all wrapped up tight. Some of them were crying. But not Lily."

"Others? What others?" Marie asked.

"The other babies. Lily was just a baby. Back then, anyway. But she was tough. She didn't cry like the others. Not even when they wrapped her tight. That's what I liked about her. She didn't seem to be afraid."

"Who wrapped her tight?" Marie asked.

He shrugged. "I don't know. But they weren't very friendly. They scared me. After a while, they refused to talk to me. At first, they were real nice, but when I asked them to help me find my mom and dad, they wouldn't help me. They were too busy fussing with those babies."

"Your parents? Do you remember the last time you saw them?"

He frowned at Marie. After a moment of silence he said, "I don't want to talk about this anymore." He vanished.

ADAM SAT AT HIS DESK, reading the local newspaper. A knock came from the open doorway leading to the hallway. He looked up. Ian Bartley stood just outside his office.

"Can I come in?" Ian asked.

With a sigh, Adam folded the newspaper, tossed it aside, and waved Ian into the office. "Are you alone?"

"Do you mean, are my parents with me?" Ian asked, walking toward Adam.

Adam stood and leaned over his desk, extending his right hand to Ian. "I assume you know?"

Ian accepted the handshake, then released it and sat down while saying, "Yes. Dad took us over there this morning, showed us his big surprise." He added with a snort, "Some surprise."

"I assume you're not happy with his purchase?" Adam sat back down behind his desk.

"What do you think?" Ian asked.

"You need to understand. I tried talking him out of it. I would have told you, but—"

"Yes, I know. Client confidentiality," Ian interrupted. "Dad told me he wanted to keep it a secret."

"When I realized he was determined to buy the property, with or without me, I urged him to let me add a contingency to view it. I figured, when he did that, you would probably be with him, and if you had any reservations, you could voice it then. But he was only interested in having it inspected. But frankly, he didn't do much of an inspection."

"I understand why you couldn't tell me. I know my dad."

"I'm really sorry, Ian. I wanted to tell you, but I couldn't." Adam leaned forward in his chair, resting his elbows on his desk.

"Walt and Danielle told me what you and Melony saw over there," Ian said.

Adam cringed. "Do you think I'm crazy?"

"Since both Lily and I saw a similar thing—as did Brian Henderson, no. Unfortunately, my parents didn't see any of it."

"I have no idea what's going on over there. Danielle came up with a theory about energy left over from spirits who lived there. Which, I suppose, is as rational a theory as anything. Especially considering what went on over there. But, Ian, I couldn't tell your father what we saw."

Ian let out a snort. "Had you told my father that story, I imagine he would have thought you were nuts and would have simply bought the property from someone else."

"But if I could have just talked him into viewing it first," Adam muttered.

Ian shook his head. "Don't beat yourself up over it. My parents have been over there a few times with me and saw nothing. So even if Dad had agreed to the contingency, it probably wouldn't have changed the outcome."

"Now what?" Adam asked.

"I figure this is something my parents are going to have to experience for themselves. I know they haven't seen anything yet, but considering what we've all seen, I can't believe one of these days my parents won't see something like we did. And after they do, how hard do you think it's going to be for my dad to unload that property?"

Adam groaned. "It will not be easy. Not unless he's willing to take a loss. They've tried to sell that property for years, off and on. I told your father that."

"Yeah, well, my father likes to think he has a special knack for seeing the diamond where everyone else just sees coal."

"And when he finally sees what we have?" Adam asked.

Ian shrugged. "I just hope he does. I know Lily is not happy with the idea of taking our son over there."

"I hate to tell you this," Adam said. "But there is another reason it might be difficult for your father to resell the property just now."

Ian frowned. "What's that?"

Adam reached for the folded newspaper and pushed it across his desk to Ian. "I assume you didn't read the morning newspaper?"

Ian looked at the paper. "No. Why?"

Adam leaned over the desk, unfolded the newspaper, and turned it around so that Ian could read the headline. *"City Dumps Cursed Property."*

Ian glanced over the headline and picked up the newspaper. He let out a sigh and began to read. A few minutes later, he refolded the newspaper and tossed it on the desk. "That's lovely. I imagine the city is relieved they didn't write a similar article before it sold."

"While most people won't believe the place is cursed—or haunted as the article suggests, when it comes to spending their money, it will make a difference, and some will see it as an opportunity to make a lowball offer," Adam said. "No way will they pay full price. They'll want a deal. Which will mean your parents will lose money if they decide to sell now."

Ian let out a sigh. "Damn. What now?"

"I don't know. But I'm really sorry," Adam said.

"DID KELLY'S PARENTS ARRIVE OKAY?" Tori Simmons asked her brother on Saturday afternoon.

"They got in last night," Joe told her. He sat alone in his office, talking to Tori on his cellphone. "Chris is taking us all to Pearl Cove tonight."

"Nice. Don't you have to work?"

Joe glanced at the clock. "I get off in a couple of hours."

"Try to pin down a date for the bridal shower. This is going to be last minute as it is, since we only have a two-week window if we want her mom to come," Tori urged.

"I don't think that will be a problem."

"Why?"

"They're moving to Frederickport. Technically, they already moved, since escrow closed on their house right before they got here," Joe told her.

"Seriously? You didn't tell me they were planning to move here."

"I didn't know," Joe said.

"Kelly didn't tell you?"

"She didn't know. She just found out today."

"Wow. You said they already sold their house?" Tori asked.

"Yes. They put everything in storage and are staying at Marlow House, but that's only temporary. They're looking for a rental."

"That would probably be a good idea. See if they like the weather. I imagine it will be a big change for them."

"Remember, her father is a contractor? He intends to build. They already bought property. You'll never guess where."

"Where?" Tori asked.

"They bought the Marymoor property," Joe told her.

"You're kidding? No!" Tori gasped.

"Oh, please, don't start with all that cursed nonsense," Joe said with a laugh.

"I wasn't... it's just that——"

"Oh, Tori, I have to go. The chief is calling."

Tori sat in silence for a few minutes after her brother said goodbye and hung up. She considered what he had just told her. Still holding her cellphone, she looked at it. A moment later she tapped her photos app, opening it. Flipping through the pictures, she found one she had taken of a woman's black-and-white photograph.

The woman had died years before Tori's birth. She had died at Marymoor Sanatorium.

TWENTY-FOUR

Lily was finally alone with her husband. June and John had gone back to Marlow House to rest and get ready for dinner. She had put Connor down for a nap, because they planned to take him to Pearl Cove with them, since all the babysitters she normally used would be joining them for dinner. She knew Marie was in the bedroom with Connor, monitoring her sleeping son and the mystery ghost. Marie would also go with them to Pearl Cove. She would keep Connor entertained during dinner. Everyone needed a nanny ghost, Lily thought. It was those other ghosts she found troubling.

Lily sat with Ian on the sofa, her bare feet propped up on the coffee table. "I have an idea. I know what we can do."

"What do you have in mind?" Ian asked.

"I can't believe your parents won't see some of the stuff all of us have. We need to encourage him to go over there every day to look at their lot and plan their house. And one of these days, something is bound to happen," Lily said. "It's going to take your dad a while to get his house plans and go through the approval process. Certainly, something will happen before then, and they'll decide not to build there."

"I told you, even if that happens, it's going to be difficult to unload that property. Adam was not encouraging. Especially if my parents do it in the next few months. I showed you that article."

"I know. Your mother called me. She saw the article over at

Dani's and thought it was hilarious. She wants to frame it and hang it in her new house." Lily rolled her eyes at the idea. "But I know how your parents can sell it and not lose a dime."

Ian looked at Lily. "How?"

"We buy it."

"I told you. There is no way my dad will let me bail him out of this. His pride would get in the way."

"He doesn't have to know you're the one buying it. We'll get Adam to bring the offer."

"My name would be on the offer. My dad would see it," Ian reminded her.

"Not if we set up some sort of shell company and buy it anonymously."

Ian cocked a brow at Lily. "You're being Lucy this time? Well, you do have the red hair for it."

Lily frowned at Ian. "What is that supposed to mean?"

"Sounds like one of those goofy Lucy and Ethel schemes you and Danielle come up with sometimes."

"Oh, hush, it is a good plan," Lily said.

"It is an expensive plan," Ian said.

"I thought you said you would buy the property from your parents."

"Yeah, if it prevented them from building on it. But if they experience what we have, they will never build on it. And if we do what you suggest, my father would be horrible to live with."

"What do you mean?" Lily asked.

"He'll be bragging about what a shrewd businessman he was. Managed to get rid of property—the property I clearly did not feel he should buy. This is complicated enough."

Lily let out a sigh. "Then there is no solution?"

"There is only one I can think of. We need to hire an exorcist."

"Not a bad idea. I wonder if they have one in Frederickport." Lily glanced at her watch.

Ian chuckled, yet silently told himself to ask Danielle to ask Eva if an exorcist could really get rid of unwanted spirits.

"I don't know why my mom had to go shopping in Portland today. She knew Chris was taking us all to Pearl Cove. I hope they get back in time."

Ian reached over and patted her denim-clad thigh. "I'm sure

they will." He was proven right twenty minutes later when the doorbell rang.

"LAURA?" Lily said in surprise when she opened the front door and found her sister standing on her front porch with her parents.

"Surprise," Laura greeted her with a cheeky grin.

Lily laughed, and the two women hugged while Sadie nosed the new arrivals, her tail wagging.

When the hug ended, Gene asked, "Are you going to let us inside now?"

"Sure, Dad." Lily grinned. As she walked in the front door with her sister and parents, she paused a moment and said, "I need to call Pearl Cove and add another person to the party."

"Don't worry about that," Tammy said, following Lily inside. "Danielle called Chris this morning."

"I can't believe we're going to dinner with that hunky and rich Chris Glandon." Laura practically drooled.

"Don't call him that, remember," Lily reminded her. Once inside the house with her family, she shut the door.

"WHAT DO you mean you aren't going with us?" Chris asked Heather when he arrived at her house. He followed her to the living room.

"I appreciate you asking me, but I really don't know those people." Heather picked up Bella, who had been napping on her recliner. She sat down and dropped the cat on her lap. Bella stood up and jumped to the floor.

"You know all of them," Chris argued.

"Yeah, Kelly thinks I'm whacko. And I can't even imagine what she's told her parents about me."

"Well, you *are* kind of whacko."

Heather rolled her eyes.

"Come on. You'll be my date," Chris said.

Heather wrinkled her nose. "Yuck. Now I'm for sure not coming."

Chris laughed. "Okay, not my date. But come as my sidekick."

"I have to admit, I like sidekick better than date. And I do love the food at Pearl Cove. But seriously, Chris, I doubt anyone really wants me to come."

"I know Walt and Danielle do. And so do Lily and Ian. Anyway, I have a feeling Danielle's going to be calling for a meeting of the mediums."

Heather frowned. "Why? Is this about the property Ian's dad bought?"

"That and the boy ghost," Chris said.

"What boy ghost?" Heather asked.

Chris went on to tell Heather what Danielle had told him on the phone earlier that day.

"Wow. Busy week for ghosts. And it isn't even Halloween," Heather said. "But we won't be able to talk about anything with Lily's and Ian's families there. Not to mention Joe."

"True. But we can figure out when would be a good time for all of us, and set it up on the QT."

HEATHER SAT ON HER RECLINER, her feet propped up on its footrest. Chris had left minutes earlier. Reaching up, she tugged the rubber bands from the ends of her two braids. She tossed them on the end table and combed her fingers through her ebony-hued hair. After removing any tangles, she reached to the side and picked up her cellphone from the end table. She dialed Brian.

"Hey, what are you doing?" Brian asked when he answered Heather's call.

"Chris dropped by. He is really bugging me to come to dinner tonight. Says it's because the mediums need to schedule a meeting to discuss ghosts."

"I assume you're talking about the Marymoor ghosts?" Brian asked.

"Yeah, that and some boy ghost hanging out with Connor."

"What?"

Heather told Brian about the new ghost playing with Connor. She then said, "Chris says he wants me there tonight so we can arrange a meeting of the mediums. But there is no way we can discuss anything with Joe and the others there. I think Chris just wants me to protect him from Lily's sister, Laura."

"Laura's here?" Brian asked. "I thought Joe said Lily's sister and brother couldn't make it."

"It was some sort of surprise. Lily's parents picked her up at the airport today. Anyway, she's coming tonight, and the last time Laura was here, she was pretty flirty with Chris. I don't think he wants to deal with her."

"How will you being there help?"

"Chris said something about me going as his date. Gross."

Brian laughed. "I don't think most women would call Chris Glandon gross. Didn't I once say I wondered if he had a thing for you?"

"Oh, shut up. Now you're being gross. Chris is like a brother to me. Anyway, I think he gets some perverse pleasure making some people think I'm his girlfriend. He did that with his uncles."

"Yeah, and that almost got you framed for murder. So, are you going?"

"I have an idea. I think you should come tonight. Have dinner with us," Heather said.

"Sure, you want me to just barge in, invite myself?" he teased.

"No. But if you happen to be at the bar, enjoying their happy hour and appetizers, and I happen to see you and then invite you in front of everyone, what can Chris say? It will serve him right for trying to use me as a buffer for Laura."

THEY ALL ARRIVED at Pearl Cove before their host, Chris Johnson, aka Chris Glandon. Chris had made the arrangements ahead of time, reserving the one ocean view spot that wasn't a booth. The restaurant staff had pushed together several tables to accommodate the larger group.

Ian sat on one end, across from his father and next to Lily. To Lily's right was Connor, and next to him was his grandma Tammy, Gene, and then Walt and Danielle.

Next to John, across from Lily, sat June. Originally, Kelly sat next to her mother, with Joe next to her, and Laura next to Joe. But Kelly and Laura kept chatting away, like long-lost friends, each leaning across Joe to talk to the other one. After a few minutes, Joe offered to switch seats with Kelly.

Lily quietly watched the commotion as everyone took their seats.

Chris and Heather hadn't yet arrived, but Lily knew why Laura had waited to see where the others wanted to sit. Her sister obviously wanted to position herself close to one of the two empty chairs where Chris would be sitting. She loved her sister, but she also knew her sister's tricks.

Lily marveled at how Laura and Kelly seemed like old friends. At her wedding, the two had hit it off despite Laura's attempt at humor, comparing Joe to the fictional Joe Morelli of the popular Stephanie Plum series. She also remembered how the two had tried to hijack her wedding, wanting to move it outdoors. It made Lily wonder, did Kelly intend to have an outdoor wedding?

Everyone had finally taken a seat and passed around menus when the host and Heather arrived.

"He brought Heather?" Laura whispered to Kelly. The two women looked toward the couple walking in their direction. Heather wore a mid-calf-length skirt, heeled boots, with layered blouses in various shades of fuchsia. She wore her hair down around her shoulders, its slight curl from her recent braid. Chris looked as if he'd stepped off the pages of *GQ* instead of his beach-boy persona.

"They work together, and she's always hanging around him," Kelly whispered. "But I don't think you have any competition there."

"He is gorgeous," Laura whispered.

Some of the men at the table stood up. They exchanged hand-shakes and hellos. Chris moved around the table, greeting everyone, while Heather extended a perfunctory greeting to all before excusing herself to use the ladies' room.

Left alone, Chris eventually found himself by the two empty chairs, with Lily's sister, Laura, grinning up at him.

"Oh, I guess I get to sit next to the host," Laura cooed. Still sitting, she reached to the empty chair next to her and pulled it out for Chris. "It was so nice of you to host this dinner. I feel like a gate-crasher." Laura giggled.

"I think she's flirting with you, Chris," Marie observed. Only the mediums at the table could hear. Chris tried to ignore Marie. He was about to suggest Heather might prefer that chair when she got back from the bathroom. But before he did, Heather showed up at the table, practically dragging Brian Henderson with her.

"Look who I found in the bar," Heather said. "It's Joe's best man."

"How did she know?" Kelly muttered under her breath.

Those at the table exchanged more greetings and handshakes.

Chris was still standing when Heather blurted, "I think he should join us, don't you, Chris? After all, he is going to be Joe's best man." Heather nudged Chris to the chair Laura had pulled out, while claiming the empty one next to him, and saying Brian could sit at the end of the table, next to her. All they would need was another chair.

The server moving around the table, taking drink orders, quickly brought Brian a chair. Danielle leaned over to Brian and whispered, "That was pretty slick of Heather."

Brian flashed Danielle a sheepish grin.

"And it is such a coincidence you happened to be in the bar. Do you come here often?" Danielle teased.

Brian's grin broadened.

Danielle glanced across the table and noticed Laura was no longer chatting nonstop with Kelly, but now focused her attention on Chris.

TWENTY-FIVE

C uriosity brought Eva to Ian and Lily's house on Saturday night. She knew they weren't home. Everyone had gone to Pearl Cove for the evening, even Marie. But she wondered if the boy ghost she had heard about would be there. Like the spirits at Marymoor, he had been uncooperative, unwilling to give Marie information to help him move on.

When she arrived in the Bartley living room, Sadie greeted her with a friendly bark, her tail wagging.

"Hello, Sadie. Are you all alone tonight?" Eva asked.

"Who are you?" a childish voice asked in awe. "You're beautiful."

Eva turned from Sadie and faced a young boy. Smiling, she said, "I guess Sadie's not alone. Hello, my name is Eva. Who might you be?"

"I'm Rupert," he said without thought.

Eva smiled softly. "Rupert. Rupert is a wonderful name." Eva took a seat on the sofa and waved to the place next to her. "Why don't you join me, Rupert?"

Without hesitation, Rupert sat next to Eva, his eyes wide as he refused to look away from her. "You are so beautiful."

The corners of Eva's smile twitched. "You are so kind. I imagine you have a most beautiful mother, considering you are such a handsome young man."

Rupert nodded. "Yes, my mother is beautiful too." His smile faded into a frown.

"What is it, Rupert? Where is your mother? I imagine she must be worried about you."

Rupert considered the question for a moment and then shook his head. "I don't really want to talk about her right now. I think I'm going to wait for Connor in his room."

The next moment, he vanished.

"Hmm… at least he told me his name." Eva looked at Sadie and said, "I have to go now, Sadie. Look after Rupert."

EVA SAVED her glitter and snowflakes for another time and arrived at Pearl Cove without fanfare. She located Danielle and the others quickly. When arriving at the table, she found Marie busily making faces at Connor, who kept giggling while his grandmothers discussed what a happy child he was, content to play alone, unaware Marie's spirit kept the boy occupied.

Eva ignored the various discussions taking place at the table. She looked at Danielle and announced, "He told me his name." All the mediums looked at Eva, silently waiting for her to tell them more.

"The child who has been playing with Connor. He told me his name," Eva elaborated.

"Why would he do that?" Marie asked. "I tried forever to get him to tell me."

Eva shrugged. "He said I was beautiful."

"Typical man," Heather muttered.

"What?" Brian asked.

Heather leaned to Brian and whispered, "Eva is here. She's standing right behind you."

"Did he tell you anything else," Danielle whispered. To those around the table, it looked as if Danielle was talking to Brian.

"I assume that was for Eva, not me," Brian whispered back.

Danielle gave him a nod and smiled.

"No. When I mentioned his mother, that seemed to upset him, and he vanished. I peeked into Connor's room and saw him sitting in a large cardboard box. I left him there with Sadie keeping an eye on him."

"The name is something. What is it?" Danielle asked, her voice still a whisper.

"I am curious to find out what you're talking about," Brian muttered.

"Rupert," Eva announced.

Danielle frowned. Rupert? Why did that name sound familiar? While certain she had never known a Rupert, someone close to her had mentioned a Rupert. She considered it a moment and then turned and looked down the table at Lily, who currently chatted with June.

"Lily, excuse me," Danielle called out.

Lily stopped talking and turned to face Danielle, as did everyone else sitting around the table.

"Didn't you used to know a Rupert?" Danielle asked Lily.

Laura started laughing.

Danielle and the others turned to Laura. Lily's sister continued to laugh.

"Oh, Laura, be nice," Tammy chided.

"What is so funny?" Danielle asked. Everyone else at the table silently waited for an answer.

"Rupert was Lily's imaginary friend," Laura explained.

"It was cute," Gene said.

"Yeah, right," Laura scoffed. "Crazy cute."

"You had an imaginary friend?" John asked Lily.

Lily shrugged. "It was no big deal. Lots of kids have imaginary friends."

"Frankly, I'm relieved. That explains a lot," June said.

Ian looked at his mother. "What do you mean, Mom?"

June smiled at Ian and then glanced at Connor. "I have to admit, I was starting to find it a little peculiar how Connor plays. Like he's playing with someone who isn't there. But if this is something that runs in the family, and I suppose Lily turned out fairly normal..."

"Fairly normal?" Lily muttered.

Laura laughed. "That sounds like something I would say."

Lily frowned at her sister.

"It was just a phase she went through," Tammy said defensively. "It's not like talking to imaginary people is something that runs in our family."

"No, just with Lily," Laura teased.

"I don't understand why we are talking about Rupert," Lily asked, sounding annoyed.

"I'm sorry," Danielle said. "Someone mentioned the name, and I thought it sounded familiar."

"It's fairly obvious Lily did not have an imaginary friend as a child. She had a ghost playmate," Eva said.

"A little like Eva was mine," Marie said.

"And then you just stopped seeing me," Eva said sadly.

"But I remember now." Marie smiled at Eva.

"That doesn't make any sense," Danielle said under her breath. Only Eva heard.

"Yes, it makes sense," Eva said. "If you want to know for certain, find out when Lily started seeing Rupert and when she stopped. Perhaps that will give us a key to help him move on."

Danielle looked at Tammy and asked, "I find the phenomenon of imaginary friends fascinating. A lot of children have them. I was wondering, when did you first notice Lily had an imaginary friend?"

Lily frowned at Danielle yet said nothing.

Tammy considered the question a moment and then said, "Honestly, I can't pinpoint when it started. Of all my children, Lily was the easiest."

"Not sure about that," Laura grumbled.

Tammy flashed Laura a smile. "I mean when she was a baby—a toddler. She would wake up from a nap, content and happy in her crib. When she was older, she would play like Connor does now. She could entertain herself." Tammy looked at Laura and said, "You and your brother never did that."

"True, but when she was older, Rupert became a problem," Laura reminded her.

"How does an imaginary friend become a problem?" John asked.

Tammy smiled ruefully. "When Lily started talking, one of the first words she said was Rupert."

"Rupert? Who taught her?" June asked. "That's an unusual name."

"I suspect it was something she saw on television. That must be it, because we didn't know any Ruperts, and I certainly don't know anyone who taught her that name."

Everyone looked at Laura. "It was you, right?" Kelly asked.

Laura looked around the table at all the faces staring in her direction. She laughed. "No. Although, that would have been a great prank. Teach your little sister to say a weird name and get her to say it's her imaginary friend. But no, I can't take credit for that one."

"I have to vouch for Laura there," Tammy said. "Rupert annoyed the dickens out of Laura. I think she was jealous of him."

"I wasn't jealous," Laura grumbled. "But dang, it was annoying, my kid sister always talking about Rupert and how he was her best friend."

"When did it stop?" June asked. "How old was she when she grew out of it?"

Tammy let out a sigh and looked over to Lily, who silently listened. "It was cute at first. But as she got a little older and started talking, she insisted we play along. We did at first. But after a while, well, like Laura said, it was annoying. Finally, one day, something happened. I just wanted the Rupert play to stop."

"What happened?" June asked.

Tammy shrugged. "I don't really remember."

"I do," Laura said. All eyes at the table turned to Laura.

"What did she do?" Kelly asked.

"One day Lily thought it would be a good idea to put all her stuffed animals in the bathtub and give them a bath."

Lily groaned.

"Mom was not happy. Lily insisted it was Rupert's idea, not hers," Laura explained.

"So what happened?" Kelly asked.

"Mom told Lily she had ruined the stuffed animals," Laura continued. "She put some of the other toys Lily had been playing with in a big cardboard box and ordered Rupert to get in the box with the toys. Mom told Lily that when she learned to take care of her things like a big girl, she could have them back."

"What happened after that?" Kelly asked.

Laura shrugged. "It worked, I guess. The Rupert play stopped. Well, not right away. But instead of Lily acting like Rupert was with her, she played along with Mom, pretending he was up in the attic with her toys. Every day Lily would ask Mom when Rupert could come back downstairs. I guess Lily finally got the message, Mom didn't want to play the game anymore."

"She said he moved," Lily blurted.

Everyone at the table looked to Lily.

"Mom told me Rupert wasn't coming to play with me. She said he moved away to another city to be with his family. That's when I stopped asking," Lily said.

"Did you get your toys back?" Kelly asked.

"Eventually, but I didn't really want to play with them anymore." Lily paused a moment and looked at Tammy. "Those are the toys you brought Connor, aren't they?"

"Yes. I never understood why you didn't want them anymore. But I thought maybe Connor would like them. Some are like new," Tammy said.

Ian playfully wrapped an arm around Lily and pulled her close. Teasingly he said, "I never knew you were such a troubled little girl." He kissed her forehead.

Lily failed to see the humor in Ian's lighthearted jest. Something about rehearing the Rupert story bothered her. She didn't have time to dwell on it. The next moment, a server showed up to clear their dinner plates and take their dessert order. A few minutes later, someone changed the topic of conversation.

When Lily excused herself to visit the ladies' room before they brought dessert, Danielle and Heather got up to go too. When the three were out of earshot of the rest of their party, Lily asked Danielle, "Why did you have to bring up Rupert? Who brought up the name? I want to kick that person. I really didn't need all that."

Lily pushed her way into the women's restroom, Danielle and Heather right behind her. Once Danielle was certain the three were alone in the bathroom, she said, "Lily, we know who the ghost playing with Connor is. Eva is the one who brought up the name."

Instead of continuing to one of the stalls, Lily stopped, turned around, and faced Danielle. "What are you talking about?"

"Eva was over at your house tonight. She got the ghost to tell her his name. It's Rupert."

Lily frowned. "Rupert?"

"I think you are the Lily he was looking for. I don't think Rupert was an imaginary friend. He was your ghost playmate. Like he is Connor's now."

TWENTY-SIX

L ily stared dumbly at Danielle, her forehead drawn into a frown. She didn't respond immediately. Finally, she said, "No way. You're saying my Rupert, my imaginary friend, was really a ghost?"

"It looks that way," Danielle said.

Lily shook her head emphatically. "No. I can't see ghosts."

Danielle grinned and reached out to Lily's hand. "Lily, you understand it doesn't work like that. Your own son——" Before Danielle could finish her sentence, Lily turned abruptly and walked from Danielle and Heather, going into one of the toilet stalls. She slammed the door and locked it.

Heather turned to Danielle and arched her brows. "Wow, Lily had a ghost friend when she was a kid?"

From the stall Lily yelled, "No I didn't!"

Heather and Danielle looked at each other, and Danielle whispered, "Yeah, I think she did."

"Stop talking about me!" Lily yelled from the stall.

Heather rolled her eyes and looked at Danielle and said, "Since we can't talk about Lily—are you pregnant?"

"I haven't bought a test yet. It's been a little crazy, having a house full of guests and dealing with unwanted hauntings," Danielle said. "But please don't ask that so loud. Someone could come in here, and I don't want to say anything until I know for sure and am ready to tell people."

They heard the toilet flush. A moment later Lily walked out from the stall and headed to the sink. Silently, she washed her hands while Danielle and Heather watched. When she turned around and faced them, she said, "I think you're right. About Rupert. How did I not see it?"

"What changed your mind?" Danielle asked.

"I remember what he looked like. In my head, I can picture him. I convinced myself I somehow imagined all that. But now… now I'm not sure," Lily said.

"What does he look like?" Heather asked.

Lily described a little boy who could very well be the Rupert who had been playing with Connor—or a hundred other little boys.

"It sorta sounds like him," Danielle said.

"You really think this ghost was my imaginary friend?" Lily asked.

"Of course he was," Eva said the next moment when she appeared in the bathroom.

"Eva's here," Danielle told Lily.

"I've been giving it some consideration. Lily might be the one to help Rupert move on," Eva said. "She's the one he's been waiting for all these years. There is a bond."

Danielle repeated what Eva said.

"How do I do that?" Lily frowned.

"We can help you later. I also came in here to tell you, you need to get back to the table; the others are wondering what happened to you," Eva said.

Again, Danielle repeated what Eva said.

"I need to use the bathroom," Heather blurted before turning and heading to a stall.

HEATHER, Danielle, and Lily returned to the table just as the server brought the plates of dessert—and just in time to hear Tammy tell June, "Lily doesn't want to go back to teaching."

Lily frowned at her mother while taking her seat. "I probably will someday," she said.

Tammy looked at her daughter. "June thought you wanted to go back now."

"Oh. Yeah, not now. Connor keeps me pretty busy." Lily grinned over at her son, who was happily eating a cookie.

"Now that we'll be living here, it won't be a problem," June said.

"Mother, not now," Ian said under his breath.

Lily frowned at Ian. "What?"

June laughed. "My son is just being silly. He didn't want me to say anything when we told you about the property. But now that's all behind us, and you've all seen it and gotten over that ghost nonsense, you can start making plans to go back to work. Kelly says school has already started, but I'm sure you can substitute."

Lily frowned. "I'm not sure I understand what you're talking about."

Tammy reached over and patted her daughter's hand. "June seems to believe you're eager to go back to teaching, and she has generously offered to watch Connor for you so you can."

Lily understood her mother and recognized the sarcasm in her voice. Fortunately, Lily didn't imagine June had picked up on the true nuance of her mother's words.

Lily giggled. "Oh my gosh, that's sweet of you, June, but honestly, I hate subbing. Thank you for the kind offer, but I'd rather be poked in the eye with a fork than sub again."

John frowned. "Odd expression."

Lily flashed John a smile. "It's something one of my friends, Lynn, used to say. She was a teacher I worked with in California. It fits."

"Are you saying you hated teaching?" June asked.

"No. I loved teaching. Subbing is something entirely different," Lily said.

"I just assumed, the extra money…" June stammered.

"Mom, we don't need the extra money," Ian said.

"I understand you make a lot of money, Ian. But women these days don't want to be taken care of like a child. They want their own money." June turned to Lily and smiled. "Isn't that right?"

"I don't imagine any adult appreciates being treated like a child," Lily said sweetly.

Fascinated by the conversation, Heather silently ate her dessert while listening to the exchange. It started to piss her off.

"She can go back to work next fall," June said. "Although, you should rethink subbing."

"Mother, Lily and I discussed this before Connor was born. We both want her to be a stay-at-home mom."

"Ian, dear, you sound so old-fashioned. Lily is a modern woman; you can't make her stay home just because it suits you. Women these days need to have a purpose and contribute to the family income."

"That's not a problem for Lily," Heather blurted.

Startled by Heather's comment, June looked down the table and frowned.

Heather flashed June a smile and said, "Lily has a purpose; she's an awesome mom. I understand she was an awesome teacher too. That's what Evan MacDonald says. He was one of Lily's students. But for now, Lily wants to focus on Connor. It's not something all women would want. Heck, I don't even want kids. But I respect her for it. And if you're worried about her feeling funny about not contributing money to the household, I guess you aren't aware of the small fortune she brought into the marriage."

Momentarily speechless, June stared at Heather. She blinked her eyes several times and then said, "Yes, I'm aware of the settlement. But it isn't just about money. I just assumed Lily would be anxious to go back to teaching, and I wanted her to understand I'd love to watch Connor for her."

"June, that is such a sweet offer," Lily said. "Really it is. But like Ian said, this is something he and I discussed before Connor was born. I understand I'm more fortunate than most women. I have a choice. I can be a stay-at-home mother or go back to teaching. Most women don't have that choice. But I do. And for now, I choose to be at home with Connor and Ian. It's where I want to be."

Ian smiled at his wife, reached over, and gave her hand a gentle squeeze.

"Since we're discussing babysitting and Connor, we should talk Ian and Lily into doing something romantic for their anniversary. After all, there are so many willing and able babysitters available," Danielle said. With the conversation turned in another direction, those who hadn't finished their desserts resumed eating.

"Wow, I've never seen Heather talk that much," Laura whispered to Kelly.

"I wonder if that guy she's dating knows she doesn't want kids," Kelly whispered back.

"She's dating someone?" Laura mouthed, not wanting Chris to overhear.

"That's what she said. Some guy who's a lot younger than her."

Laura glanced down the table at Heather, who was talking to Brian and Chris.

"Do you know the guy she's seeing?" Laura whispered.

Kelly shook her head.

"They seem pretty friendly." Laura nodded to Brian.

Kelly frowned. "You mean Brian and her?"

Laura nodded.

"They developed some weird bond after the kidnapping. Your sister told you about that, right?" Kelly asked.

"Yeah." Laura ate her last bite of dessert and looked away from Heather.

Meanwhile, the mediums did their own whispering around the dinner table. They all agreed to meet at Chris's house in the morning, to discuss what they might do to help exorcise the spirits haunting the Marymoor property while helping Rupert move on.

ACROSS TOWN, while Joe Morelli had dinner with his fiancée's family and friends, his sister, Tori Simmons, sat stoically in her recliner, flipping through photographs on her iPad.

"What's with the frown?" her husband, Craig, asked when entering the room.

Tori glanced up from her iPad and watched as Craig sat in the recliner next to hers.

"I was looking at the pictures I took over at the museum. Do you realize how bizarre this all is?" she asked.

"It is pretty weird."

"I thought putting something together on Joe's family history would be a cool shower gift. A way for her to learn more about our family. Especially if they have kids someday." Tori let out a sigh.

"Have you told your brother?" Craig asked.

Tori flashed her husband a frown. "No."

Craig chuckled. "Come on, you're making way too much of this. I imagine everyone has someone in their family tree they would rather keep hidden. Go back, like, ten generations and we have over a thousand great-great-grandparents. What is that, seven greats or something? What are the chances none of them are crazy?"

"This is a great-great-grandmother. Joe and I only have sixteen of those, not a thousand."

Craig shrugged. "Still, one out of sixteen, seems like reasonable odds."

Tori looked back to her iPad and started flipping through the photographs again. "I looked them all up. They were all wealthy. Just like Caroline."

"What is it they say, money doesn't guarantee sanity," Craig said.

Tori looked to him and frowned. "Nobody says that."

"They should. It's true. Considering what you're looking at." He nodded to the iPad.

"What I find strange, their pictures were all together."

Craig shrugged. "Why is that strange? They were patients of Marymoor, right? You got those from the Marymoor file at the museum."

"Yes. But I don't believe all the patients at Marymoor were wealthy. And why did they keep these photos in a separate envelope? Millie told me the museum didn't put them in the envelope. They were like that when the museum got the files."

"Think about it, Tori. Marymoor administration probably considered those women special patients. All from wealthy and influential families of the time. Like VIPs."

"VIPs in a mental institution?" she said with a snort.

Craig shrugged again. "Something like that."

"I wonder if I should show these to Ian," Tori muttered, still focused on the images.

"Why?" Craig asked.

"His parents did buy Marymoor; I imagine he's interested in the property. There could be a story here."

Craig laughed.

"What?"

"One minute you act like you don't want anyone to find out about her; the next you're talking about turning the story of your great-great-grandmother dying in a mental institution over to a famous journalist."

TWENTY-SEVEN

"That was an interesting dinner," Walt said when he and Danielle were alone in their bedroom later that evening. Downstairs, their guests had gone to their rooms for the night.

"I was proud of Tammy. There were a couple of times tonight I thought she wanted to smack June," Danielle said as she sat on the edge of their bed and slipped off her shoes.

"Heather surprised me, standing up for Lily like that," Walt said.

"I noticed Lily gave Heather a hug when they said goodbye at the restaurant. Lily and Heather normally don't hug," Danielle said with a chuckle. "At least, not each other."

"It was hard for me to keep up with everything." Walt sat on the end of the bed, next to Danielle.

"There was just too much going on tonight. I feel like my head is going to explode."

Walt reached over and gave Danielle's knee a pat. "Something a good night's sleep will fix."

"I can't go to bed right now; I have an idea."

Walt groaned.

Ignoring Walt's reaction, Danielle asked, "Can I use your computer? I left mine in the parlor, and I really don't want to go back downstairs and chance one of them getting up and asking me what I'm doing. With Ian's parents staying in the downstairs bedroom, with my luck it would be June."

"Can't this wait until tomorrow? When we go over to Chris's in the morning, you can share your idea with everyone."

"It won't take long," Danielle promised.

With a sigh, Walt looked at Danielle. "Okay, what's your idea? What are you so determined to look up?"

"It's about Rupert. I have an idea how to figure out who he is," Danielle said.

"I thought we already determined he was Lily's imaginary friend."

"I mean before that. Something that might help him move on."

Walt studied Danielle for a moment and then said, "Go on."

"I was thinking about what Rupert told Marie. He first met Lily when she was a baby. Younger than Connor, he said. Somewhere where women were wrapping up other babies. What does that sound like to you?"

Walt stared at Danielle and then shrugged. "Where?"

"A hospital, silly. The maternity ward. That's where Rupert first saw Lily. And why does a ghost typically hang out at a hospital?"

"Because they died there?"

"Exactly! So I was thinking, one of the genealogy sites I use has a comprehensive California death certificate data base. I could look for someone named Rupert who died around the time Lily was born. And if he died in the same hospital—well, not sure the death certificate will say the hospital, but it will the county—then maybe we found our Rupert."

"Danielle, while you're probably right, what Rupert described to Marie is likely a maternity ward, and it stands to reason he died in that hospital. It doesn't mean he died around the time of Lily's birth. He might have been wandering the halls of that hospital years before Lily was born."

"No. I remember Tammy once telling a story about Lily's birth. The hospital was brand new, and when she went into labor, Gene was so flustered, he started driving to the hospital Laura had been born at, and Tammy had to tell him to turn around. That hospital opened the year before Lily was born. Now, it is possible Rupert died in the area, and for whatever reason, got stuck in the hospital, like Lucas did in that office building. And considering his name— not exactly a name my parents' generation commonly named their kids—so it is entirely possible I won't find anything helpful. But I want to at least try. I doubt it will take thirty minutes."

Walt let out a sigh and said, "Go on, use my computer. Do you want to take your shower first?"

Danielle shook her head. "No. Go take yours. I'll take mine after you."

WHEN WALT GOT out of the shower, he found Danielle sitting at his computer, intently focused on the monitor while her right hand fiddled with the mouse. Shirtless and wearing plaid pajama bottoms, his hair wet and combed back, Walt sat in a chair next to her and said, "You can take your shower now."

She looked at him. "I found something."

"Really?"

Danielle nodded and looked back to the computer. "Yes. I found the death certificate for an eight-year-old boy named Rupert Peterson, who died the same day Lily was born, in the same county. I'm looking for anything else on him. Considering when he died, there really wasn't the internet back then. At least, not like it is today. So I'm looking in one of the newspaper archives. I had to renew my membership."

Walt silently watched as Danielle continued to surf for information. After a while, Walt stood up and walked to his nightstand. He picked up his cellphone and looked at the time. Danielle had been at the computer for over forty minutes now. He was about to suggest she call it a night when she cried out, "Oh my gosh, it's him!"

Walt walked to the computer as Danielle turned the monitor slightly so he could get a better view. On the screen was the image of a newspaper article with a black-and-white photograph of a little boy. He looked just like the ghost they had met across the street.

"It's so sad," Danielle said. "His name was Rupert James Peterson. He was just a few weeks shy of his eighth birthday when he died. He died at the hospital the same day Lily was born."

"How did he die?" Walt asked, sitting back down.

"He had some sort of congenital heart condition. Reminds me a little of Eva. Except in his case, it had gone undetected. He was playing baseball with some friends and collapsed. They brought him right to the hospital, but they couldn't save him."

"And that poor boy got lost at the hospital," Walt said. "I wonder if his parents are still alive."

"It's entirely possible. He didn't have any siblings. But his parents could have had more kids after he died. If his parents are still alive, there may be grandparents who've moved on, waiting for him." Danielle stood up from the computer and walked to the window. She pulled open the blinds and looked outside.

"What are you doing?" Walt asked.

"I'm hoping Lily is still awake."

"Why?"

Danielle turned to Walt. "Eva is right; Lily is the best one to reach him. She needs to do this now before he wanders somewhere else and stays lost."

"How is Lily supposed to do that?" Walt asked. "She isn't a medium."

"But she can talk to him," Danielle reminded him. "The lights are on over there. I'm going to call her."

Walt didn't try arguing with Danielle. She had made up her mind.

"ARE YOU COMING TO BED?" Ian asked Lily when he walked into the living room and found her sitting on the sofa.

"I can't sleep. Not after what Dani told me tonight," Lily whispered, looking toward the nursery.

Lily's cellphone rang. She picked it up off the coffee table, looked at it, and said, "It's Dani."

Ian let out a sigh, walked to his recliner, and sat down.

"Hi, Dani," Lily said a moment later.

"Where are you?" Danielle asked.

"I'm sitting in the living room with Ian." Lily glanced at Ian and smiled.

"Where's Connor?" Danielle asked.

"He's sleeping. Marie's in there with him. I assume Rupert's in there too." Lily let out a groan and said, "I don't believe any of this."

"I have his picture," Danielle blurted.

"Whose picture?" Lily asked.

Danielle told Lily all she had learned that night. Across the room, Ian curiously watched as Lily listened to what Danielle had to say. He wondered what Danielle was telling his wife.

When Danielle finished her telling, Lily blurted, "Send me the picture!"

"Rupert's?" Danielle asked.

"Yes. I still have a hard time believing this."

"Okay. I'll text it to you. After you look at it, call me back on my cellphone and tell me if it's your Rupert."

When Lily got off the phone, Ian asked, "What was that all about?"

"Danielle is sending me a picture. Hold on. I'll tell you in a minute." Lily looked at her phone, waiting for Danielle's text to arrive.

IAN WANTED to go to bed. It had been an exhausting day. He watched as Lily stared at her phone. After whatever Danielle had sent arrived, she hurriedly opened her messages. She stared at the cellphone, not saying a word. Suddenly, Lily broke into tears.

Ian jumped from his chair and rushed to Lily. "What is it?" She threw herself on the sofa, facedown, and cried unconsolably. Her cellphone rang. Lily ignored her phone, but Ian answered the call. It was Danielle.

"What the hell did you send Lily?" Ian asked angrily.

"What's wrong?" Danielle asked.

"Can't you hear her? She's sobbing. What did you send her?"

"I'll be right there," Danielle said.

LILY, Ian, and Danielle sat in the Bartley living room. Lily had finally stopped crying, and now sat next to Ian, his arm wrapped around her shoulder.

"Please tell me if he comes in here," Lily whispered.

"Who?" Ian asked.

"I'm pretty sure she means Rupert," Danielle said.

Lily nodded.

"Will someone tell me what's going on?" Ian asked.

With a sniffle, Lily turned to Ian. "He really was my imaginary friend. But he was never an imaginary friend. He was a ghost. And he was my best friend, my constant companion for the first six years of my life."

Ian glanced toward the nursery. "It's really him?"

Lily nodded. "In my head, I could visualize what he looked like. Of course, over the years, I believed my imagination made it all up. But when Dani sent me his picture… it was him. And he was just a frightened little boy. And they locked him in our attic for all those years, frightened and alone." Lily began to cry again.

"Lily," Danielle said gently, "spirits don't have the same sense of time as living people. Not even little-boy ghosts. Ask Walt. You need to pull yourself together, because you can't help Rupert move on if you keep crying."

A few minutes later, Lily sniffled and wiped the tears from her eyes with the back of her sleeve. "How do I do that? How do I help him move on?"

"You need to talk to him," Danielle said.

"But I can't see him."

"You talked to Cheryl and helped her. And you couldn't see her," Danielle reminded.

Lily smiled at the memory. "Yeah, I did, didn't I?"

"And with Rupert, you know things that no one else does. If you want to help him, this is how you can. Help him come to terms with his reality, and then he can move on. He will be happier."

Lily nodded. "I can do this."

TWENTY-EIGHT

Marie heard them in the living room. Sitting on the rocking chair in Connor's room, she glanced to the crib. Connor had fallen asleep before they had gotten home from the restaurant. Rupert had retreated to the cardboard box with Lily's old toys. She heard him humming softly.

Frowning, Marie wondered what was going on. It sounded like someone was crying. Glancing back to the box and then to the crib, Marie instantly moved from the rocking chair to the living room just in time to see Danielle leaving. Danielle's back was to her, and she didn't notice Marie standing there. Marie was about to say something to Danielle, but she noticed Lily going to Connor's room. Instead of following Danielle out, Marie returned to the rocking chair in the nursery. The next moment, Lily eased open the bedroom door and stood there, looking in. The room's night-light provided the only lighting.

Connor stirred in the crib. Lily walked to it and looked down at her son. He fussed.

"I bet you need a diaper change," Lily whispered. The next moment, a diaper floated over to Lily. "Thank you, Marie."

Quietly, Lily changed Connor's diaper. She picked him up and looked at the rocking chair.

"Marie, if Rupert is still here, please rock the chair."

The chair rocked, and Connor fussed some more.

"Marie, I'd like to sit on the rocking chair with Connor," Lily whispered.

"Certainly, dear," Marie said, moving from the rocking chair. She watched as Lily sat down with Connor, holding him in her arms.

"Connor," Lily said, "I would like to tell you a story about Marie and Rupert."

Rupert popped out of the box. "Is she talking about me?"

"I imagine so," Marie said. "Why don't you come sit next to me, and we'll listen."

Rupert scampered out of the box and sat down next to Marie, his eyes on Connor and Lily.

"Once upon a time," Lily began. She brushed her fingertips along Connor's forehead as she gently rocked him in the chair. He looked up at Lily and smiled. "Before you were born, I moved to Frederickport and met your daddy. I also met a very nice lady name Marie. When Marie was a baby, like you, she lived in this house. This was her room."

Rupert looked to Marie. "Is she talking about you?"

Marie nodded. "Yes, dear. She is."

"Marie became a very good friend to me and your daddy. She even sold us this house." Lily smiled down at Connor. "But one day something sad happened, Marie died."

Rupert looked to Marie and frowned. "What is she talking about?"

"Just listen," Marie whispered.

"We were all very sad; we were going to miss Marie. When people die, they usually move on in their journey. They go some- where—I guess it is heaven—where they see all the friends and family who died before them. It's like a big reunion party."

"I don't understand," Rupert said.

"Shh… listen," Marie whispered.

"But Marie was not ready to move on in her adventure. No, she wanted to stick around because she has a grandson she wanted to see married. And she was afraid if she moved on, he might never get married."

"That's not exactly accurate," Marie muttered.

"So Marie stayed," Lily continued. "Her spirit decided to stick around with all of us. Some people call the spirit who sticks around a ghost. Some people think of ghosts as scary things, but Marie isn't scary."

Rupert looked to Marie, his eyes wide. "You're a ghost?"

"Normally, I can't see ghosts," Lily said. "But I know Marie is here because we have some friends who can see ghosts. And sometimes, well, sometimes babies can see ghosts, like you can see Marie."

Rupert looked back to Lily, fascinated with her tale.

"But guess what? When I was a baby, I could see ghosts, just like you," Lily whispered to Connor.

"You could?" Rupert asked.

"She can't hear you," Marie reminded him.

Ignoring Marie, Rupert continued to stare at Lily.

"Connor, while Marie chose to stick around and watch you grow up and see that her grandson gets married, not all ghosts—or spirits —stay because they made a choice. Some stay because they're confused, and they don't realize they're dead."

Connor kicked his feet and let out a babbling sound. He stared up at his mother.

"When my mommy was pregnant with me, she went into labor, and Daddy took her to a hospital. That's where I was born, in a hospital. Before my parents took me home, a little boy died in the hospital. He was very sick, but he didn't understand. Even his parents didn't. They were all very shocked when he died suddenly. It was very sad."

"What little boy?" Rupert asked.

"He was confused, because he didn't expect to die. He found me in the nursery with the other newborns, and for some reason he decided to go home with me. I think because he couldn't find his parents. Like you can see Marie, I could see him. And as I grew up, he stayed with me. He was my best friend. He was my special friend. We had so much fun together. I never got lonely because he was always there. And since he could not pick up toys like a living boy, he never stole my toys." Lily chuckled at the memory while silent tears rolled down her face.

"He taught me to build sandcastles at the beach. He couldn't do it himself, but he told me how. My sister teased me. Said he wasn't real. So did my parents. Sometimes they would pretend he was real, but to them, it was a game."

Rupert stood up, his eyes still on Lily.

"One day, Rupert suggested I give my stuffed animals a bath. I got in trouble. And when I said it was Rupert's idea, my mother got angry. She gathered up some of my toys, put them in a box, and said until I proved I could take care of them, she was putting them away. She ordered Rupert to get in the box with them. Mom didn't think Rupert was real. She was just trying to get me to give up what she thought was my imaginary friend. But I think she scared Rupert, so he did as she told him. He got in the box. And I never saw my friend again."

Tears streamed down Lily's face. She closed her eyes and lowered her head. "I'm so sorry, Rupert. I never meant to hurt you."

"Lily!" Rupert gasped. "It really is you, my Lily!"

Gently, Marie lifted Connor out of Lily's arms and carried him over to the crib. Lily remained sitting in the rocking chair, tears still sliding down her cheeks.

Rupert moved closer, sitting by her side. He looked up at her. "It really is you?" he whispered.

Marie set Connor on the mattress and turned to Rupert and Lily. "Remember, she can't hear or see you."

"But she used to," Rupert said.

"Yes. When I was a baby, a spirit named Eva Thorndike used to visit my crib. I could see her. She would sing to me. But as I got older, I could no longer see her. But now that we are both spirits, we're friends. And I can see her again. She, like me, decided not to move on yet."

Rupert looked at Marie. "I'm dead, aren't I?"

Marie nodded.

"I'm the sick little boy who died in the hospital."

"I'm afraid so," Marie whispered.

Rupert let out a sigh. "I sort of always knew." He looked toward the crib. "Does this mean someday Connor will stop seeing us?"

Marie shrugged. "I'm not sure. I suspect I stopped seeing Eva because no one around me could see her. With Connor, there are several adults in his life—including his parents—who acknowledge I'm here. So it's possible with them acknowledging my existence, he won't stop seeing me. But I'm not sure."

"Will Lily let me stay with Connor?" Rupert asked.

"I think Lily would rather you do what's best for you," Marie said.

"What's that?" Rupert asked.

"Move on in your journey. I imagine there is someone waiting for you."

"Like my mom and dad?" he said hopefully.

"It depends. Your parents might be around the same age as Lily's parents, perhaps a little older. Lily's parents are still alive. Do you remember your grandparents?"

"Yeah. I loved my grandparents. I miss them."

"Were they still alive the last time you remember?" Marie asked.

Rupert nodded.

"Marie, is Rupert still here? If he is, will you move something," Lily whispered.

Marie looked at the box Rupert had been sitting in. It lifted into the air, then dropped back to the floor.

"I need to know if Rupert is okay. If he understands. Can you lift the box if he does?" Lily asked.

Marie looked at Rupert. "Are you okay?"

Rupert nodded.

LILY CRAWLED into bed with Ian. When she did, he rolled over and took her in his arms.

"Are you okay?" Ian asked in a whisper.

"I think so. Drained. I have no idea what Rupert understood, or where we go from here. This has been the craziest day!"

Just as Ian pulled her closer, the cellphone on the nightstand rang.

"Who is calling this late?" Ian grumbled.

Lily pulled away from Ian and picked up the phone. She looked at it. "It's Dani."

Lily answered the phone. Ian watched as Lily listened to what Danielle was telling her. Finally, Lily hung up.

"What was that about?" Ian asked.

"Marie popped over to Walt and Danielle's to convey a message to me."

"We lead the weirdest life," Ian muttered and then asked, "What did Marie say?"

"Rupert listened to what I said, and he accepted everything. He is ready to move on—"

"Thank God," Ian blurted.

"But first he needs our help."

"Of course he does," Ian groaned. Flopping his head back on his pillow, he stared up into the darkness. "What does he want?"

"To find out where his parents are. If they're still alive, he wants to find them before he moves on, to make sure they're okay."

Ian let out a sigh. "I suppose I can help find them."

"Once we help Rupert, then we can focus on our other issue."

Ian drew Lily back into his arms. He held her for a few moments and then said, "You know what always drives me crazy?"

"Yes. The best stories of your life are the ones you can never write."

Ian pulled away and looked at her. "How did you know I was going to say that?"

"Because you basically say the same thing each time one of these things happens." Lily snuggled closer.

"Maybe I should start writing fiction," Ian said after a few minutes.

"Fiction?"

"It wouldn't really be fiction. But everyone would think it was."

Lily chuckled and gave Ian a quick kiss. "Go to sleep. I have a feeling this is going to be a long two weeks."

"I hate to remind you," Ian said. "It's going to be longer than two weeks. My parents aren't leaving, remember?"

Lily groaned and then rolled out of Ian's arms, her back now to him as she hugged a pillow. "I love you, Ian, goodnight."

"Night, Lily. I love you too." Ian rolled over, his back now touching Lily's.

TWENTY-NINE

Something licked his mouth. Chris opened his eyes and found his pit bull, Hunny, staring into his face. The next moment, the dog swiped her wet tongue over his nose. Pushing Hunny away, Chris grunted. "Really, Hunny?" Glancing over at the clock on his nightstand, he saw it was almost 7:30 a.m. Chris could normally sleep in on Sunday morning, but in that moment, he remembered the mediums were all meeting at his house in an hour and a half. Instead of jumping out of bed, he wiped the back of one hand over his mouth and nose to remove the dog slobber.

Hunny remained by Chris's side, sitting on the floor next to the bed, staring intently at him. The dog whimpered, never taking her eyes off her human.

Reluctantly, Chris sat up in bed and looked down at the dog. "What is it, girl? You need to go out?" Hunny whimpered again.

Letting out a sigh and about to climb out of bed, Chris paused when he heard it—the sound of running water. The next minute Chris was up, out of bed, and in his kitchen, cursing. A small river traveled through his kitchen and into the living room, its source a broken pipe under the sink. It took him a few minutes, but he finally got the water turned off.

"This isn't supposed to happen with a new house," Chris grumbled as he mopped up the mess while Hunny watched. He looked over at the dog and smiled. "Is this what you were trying to tell me?"

After cleaning up the water, Chris got Bill Jones on the phone, who agreed to be at the house in half an hour. Once off the phone with Bill, Chris sent two text messages, one to Heather and one to Danielle. He considered calling, but he wasn't sure they were up yet, and he saw no reason to wake them.

The messages read: *I had a water pipe break. Bill is coming over to fix it. We can't talk while he's here. Let's meet at Heather's instead, same time. See you at 9.*

HEATHER ROLLED over in bed and bumped into Brian. He stared into her face and smiled.

"Good morning," Heather greeted him. "What time is it?"

"I think you're going to be late for Chris's. It's almost nine." Brian grinned.

"Dang!" Heather jumped out of bed. "Why didn't you wake me?"

Brian chuckled. "I just woke up a couple of minutes ago. Did you know you snore?"

"I do not!" She snatched her robe off the end of the bed and hastily put it on.

"You do," he teased, sitting up in bed.

"Well, maybe I do." She glanced around the room.

"What are you looking for?"

"My cellphone. I need to text Chris and let him know I'll be a little late." She glanced at the clock. It was just a few minutes until nine, and then she remembered. "It's downstairs. I left it in the kitchen."

Brian started to get out of bed. "You get dressed, and I'll run down and get it for you."

"No." Heather pushed him back in bed. "You don't have to get up. I'll run down, send him a quick message, and then get dressed. You go back to sleep."

"Why would I do that?" He frowned.

Heather shrugged. "It's Sunday. Sundays are to sleep in. Anyway, I should be back in an hour, and you promised to make me breakfast."

Brian laughed. "Fine." He leaned back on his pillow and watched as she dashed out of the room.

WHILE GOING TO THE KITCHEN, Heather heard someone knocking on her front door. She walked to the door and peeked out the side window. Chris, Walt, and Danielle stood on her porch. With a frown, she opened the door.

"What are you guys doing here?" Heather asked.

"Didn't you get my message?" Chris asked, walking into her house without waiting for an invitation. Walt and Danielle followed him. Once inside, Chris paused a moment and looked Heather up and down, noting her messy just-out-of-bed hair and the way she clutched the belt of her robe tighter.

"You aren't even dressed yet," Chris observed. "And your hair… didn't you get my text?"

"What text? I overslept and just came downstairs to send you a message to let you know I was running late. I left my phone in the kitchen last night. Why are you here?"

"Chris woke up to a broken pipe," Danielle explained. "Bill is over there working on it. And we really couldn't do this at our house, with Ian's and Lily's parents there."

"I'll go make coffee while you put something on," Chris said, turning and heading for the kitchen. But when he did, the sound of someone on the stairs stopped him. He turned and looked up into the face of Brian Henderson—a startled Brian Henderson— wearing just boxers.

"Oh crap," Heather groaned.

"BRIAN? SERIOUSLY?" Chris said for the third time.

"I'm surprised it took you this long to figure out." Walt chuckled. The four sat in Heather's kitchen, drinking coffee.

After Brian had barged in on Heather's unexpected guests, Danielle ushered Walt and Chris in the kitchen, where she made coffee and left Heather to deal with Brian, who quickly dressed and made a hasty exit.

"You knew?" Chris asked Walt.

183

"Sure. I'm not stupid." Walt took a sip of his coffee.

Chris frowned at Walt, and Danielle chuckled. "Chris, you might say they bonded on their little adventure in the woods."

Chris looked from Danielle to Heather, who just shrugged and took another sip of coffee. After seeing Brian off, Heather hadn't bothered changing out of her robe, but she had combed her hair.

"He's old enough to be your father," Chris told her.

"If he were my father, then it would be an issue," Heather said.

"But it's Brian Henderson," Chris said.

Heather frowned. "You seriously don't like Brian?"

"He did try to arrest me—and Danielle," Chris said.

"That was, like, a million years ago," Heather reminded him.

Chris sighed. "True. And I must admit, he's been an alright guy lately. And he handled the ghost thing impressively well. So that's why he's been around so much lately?"

"You're okay with me dating him, then?" Heather asked.

"I guess when it comes right down to it, it really is not my business. As long as he's good to you, and you're happy, then I suppose I'll have to get used to it."

"You do know, I don't really care if it is none of my business, if you start dating someone I don't approve of, I will say something," Heather told Chris.

"Yeah, I know." Chris took a drink of coffee and then asked, "Joe doesn't know, does he?"

"Oh, gawd no." Heather cringed.

Chris frowned. "Why not? Why is Brian keeping it a secret from him?"

"Brian's not keeping it a secret. I am."

WHEN THE DISCUSSION of Brian and Heather ended, the four turned to the business at hand. Danielle started by filling Heather and Chris in on what had happened between Lily and Rupert the night before.

"Wow, that is amazing," Chris said.

"Fortunately, I don't think Rupert is going to be a problem. Ian is trying to see what he can track down on his parents, and then we can figure out what to do next. But the biggest issue we have right now is Marymoor," Danielle said.

"I might get some perverse pleasure thinking of Joe and Kelly visiting her parents after they build a house there, if it weren't for Connor," Heather said.

"There is always a chance June and John will witness some of the things we have and not build on the site, but according to Adam, it's going to be hard to resell that property," Danielle said.

"Do you have any ideas?" Heather asked.

"We need to find some way to convince the spirits to move on," Danielle said.

"I know that. But according to Marie and Eva, they aren't being very cooperative. Sounds to me like what we need is an old-fashioned exorcism," Heather said.

"We need to learn more about them. Find out why they haunt that place," Chris said.

"Because they're ghosts of crazy people," Heather suggested.

"Eva thinks there's something else," Walt said. "Something that's keeping them here."

"She also thinks there are more than three spirits over there. They've seen three so far, but they feel there's more who refuse to show themselves," Danielle said.

"A couple of us need to go over there," Chris suggested. "They are obviously not showing themselves to Eva and Marie, who tried talking to them. But I wonder, perhaps if a medium goes over there —doesn't attempt to communicate with them, pretends not to see them. It's possible others will show themselves."

"Kinda like eavesdropping?" Heather asked.

"Something like that," Chris said. "It may not work, but we could give it a shot."

"Walt and I could drive over there," Danielle suggested.

"No!" Heather blurted. "You can't do it. Let me do it with Chris or Walt."

"Why can't Danielle do it?" Chris asked.

"Too much negative energy. It might not be good for you right now. There is no reason to take that chance," Heather insisted.

Chris frowned. "What are you talking about?"

"I'm sure it will be okay," Danielle said.

"Hey, if you aren't drinking caffeine just in case, I think you should avoid negative energy, too. You don't know how that could affect the baby," Heather said.

"What baby?" Chris blurted.

Danielle groaned. She looked at Chris. "We don't know if there is a baby."

"But there might be," Heather reminded her.

Danielle glared at Heather. "It was supposed to be a secret."

Heather shrugged. "Chris knows about Brian, so why can't he know about a maybe baby?"

"What baby?" Chris snapped. He looked at Danielle. "You're pregnant?"

"Maybe," Danielle said.

"She needs to take a pregnancy test," Heather said.

"I agree with Heather," Walt said. "One of us can do this, but not Danielle. Just in case."

Chris looked from Walt to Heather to Danielle. "Why am I the last to know everything around here?"

"If it makes you feel any better, the only other one who knows I might be pregnant is Lily," Danielle told him.

"You seriously don't think Lily told Ian?" Heather asked.

Danielle shrugged. "Okay, then Lily and Ian."

"Does Lily know about Heather and Brian?" Chris asked.

"I never told her, but I think she might have figured it out," Danielle said.

Heather arched a brow at Danielle. "Really?"

"It's possible." Danielle shrugged.

"Marie also knows about Heather and Brian," Walt said.

Chris considered all that he had just learned. Finally, he smiled and looked at Walt. "Wow, you might be a dad?"

Walt grinned. "That's what my mom tells me."

"Your mom?" Chris frowned.

"Let's talk about that later. First, we need to figure out who's haunting Marymoor, and why," Danielle said.

PEARL HUCKABEE STOOD at her bedroom window, looking down at the sidewalk below. She watched as the Marlows and Chris Johnson walked down the street. The three had just left Heather Donovan's house. Earlier that morning, as she was getting her newspaper, she'd caught Brian Henderson sneaking out from the back of Heather's house. It was obvious he had spent the night—again.

There were several vehicles—ones she had never seen before—

parked in front of Marlow House. Someone was staying over there. People had been coming and going for the last couple of days.

Pearl considered calling the police and letting them know the Marlows had likely reopened their illegal boardinghouse. But why bother calling the police? The officer she normally called had just slunk out of Heather's house right after the Marlows' arrival. They were all in cahoots with each other. With disgust, Pearl closed her blinds.

THIRTY

L ater Sunday morning, Chris drove over to Heather's and picked her up. They headed over to the Marymoor site. After talking to Ian earlier about what they planned to do, Ian promised to keep his parents entertained that morning so they wouldn't drive by their property and run into Heather and Chris.

Pulling up in front of the site, Chris parked and turned off the engine. They remained sitting in the car, seatbelts on, with Chris's hands resting on the steering wheel.

"Last night was a setup, wasn't it?" Chris asked.

Heather frowned and looked from the Marymoor property to Chris. "What are you talking about?"

"You asked Brian to meet you at the restaurant."

Heather grinned. "Yeah. I told him to meet me in the bar."

"You know, he tried to pay for his dinner last night. I wouldn't let him," Chris said.

"Yeah, I know. He told me. I think he felt funny having you pay, since you hadn't invited him. But I figured it served you right."

"Served me right for what?" Chris frowned.

"Oh, fess up. The only reason you wanted me to come is so that I'd be protection from Laura," Heather said.

"I don't need protection," Chris said with a snort.

"Okay, not protection. But a buffer."

Chris sighed. "Okay, maybe a little. But I still wanted you to come."

"Chris, you sort of have a habit of using me for shock value. I don't think you mean anything by it, but sometimes it's irritating."

"What do you mean shock value?" Chris asked, sincerely confused.

"You did it with your uncles. You wanted them to think we were dating. Because you found it funny that they thought you were seeing someone like me."

Chris frowned. "What do you mean someone like you?"

Heather rolled her eyes. "Oh, come on. Don't play stupid. I'm happy with myself. I'm who I am. I think I'm happier with myself than I have been in years. And part of that has to do with you. So I thank you for that. But I also see how other people look at me."

"I still don't understand."

"Yes, you do. But you're too embarrassed to admit it."

Chris studied Heather. Before he could respond, Heather looked past him to the Marymoor property and called out, "Look!"

Chris turned around to see what Heather saw. Standing behind the fence stood a row of women. At least they had been women during their lives. Considering their transparent nature, he knew they were spirits. Silently, he counted. There were eight of them.

"I wonder who they are," Heather whispered.

"I doubt they can hear you from here," Chris said.

"Are they wearing nurse uniforms?"

Narrowing his eyes, Chris studied the apparitions. "I don't think so. It looks like something patients wore."

"Ready?" Heather unfastened her seatbelt.

Chris unfastened his. "Okay. Let's walk over there. But remember, we don't want them to know we can see them."

"I DON'T BELIEVE I've seen them before," Caroline said as she watched the two people get out of the car.

Elsie studied the pair and frowned. "I hope they're not coming over here. Maybe they're going to one of the other houses."

"No. They're heading our way. Ignore them; hopefully they won't notice us," Rose suggested.

The eight women—or more accurately, spirits—watched as the

189

man and woman walked toward them, chatting amongst themselves. They stopped when they reached the gate, making no attempt to enter.

"This is a nice piece of property," the woman said. "It is a nice neighborhood."

"Yes, it is," the man said. "But I'm a little spoiled. I like where we live better."

"That's just because your house is right on the water," the woman retorted.

"I heard someone bought this property. I wonder what they're going to do with it," the man said.

"Sounds like they're just lookers," Florence said. "Rose, I don't think they're someone we need to worry about."

"I wouldn't mind if he was staying," Gertie said.

"Oh, Gertie!" Caroline laughed.

"Caroline, I have to agree with Gertie. He is rather delicious," Viola said with a sigh.

"Ladies," Molly said, when she appeared by the gate the next moment, "what are you doing out here?"

"We're watching the lovely scenery. Who do you think he is? Can he stay?" Gertie asked.

"You aren't supposed to talk to strangers. Randal will get mad," Molly reminded her.

"Randal is always mad," Edna snapped. "And we haven't talked to them; we're just looking. Anyway, Randal hasn't been here since —since before Sean left."

"We don't want to give him any reason to return right now," Molly said.

"I want to go home," Viola said. "Why can't we just go home? Everyone else could go. It's just us, Waylon, and Sid now. Sid is always angry, and Waylon is always afraid. And neither of them looks like him." Viola pointed to the stranger standing beyond the gate with the woman.

The sound of a car driving down the street caught their attention. They all turned to see where it was going.

CHRIS AND HEATHER watched as the car parked behind Chris's vehicle. A moment later, two women got out. It was Laura and Kelly.

"Here comes your girlfriend," Heather whispered.

"I thought Ian promised to keep them away," Chris whispered back. He looked over at the spirits. They were no longer there.

"Drat, they scared them off," Heather whispered to Chris.

"Well, hello, what are you guys doing here?" Kelly asked when she and Laura walked up to them.

"We were on our way to the office," Heather lied, "and we thought we'd stop and have a look at the property your parents bought."

"You're working on a Sunday?" Laura asked.

"Yeah, Chris is a slave driver," Heather said.

"We're just going in for a few minutes," Chris lied.

"Laura wanted to see the property," Kelly told them.

"Kelly was telling me how it's haunted," Laura said with a giggle.

"We really need to stop saying that. I have a feeling your sister is starting to believe it," Kelly said.

"Oh, Lily will get over it," Laura said. "But she's like Mom. Believes all that stuff is possible. Mom even claimed Grandma came to her after she died. Grandma told her everything was okay, that she was going to be with Grandpa."

"And you didn't believe her?" Heather asked.

Laura frowned at Heather. "Seriously?"

Heather shrugged. "I just think anything's possible."

"We need to get going," Chris said.

When Chris and Heather drove off in the car a few minutes later, Kelly said, "Don't you know? Heather once claimed she can see ghosts."

"I CAN'T BELIEVE IT; even ghosts hit on you," Heather scoffed.

"No ghost hit on me," Chris argued.

"They would have had they known you could see them," Heather said.

"Hey, you're making me feel like a piece of meat."

Heather glanced out the back window and watched as Laura

and Kelly stood in front of the property, watching them drive away. "I hope one of those spirits throws something at them. I know she's Lily's sister, but she irritates me."

"So does Kelly," Chris reminded her. "Irritates you, that is."

Heather turned around in the seat and looked out the front windshield. "True. Hey, where are we going? This isn't the way home."

"You told them we were going to the office," he reminded her.

"Well, I don't really want to go," Heather said.

"Don't worry, I'm turning up here. I just didn't want them to see us going the other way."

"We need to tell Danielle and Walt what we found out." Heather picked up her purse off the floor and removed a piece of paper. She started writing.

Chris glanced over. "What are you doing?"

"I don't want to forget. Some of them called the others by names."

WALT AND DANIELLE sat in Heather's living room with Heather and Chris.

"Eva was right; there are more than three spirits haunting the place. My bet, there are eleven spirits over there," Chris said.

"Eleven? How did you come up with that number?" Walt asked.

"We know Eva and Marie saw two men and Molly the nurse. I'm certain we saw Molly today, too. She was wearing a nurse's uniform with the bloodstain," Chris said.

"But there were eight women there before Molly showed up," Heather said. "We're pretty sure they were patients, not nurses, because of how they dressed. And when Molly showed up—or who we assume was Molly—she was kinda bossy with them."

"While we didn't see the men, one woman mentioned the two men. She called them Waylon and Sid," Chris said.

Danielle frowned. "Waylon's the name of the patient who killed Molly."

Heather glanced at Danielle. "Sounds like he's one of the spirits haunting the place."

"But why are you so sure there are only eleven spirits?" Walt asked.

Chris looked to Walt. "It was something one of them said."

"But they also mentioned someone else. They talked about a Randal," Heather reminded Chris.

"I know, but it didn't sound like he was still there," Chris said.

Danielle let out a sigh. "I wonder who the women were, and why they haven't moved on."

"I don't know. But I caught a couple of the names. I wrote them down." Heather picked up her purse and removed the small notebook. She opened to the page she had written on and read, "Rose, Gertie, Caroline, Randal, Waylon and Sid. Of course, we already mention the guys' names." Heather looked up and then said, "One of them said she wanted to go home. Then she said something about how everyone had left, and there was just them, Waylon and Sid."

"She also said Sid was always angry and Waylon was afraid," Chris added.

"Interesting," Danielle murmured. "I would expect Waylon to be the angry one; he's the one who killed Molly."

"Now what?" Heather asked.

"I'd like to find out who they were—it could give us a clue why they stuck around. And if we can find something about their families, people they cared about who have moved on, it will be easier to convince them to continue in their journey."

"By what they said, I'm fairly certain they don't understand they're dead," Chris said. "While they seem to know that not everyone can see them, I don't think they have figured out why."

"Well, they are crazy, so there is that," Heather said.

THIRTY-ONE

Danielle's cellphone rang. Picking up the phone, she glanced at it and said, "It's Lily," before answering. A few minutes later, after updating Lily on Heather and Chris's visit to the property, Danielle got off the phone and said, "Ian's parents are taking Tammy and Gene out to lunch over in Astoria. Laura and Kelly are going with them."

"Not Ian and Lily?" Walt asked.

Danielle shook her head. "No. Ian made an excuse about having to do something for his editor. He wants to do a little online sleuthing, hoping to find something on Rupert's parents."

"What about Lily?" Heather asked.

"She's staying home with Connor. Made some excuse why she couldn't go."

"Now what?" Heather asked.

"While Ian is looking into Rupert's parents, I think the four of us should go down to the museum, check out the files on Marymoor, and see if we can find out who those women were. Hopefully, we can find some information to help us get them to move on," Danielle suggested.

Heather glanced at the time. "If we're going to do that, we'd better leave now; the museum closes early on Sunday."

"If it's closed, we can always stop at the Catholic church; I understand they're open all day on Sunday," Chris suggested.

"Why would we stop at the Catholic church?" Danielle asked with a frown.

"Don't they still do exorcisms?" Chris joked.

"PERHAPS THE BOARD needs to consider a temporary exhibit on Marymoor Sanatorium, with all the recent interest in the place," Millie Samson said after Walt asked her if they could go back in the storage room and look through the files. She stood behind the counter at the museum gift store, while another docent chatted to several visitors in the exhibit area.

Walt had told Millie he was researching for a book, and considering the lateness in the day, Danielle and his friends had offered to help go through the files to speed up the process. They knew Millie would never deny Chris access to the museum files, considering she knew his true identity, and that identity, Chris Glandon, was the museum's major benefactor.

"Others have asked to see the files?" Danielle asked.

"Ever since the city announced they were listing the property again, a number of our members have asked about the sanatorium. Many had never heard of it. Only one person asked to see the files. That was Tori Simmons. But now that I think of it, that was a few weeks before there was any talk about listing the property."

"Tori Simmons? Joe Morelli's sister?" Danielle asked.

"Yes. She was doing some genealogy research." Millie added in a whisper, "One of her ancestors was a patient there."

"Really?" Danielle said, while Heather, Chris, and Walt silently listened.

"I think she wanted to find out why she was sent there."

"Because she was crazy?" Heather suggested.

Millie turned a smile at Heather and said, "Not necessarily by today's standards. No, back then they could lock women away simply for not behaving as society deemed proper."

Chris glanced over to Heather and arched a brow. Heather noticed his silent commentary and frowned. She reached over and gave his arm a pinch.

"Ouch!" Chris rubbed his arm. "I thought you weren't going to do that anymore."

"I didn't say anything about pinches." Heather shrugged.

195

Millie flashed a smile at Heather and Chris and continued, "Or, if someone was a lesbian, they could commit her. Not even a lesbian, just a woman who did not act feminine enough, like we used to call tomboys. If a man in her life did not approve, he could get her committed. Of course, medical conditions, like epilepsy, also got people committed back then, or postpartum depression."

"That really sucks," Heather grumbled.

"THEY BURNED us at the stake; they committed us to mental institutions," Heather snarked as she walked into the storage room with Walt, Danielle, and Chris. Chris flipped on the overhead light while Walt closed the door behind them.

"I wonder why Joe's ancestor was sent to Marymoor," Chris said.

They followed Danielle. The museum hadn't moved the boxes since she had gone through them when searching for information on Sean Sullivan. Walt used his energy to move the boxes to the long table in the center of the storage room. The boxes floated to the table while each person took a seat.

"Photographs," Chris said after a few minutes of sorting through a box. Black-and-white photographs slid from a large envelope, scattering on the table. Heather stood up to get a better look.

"That's them!" Heather said excitedly. She picked up the photos, sorting through them.

"You saw all of those women today?" Danielle asked.

Heather handed Chris the photos, who counted them, then flipped through each one, looking at the faces of the women. He nodded. "Yes, it's them." He turned the photographs over and looked at the back side of each one. "There are no names on any of them, but they're all numbered."

"Can I see?" Walt asked, holding out his hand. Chris passed the stack of photos to Walt.

"Viola Hawkes," Walt said, looking at one photograph.

"You knew her?" Danielle asked.

"I knew who she was. She lived in Portland, a very wealthy family. A patron of the arts. While I can't say I knew her personally, Eva once pointed her out to me. I don't think they were friends, but

Eva knew who she was." Walt looked up from the photograph. "She was a patient at Marymoor?"

"It looks that way," Chris said.

Still holding the photo and studying it, Walt shook his head. "I remember when she married; it was quite the news. She was a wealthy heiress, a socialite. And then, less than a year later, she went abroad with her new husband, and I heard she died in Paris. He returned to the States. When was she at Marymoor?" Walt frowned.

"She must have died at Marymoor," Heather said. "That's where her spirit is. I saw her there this morning. She obviously didn't die in Paris."

Walt frowned and flipped through the rest of the photographs. "I recognize some of these other women. I never heard about any of them being at Marymoor. But they were all from wealthy families."

"And they were all sent to Marymoor?" Danielle asked.

"It looks like it," Chris said.

The eight photographs eventually went to Danielle, who snapped a photo of each one with her cellphone. She returned the original photographs to their envelope and resumed going through the boxes with Walt, Chris, and Heather. They stayed for another hour, occasionally snapping photos of pertinent documents or photographs.

WALT AND DANIELLE stopped at Ian and Lily's after leaving the museum. The parents and sisters had not yet returned from lunch.

"You won't believe what Ian found," Lily said when she opened the front door for Walt and Danielle.

"Sounds like we both had an interesting day with research," Danielle said.

"What did you find out?" Lily asked, leading Walt and Danielle back to Ian's office.

"First, tell us what Ian found," Danielle urged as she walked down the hallway. She glanced over to Connor's bedroom, noticing its closed door.

"He's not sleeping," Lily whispered. "But he's in there with Marie and Rupert. I really don't want to discuss this around Rupert."

When Walt and Danielle walked into Ian's office, Ian looked up and smiled. "Glad you're here. Now Marie doesn't have to tweak Lily's ear."

Danielle frowned. "Why is Marie tweaking your ear?"

"To get us a message," Lily explained. "How else is she going to let us know if Rupert has come in the room?"

The next moment, Lily let out a yelp and grabbed her right earlobe. She looked around. "Marie?"

Walt chuckled. Danielle glared at her husband. "That was not nice."

Lily frowned at Walt. "Did you do that?"

"Sorry. I couldn't resist," Walt said sheepishly.

"Brat," Lily muttered.

"Lily said you found something interesting on Rupert," Danielle asked Ian.

"Yes, but I'm not sure it's our Rupert," Ian said.

"It has to be," Lily said. "But it is bizarre."

Curious, Walt and Danielle looked to Ian.

"The article you found had the name of Rupert's parents. But I couldn't find anything on them in California. Nothing after the article on Rupert's death," Ian began.

"But Lily said you found something?" Danielle asked.

"Yes. I found an obituary for a woman in Salem, Oregon, who would have been about the same age as Rupert's mother—with the same name."

Danielle frowned. "I doubt it's Rupert's mother. Peterson is not that uncommon a surname. And Salem, Oregon? They lived near Sacramento. What's the chances they moved to Oregon? Heck, if they decided to move out of state, there are forty-nine states to choose from."

"You know how obituaries list family members who already died?" Lily asked.

"Yeah," Danielle said.

"Her deceased husband's name is the same as Rupert's father. Plus, she had a son who died before her—a Rupert Peterson. It didn't list the middle name, but still, Rupert is not that common a name," Ian explained.

"Really?" Danielle frowned.

"If it isn't Rupert's mother, then it's some bizarre coincidence," Lily said.

"And she's being buried in Salem?" Danielle asked.

"Her funeral is on Friday," Ian said.

"This week? You aren't serious?" Danielle asked.

Lily nodded. "I know, isn't it insane? You're always telling me it's common for someone who's just died to show up at their own funeral before they move on. If that happened, it would be perfect, because we could take Rupert to her funeral, and when he and his mother see each other there, well, he would definitely move on."

Danielle leaned back in the chair; her forehead furrowed as she considered what Lily had just told them. After a few moments, Walt asked Danielle, "What's bothering you?"

"It seems a little… I don't know… too convenient? Rupert's parents not only moving to Oregon, but his mother's funeral is Friday. Not only close enough to attend, but just in time to take Rupert?" Danielle looked up into Walt's eyes. Their gazes locked.

Ignoring Walt and Danielle's silent exchange, Lily said, "I know. It's crazy, isn't it? I hope it's his mom. It does seem farfetched. What are the chances we might actually find her spirit close by?"

"Oh, it's Rupert's Mom," Danielle said.

Lily frowned. "But I thought you just said it was a little too convenient?"

"I think Danielle just figured it out," Walt said.

"Figured what out?" Lily asked.

Danielle let out a sigh. "It probably is Rupert's mother. Because for all those things to fall into place so nicely—Rupert's mother moving up to Oregon, Rupert finally getting out of that attic, and he comes to Oregon just in time for his mother to be buried. Not to mention the fact he has encountered mediums to help him along the way. No. That is beyond coincidence. It is a grand plan."

"You mean a grand plan from the Universe… God?" Lily asked.

"Not in the sense it's something preordained," Walt said. "But an opportunity the Universe presents to set things right. Rupert should have moved on after he died, but he got confused, stayed with you, and then stayed trapped in the attic. Of course, he was never really trapped in your parents' attic. He could have left at any time. He just didn't know how."

"And who knows, it is possible his time with you was also an opportunity the Universe presented," Danielle suggested.

Lily frowned at Danielle. "How so?"

"Think about it. He was robbed of his childhood, but then he found you and was able to be that little boy—with you—until it was time to move on," Danielle suggested.

"Yeah, but then he was stuck in that attic for years," Lily reminded her.

Danielle shrugged. "Like I told you before, time for a spirit is not the same as for a living person. Plus, I don't believe he was trapped in that attic, not like Walt was in Marlow House."

"I had a choice," Walt reminded her. "I could have left."

"True. And Rupert could have, too. He just didn't realize it at the time. Maybe he was waiting for his mother," Danielle suggested.

"Like I waited for you," Walt whispered. "And like Rupert, I didn't realize what I had been waiting for all that time."

THIRTY-TWO

Danielle hadn't made breakfast for her guests the previous morning. Instead, they all agreed something simple like cereal would be easier, especially after the big dinner the night before. Danielle didn't need to buy the cereal. June had cleaned out her pantry before moving, and she had several open boxes of cereal in her car that hadn't been put into storage. But on Monday morning, Danielle made a large breakfast, and this time she invited Lily, Ian, and Connor to join them, along with Kelly and Joe.

Normally, Danielle would have Joanne, her housekeeper, help prepare and serve the meals when guests stayed at Marlow House. Yet they were no longer a bed-and-breakfast, and Danielle did not want Lily's and Ian's parents to feel obligated to offer payment for their room and board. While they had already offered to pay, she feared having Joanne help prepare and serve those meals might make the parents feel awkward and then insist on paying her. She opted for a less formal route by giving them the option to help prepare breakfast.

On Monday morning, Danielle soon learned not to expect any help from Lily's sister. Laura sat leisurely at the table, chatting with Kelly and Joe, while oblivious to the surrounding activity. Both mothers set the table; Lily's father flipped flapjacks on the griddle, while John stood in the kitchen, talking about his upcoming building project. Lily helped Danielle prepare the rest of the food, while Walt served coffee, juice, and eventually helped bring platters of food to the table. Danielle hadn't expected Joe and Kelly to pitch in, considering they weren't staying at Marlow House. Meanwhile, Ian entertained Connor.

"I swear, that is so typical Laura," Lily whispered to Danielle.

"What do you mean?" Danielle asked.

"She really loves being waited on."

"Well, she probably feels like this is her vacation," Danielle suggested.

"I thought she might at least offer to watch Connor while we get breakfast together."

"We could shake things up a bit," Danielle whispered. "Ian could give Connor to Marie, and she could walk him around the dining room while we eat."

Lily giggled at the suggestion.

"YOU HAVE A HIGHCHAIR JUST FOR CONNOR?" Laura asked later that morning while they all sat around the breakfast table.

"I imagine she bought it when she ran the bed-and-breakfast," June said.

"No. Actually, I bought it for Connor," Danielle said while passing a basket of cinnamon rolls down the table.

"I think I'm jealous," Laura grumbled as she snatched a cinnamon roll out of the basket.

Tammy laughed. "Why, because you don't have your own highchair?"

Laura looked at Connor, who sat in his highchair, pushing Cheerios around on its tray. "Kelly gets to see Connor all the time. And Danielle gets to see him so much she even bought him his own highchair for when he's over here. I should move to Frederickport, like June and John."

"What about your job?" Tammy asked.

"Oh, pooh on my job. I want to live closer to my sister!" Laura paused a moment, cringed, and looked at Danielle. "I forgot to ask you. Is it okay if I hook up to your Wi-Fi? If it is, I need the password. I brought my laptop with me; I promised my boss I'd do some work remotely. It's the only way he'd give me the time off."

"Sure, no problem," Danielle said.

AFTER BREAKFAST, while Lily helped clear the table, she told Danielle, "Now I feel like an ungrateful rat."

"What do you mean?" Danielle asked, piling the dirty dishes in the sink.

"Laura went to all the trouble to make it up here for Connor's birthday. And all I do is bitch."

Danielle flashed Lily a grin. "We all complain about those we love."

Lily turned to Danielle. "I never hear you complaining about Walt."

"No. But I bitch about you all the time," Danielle teased.

Lily laughed and swatted Danielle with a dishtowel.

Laura walked into the kitchen with Kelly.

"Joe had to leave," Kelly told them. She looked at Danielle and said, "He told me to thank you for breakfast, but he had to get to work."

"Glad you could make it," Danielle said as she rinsed the plates.

"I'm going to help Kelly plan her wedding," Laura announced.

"Laura has some great ideas," Kelly said. Laura and Kelly started chatting amongst themselves and then walked out to the side yard, without another word to Lily or Danielle.

"Well, gee, we don't need your help," Lily called out, knowing neither one could hear them.

Danielle giggled. "Remember, you're just happy they came."

"Yeah, yeah, yeah. Doesn't mean I can't complain about them."

AFTER BREAKFAST, instead of joining the others and going across the street to Ian and Lily's house, Walt headed upstairs to research Marymoor Sanatorium and the women in the photographs. Meanwhile, Danielle decided to run down to Old Salts Bakery to replenish her cinnamon roll supply. Her houseguests had cleaned her out.

When Danielle walked into the bakery, she spied Joe Morelli's sister, Tori Simmons, sitting at a table alone, eating a pastry and drinking a cup of coffee while reading the news on her iPad. Tori's husband, Craig, had initially introduced Danielle to Joe not long after she moved to town. Back then, Craig had been cleaning up the overgrown yard at Marlow House when he noticed someone had broken into her house. Craig had called his brother-in-law, Joe Morelli, an officer on the local police force, to investigate.

"Morning, Tori," Danielle greeted her when she walked up to her table.

Tori set her iPad on the table and smiled up at Danielle. "Hello, Danielle. You caught me at my guilty pleasure."

"Guilty pleasure?" Danielle frowned.

"I like to sneak over here and enjoy their decadent pastry and a cup of coffee, with no one bugging me."

"Then I should probably go," Danielle said with a chuckle.

Tori laughed and then reached out for Danielle. "No. I didn't mean you. I meant from the kids. Thank God they're back in school! Why don't you grab a cup of coffee and join me? I have more pastries." Tori lifted the sack on the table and gave it a little jiggle.

"Thanks. But I'll bring my own."

FIVE MINUTES LATER, Danielle and Tori sat together at a table in Old Salts Bakery, each one drinking a cup of coffee. Tori nibbled on the remaining piece of her pastry, but Danielle kept her recent purchase in its bag.

"I'm still stuffed from breakfast," Danielle explained after Tori asked if she was going to eat anything.

"Joe mentioned he and Kelly were going over there this morning for breakfast. It must be rather hectic, having Ian's and Lily's families staying with you."

"It's fun. And I miss the B and B, so it gives me my hostess fix," Danielle said.

"I'm not much on the hostess thing, but it looks like I'll be playing hostess for Kelly's bridal shower. I hope I'm giving everyone enough time," Tori explained. "The invitations went out this morning; you'll be getting yours."

"When are you having it?" Danielle asked.

"I sort of decided at the last minute to have it while Ian's parents were in town so his mom could go. But now I understand they're moving here, so I could have had it a little later. But Kelly mentioned she wanted to invite Lily's sister and mom, so…" Tori shrugged.

"It'll be fine," Danielle assured her.

"I'm great at deciding to do something at the last minute. I started a family history book for Kelly's shower gift. My way of introducing her to Joe's family tree. But it doesn't look like I'm going to finish it in time." Under her breath, Tori muttered, "Too many unanswered questions."

Danielle looked at Tori for a moment and then said, "Um… I sorta heard about your project."

Tori frowned. "You did?"

"Walt's doing some research on the Marymoor Sanatorium for a book he's writing," Danielle lied. "When we were over at the museum, Millie let us go through the boxes they have on the sanatorium. And Millie told us—"

"About my great-great-grandmother?" Tori finished for her.

"Is that who she was?" Danielle asked.

"Yes." Tori picked up her iPad and opened the photos app. She found what she was looking for and handed it to Danielle.

Holding the iPad, Danielle looked down at the black-and-white image of a woman, her expression somber as she looked off past the camera. Danielle recognized the photograph from the museum. "She was beautiful."

"Yes, she was," Tori said, taking back the iPad.

"I saw her picture when I was over at the museum. It was in an envelope with seven other photographs," Danielle said.

"Ahh, the Forgotten Women of Marymoor," Tori said.

Danielle frowned. "What do you mean?"

"That's just what I call them. Do you know how I found out she was at that place?"

Danielle shook her head. "No. How?"

"I was looking through the census reports, trying to track down ancestors. I found her on a census roll. She spent the last three years of her life in Marymoor and died there. She was only twenty-six."

"What did she die of?" Danielle asked.

"I don't know."

"Why do you call them the Forgotten Women of Marymoor?"

"Unlike many people who died there, they weren't buried in the Marymoor section of the local cemetery. Are you familiar with that?" Tori asked.

"Yes, I am."

"From what I've found, after they died, they were returned to their families. Most had family plots at various cemeteries, where they were quietly buried. When I was in Portland a few weeks ago, I visited several of the cemeteries and the graves of those women. There was nothing on any of their markers that said where they died."

"How do you know where they died?" Danielle asked.

"If you go through those boxes again, pay special attention to one ledger. There's a page that lists eight patients. No names, just a number and initials for each one. Along with birth dates and death dates. Caroline, that was my great-great-grandmother, the number by a patient with her initials matches the number written on the back of her photograph. Plus, the birth dates and death dates on that patient are hers."

"I saw that page. I even took a copy of it, but I haven't looked at it closely," Danielle said.

"I wanted to find out who the other women were. I thought it might be a clue as to why she was there. With some digging, I discovered who each one was. Their initials match what is in that ledger, along with their birth and death dates. There is also a column for when the body was picked up by the family."

"If you have all their names, would you mind emailing them to me?" Danielle asked.

"Sure. I can do it now." Tori picked up her iPad again and looked for the file with the women's names.

"I'm still not clear why you call them the Forgotten Women of Marymoor," Danielle said.

"Because I don't think anyone today knows they were ever there. Well, aside from me—and now you. But from what I've learned, back then most of their friends and family didn't know they had been sent there. My family never seem to know Caroline spent any time at Marymoor, much less died there."

"I assume you've gathered most of that information from old newspaper articles?" Danielle asked.

"Yes, and obituaries. None of those articles or obituaries ever mentioned them being sent to Marymoor. But they were all on the census reports. They were all there," Tori said. "Their photographs in that file, along with their initials in that ledger, prove it."

"Why was Caroline sent there? According to Millie, and I've

heard it before, back then a woman could be sent away simply for being outspoken," Danielle asked.

"I have no idea. When I was younger, after church our family would visit the cemetery and put flowers on the graves. We have quite a few family members buried at the Frederickport Cemetery. Before I found her on the census, I already knew how old she was when she died, but I always assumed she died at home."

THIRTY-THREE

L ily had to admit, Connor having a ghost playmate was not such a bad thing. Rupert entertained Connor, as he had once entertained her. Marie had explained to Rupert why removing Winnie's stuffing or giving stuffed animals a bath was not a good idea, and he seemed sincerely contrite for his behavior. He admitted to Marie he had been jealous of Winnie and of Lily's stuffed animals. But now that he understood his reality, he simply wanted to move on and be with his parents again.

Even though she couldn't see Rupert, Lily was no longer anxious about the two boys playing together. She had conveyed to Marie that it was unnecessary to stay by Connor's side because of Rupert's presence.

Lily knew Rupert would not be staying indefinitely. The plan was for her and Danielle to drive to Salem on Friday, to attend his mother's funeral. If she was, in fact, his mother—they still weren't certain. Rupert had already agreed to go with them. But leaving with Danielle without her mother or Laura trying to tag along was the challenge.

"The only problem with a beach wedding, the weather," Kelly said.

Lily glanced over to where Kelly and Laura sat on nearby beach chairs. After breakfast, they had all retreated outside, behind Lily and Ian's house. Everyone sat in beach chairs, aside from Lily, who

208

sat on a large blanket with Connor while he played with his sand toys.

Conversation between the women was Kelly's upcoming wedding, while the men sat some distance away, involved in their own discussion. Lily just listened, so far resisting comment.

"Which is why Lily and Ian should have gotten married outside," Laura said. "I tried to get her to, but she is so stubborn."

They all turned to Lily. She smiled at her sister and said, "I had the wedding I wanted."

Laura raised her hands and said, "Just look at this weather. It is amazing today. This is how it would have been at your wedding!"

Lily shrugged. "Hey, I live on the beach. I can enjoy this whenever I want."

"You are spoiled," Laura teased.

Lily laughed. "True."

"Have you and Ian decided what you're going to do for your anniversary?" June asked.

"They should go away for the night. Find a nice little romantic place along the ocean," Tammy said.

Lily laughed again. "Mom, didn't I just say I live on the beach already? Why would we want to spend money to rent a place on the beach?"

"Gosh, Lily. Have you and Ian been married a million years, or what?" Laura scoffed.

Lily frowned at Laura. "What is that supposed to mean?"

"Oh, stop picking on your sister," Tammy chided Laura. "Lily is just comfortable. Although, a married couple should take time for themselves." She looked at Lily and said, "And it is your anniversary. Back when you were little, I would have loved to have both sets of grandparents offering to watch you kids so we could take a little time for ourselves."

"I appreciate that, Mom. But Ian and I can go away anytime. And you're only going to be here for a couple of weeks," Lily said sweetly.

"You can't get away without Connor," Tammy reminded her.

Lily shrugged. "Danielle and Walt are always willing to watch Connor, and there is Heather."

"What about me?" Kelly interrupted.

"I was going to say you," Lily lied.

"Lily doesn't need to be bothering that Heather again," June said, "now that we're moving to town."

"Let's talk about Kelly's wedding," Lily suggested. She looked at Kelly and said, "Ian and I talked about it, and if you want to have your wedding here, you guys are more than welcome to."

"Unless they have it in the next week, they might be getting married in the rain," June said. "And even then, there is no guarantee." June glanced up to the clouds gathering overhead.

"Thank you, Lily. I appreciate your offer. I'm going to be talking to Joe about it," Kelly said.

"If you and Joe would wait a year," June began, "you could have your wedding at our new home. I have so many ideas for the gardens. There is so much room!"

"IMAGINE JOE and Kelly getting married at Marymoor?" Lily told Danielle and Heather Monday evening. She had slipped over to Heather's house after the parents and Laura had returned to Marlow House to get ready for dinner, and after Danielle had sent her a text message telling her to meet her at Heather's.

"Are they really going to?" Heather asked. The three sat around her kitchen table.

"I doubt it. I don't imagine Kelly wants to wait that long," Lily said.

The teapot on Heather's stove began to whistle. She stood up. "Do you guys want some tea?"

"I'd love some," Lily said.

"No, thanks. But I would love a glass of iced water," Danielle said.

Heather paused for a moment and looked at Danielle. "Do you not want tea, or can't you have it?"

Danielle shrugged. "Not sure."

"You haven't started your period?" Heather asked.

"No."

"Why haven't you taken a test yet?" Heather prodded.

"I just haven't bought one yet. No time. Are you going to let that teapot whistle forever?"

Heather rolled her eyes and turned from the table. When she returned with a cup of tea for Lily and water for Danielle, she said,

"If you stopped at Old Salts this morning, you could have gone to the pharmacy."

"Yes, Mom," Danielle teased, taking the water.

A few minutes later, they returned to their previous topic. Heather said, "I doubt that house will get built. Ian's parents will eventually see something over there to make them change their minds."

Lily shook her head. "I don't understand it. They drove by again this morning, and they still saw nothing. At least, nothing they told us about. And when Kelly took Laura over there, nothing unusual happened."

"I assume that's when Chris and I were there, and the Forgotten Women of Marymoor made an appearance," Heather said.

"The what?" Lily frowned.

"You haven't told her what Tori said?" Heather asked Danielle.

"I haven't had a chance to tell her," Danielle said before telling Lily about her conversation that morning with Joe's sister.

"Wow. If they're the ones haunting that place, it sounds more sad than creepy," Lily said.

"I don't know about that," Heather said. "Why were they committed? Perhaps a couple of them went Lizzy Borden on their families."

"At least one of those spirits was a killer—Waylon," Danielle reminded.

"Have you or Walt found anything about the other guy, or something about any of the women? Ian hasn't been able to do any online research with his family here. I'm not sure what excuse I'm going to come up with to get away with you on Friday to go to Salem."

"We'll figure out something for Friday. But Walt was saying we need to all get together and do some more brainstorming, especially now that we've learned a little more," Danielle said.

Lily groaned. "You do not know how hard it was for me to sneak over here without someone seeing me."

"I was thinking about your anniversary," Danielle said.

"I told you, Ian and I decided we aren't going to do anything now with all the family here."

"Yes, you are," Danielle disagreed. "You're going to the Glandon Foundation for your anniversary."

Lily frowned. "I am?"

"Yeah, but tell them you're going to some restaurant out of town," Heather said. "I'll be picking up burgers, so you won't starve."

"I don't understand." Lily frowned.

"We're having a meeting of the mediums on Wednesday evening at the Glandon Foundation, and you and Ian need to be there."

"After six thirty," Heather said. "Everyone will be gone by then. We really can't do it at my house or Chris's. Someone might notice your car."

"Then we can figure out what to do next," Danielle said.

"THANKS FOR DOING MY HAIR," Lily told Danielle on Wednesday evening. She sat on a chair in her bedroom while Danielle stood behind her, weaving her long red hair into a fishtail braid.

"Hey, I'm happy to do it. Consider it my anniversary gift to you."

"I always felt anniversary gifts were supposed to be between the couple, not from other people. But in this case, I will happily accept your gift." She then added in a whisper, "Although this all seems silly since we're not really going out."

"We have to make this look good. And about anniversary gifts, it looks like June got you guys something. I'm sure she's planning to give it to you before you leave," Danielle said.

"That's nice of her, but I wish she wouldn't have." Careful not to move, Lily stared into the dresser mirror, watching Danielle finish up her braid.

"There. I'm done!" Danielle announced.

Lily smiled and leaned closer to the mirror, examining the finished product. "It always amazes me how easy you make that look."

"It's beautiful on you. You should let me braid your hair more often."

Lily stood up and gave Danielle a hug. "Thanks. I guess I won't worry about Connor. With both sets of grandparents watching him, he should be okay—as long as my mom and June don't kill each other before we get back."

"And when all of this is over, Walt and I will watch Connor so you and Ian can have a real anniversary date."

When Danielle and Lily walked out into the living room ten minutes later, they found the two grandmothers sitting on the sofa chatting, while Connor sat on the floor playing with his toys. The grandfathers were in the dining room with Walt and Ian. John had drawn up some ideas for their new house, and he was showing them the plans. But when Lily and Danielle walked into the living room, June and Tammy started complimenting Lily on her hair and outfit. The men stopped what they were doing and walked into the living room.

"I have something I want to give you before you go," June announced. She stood and picked up a wrapped package from the floor next to the sofa and handed it to Lily. "This is for both of you, for your anniversary."

"Thank you, June. That's sweet," Lily said before handing Ian the gift and insisting he open it. They all watched Ian open the package. Inside was a piece of luggage.

"It's leather," June announced after Ian removed the small suit-case from the box. "The third anniversary is leather. If you were spending the night in Astoria, you could use it."

"It's lovely, Mom. But like we said, we're just going out for dinner," Ian said.

"But it's your anniversary, and there are plenty of sitters. You two could enjoy a nice little second honeymoon," June said.

"We appreciate the offer. But on our next trip, we will definitely use this," Ian promised.

―――――

"JUNE REALLY WANTED to get rid of us for the entire night," Lily whispered to Danielle as she got into the passenger side of the car, and Ian got into the driver's side. She glanced back to the front porch. Her parents stood with Ian's, with John holding Connor. They waved at her.

"I'll see you guys over at the foundation offices," Danielle whispered to Lily as she shut the car door.

THIRTY-FOUR

"Why do I feel like a teenager sneaking out of the house to go to a party?" Lily asked Chris and Heather when she and Ian walked into the front office of the Glandon Foundation. Hunny greeted the two with a wet nose and wiggling butt while Chris stood up and shook Ian's hand. Heather remained in her swivel office chair, her back to her desk. She gave the pair a wave.

"How you doing, ferocious?" Ian greeted Hunny after shaking Chris's hand. He gave the dog a vigorous pat along her broad shoulders. Hunny replied by swiping a wet tongue over his mouth.

"Yuck," Heather said. "I hate when she does that."

"I'm used to dog spit," Ian said as he wiped his mouth and took a seat.

"Where's Walt and Danielle?" Heather asked.

"They should be right behind us. Dani was leaving our house when we drove off," Lily explained.

Ten minutes later, Walt and Danielle showed up. Before they got down to business, Heather brought out the food she had purchased and passed it around.

"Happy anniversary," Chris told Ian and Lily as he lifted a can of beer in toast.

"I have to say, I feel overdressed," Lily said as she glanced down at her outfit.

"You look cute. And I love your hair," Heather said.

Lily flashed Heather a smile. "Thanks. Dani fixed it for me."

"Some mornings I'm tempted to knock on Danielle's door and ask her to braid my hair like that," Heather said.

"I don't believe that," Walt said.

Heather frowned at Walt. "Why?"

"Because you never knock, you just walk in."

Heather threw a french fry at Walt. Instead of hitting him, it boomeranged back to her, bouncing off her nose. "You cheat," she told him as she grabbed the fry before it fell to the floor.

They all laughed and continued eating while rehashing some of the information they all knew. When they finished dinner, Heather picked up the trash, and Chris passed around more beverages.

"Walt knew some of the Forgotten Women of Marymoor," Danielle began after Heather returned to her seat. "That list Tori sent me helped him find more information."

"Back then, you didn't hear about any of them being sent to Marymoor?" Heather asked Walt.

"No. I guess if they had, then they wouldn't have been the Forgotten Women of Marymoor, as Tori called them," Walt said. "But they were all from wealthy families."

"Were they all married?" Heather asked. "Did their husbands send them to Marymoor to get their hands on their money? You said they were from wealthy families. I could see some gold digger doing that. Hooking a rich woman and then having her locked up to get her money."

"I don't know why they were sent there," Walt said, "but they weren't all married. Several were considered spinsters."

"I hate that term," Danielle said. "And for one thing, they were not all that old."

"Understandable," Walt said. "But a woman who didn't marry by the age of twenty-three was considered a spinster."

"Hmm, Laura is a spinster? She might smack me if I called her that," Lily said.

"Actually, she is a thornback," Ian noted.

Lily frowned. "What's a thornback?"

"Oh, I've heard of that!" Heather laughed. "It's worse than a spinster—it's a woman who is still unmarried at twenty-six."

"So both of our sisters are thornbacks?" Lily asked Ian.

"So am I," Heather said. "I rather like the term. It's like something you shouldn't mess with. And I hate to remind you, but until you married Ian, you were a thornback."

Lily rolled her eyes.

"So we don't really know why those women were sent to Marymoor. We just know they died there, and they all came from wealthy families. Some were married, some weren't?" Danielle said.

"That's about right," Walt agreed.

"Considering they're haunting the site, they obviously have unresolved issues," Chris said.

"Duh," Heather snarked.

"We know who Molly is, and Waylon. Any idea who this Sid and Randal are?" Lily asked.

"The name Randal sounded a little familiar to me," Walt said. "I looked through some of the documents from Marymoor."

"Did you go back to the museum?" Chris asked.

Walt shook his head. "No. Remember the pictures Danielle took of the documents? We found the one Tori mentioned, and I must agree with her, Tori, that is. I believe those initials were the women in the photographs. Not only their initials, but their birth and death dates matched. I also found papers on Randal. I wondered why the name sounded familiar. He was the head of the sanatorium. At least, a Randal Snide was."

Heather cringed. "Snide? That sounds like a villain's name."

"Is he haunting the place too?" Lily asked.

"We didn't see him," Heather said. "But the ghosts mentioned him."

"I looked him up online, using one of the genealogy sites Danielle likes," Walt began. "Looks like he retired right after they closed Marymoor. And he retired a very wealthy man, considering where he was living. He died in Salem and is buried in the same cemetery where Rupert's mother is being buried."

"If his grave's at Salem, would he really be haunting in Frederickport?" Lily asked.

"Eva and Marie often visit other cities," Danielle reminded her.

"Yeah, but they aren't haunting them," Heather said.

Chris turned to Heather. "Remember that old adage? Beauty is in the eye of the beholder?"

Heather frowned at Chris. "What does that have to do with this?"

"Kind of the same thing. What is simply a friendly ghost stopping by to one person is a frightening haunting to another. Look at Walt," Chris explained.

"Why look at me?" Walt asked.

"I'm sure when you pitched that croquet set at Adam and Bill, they didn't see it in the same light as Danielle's encounter with you."

"Are you suggesting we might not really have anything to worry about regarding the Marymoor spirits?" Ian asked.

"Unfortunately, no," Chris said with a sigh.

"The Marymoor spirits are obviously confused, and by things they've said, I doubt they understand their reality," Danielle said.

"That's one thing I don't get," Lily said. "How does a ghost not realize they're dead when people can't see or hear them?"

"Ahh, Lily, you remember Cheryl. You helped her," Danielle reminded her.

"I'm not sure how much I helped her. And yes, I remember. But I still don't understand how she couldn't figure it out herself. Practically no one could see her. She was walking through walls." Lily shrugged.

Walt looked at Lily and chuckled. "How soon you forget."

"What are you talking about?" Lily frowned.

Danielle laughed with Walt and looked to Lily. "He's right. Remember how it was for you? Think back. You made it all the way from Palm Springs to here without a car, and you didn't even find that odd back then."

Lily stared at Danielle and then let out a sigh. She slumped back in the chair. "The truth is, I still don't get how I did all that without finding it bizarre."

"It just is what it is. You can question it all you want, but it's how it all works," Danielle said.

"Back to this Randal, does he haunt Marymoor?" Ian asked.

"It's possible, but I have to wonder, why?" Danielle said. "Eva and Marie have the ability to move around like that, but they also have accepted their reality. I'm not sure why a clear-thinking spirit would go back to a site where the other spirits are obviously confused and unable to move on."

"Maybe he goes back to try to help them move on," Lily suggested.

"I'm not convinced he haunts the place, but when the other spirits were speaking about him, it wasn't like they wanted him around," Heather said. "It's like he intimidated them."

"I agree. I don't believe they liked Randal," Chris said.

"What about the other spirit, Sid?" Lily asked.

"I found two Sids—one a patient and another an orderly who worked there," Walt said.

"We didn't see Sid, so I have no idea if he was a patient or someone who worked there," Heather said.

"What now?" Lily asked.

"I want to talk to Eva about this. In the meantime, I believe we've resolved your imaginary friend issue. That's if things work out for us on Friday," Walt said.

"I still can't believe he's actually my Rupert." Lily sighed.

KELLY AND LAURA sat in Ian and Lily's living room with their parents. Minutes earlier, the grandmothers had put Connor down for the night.

"I can't believe how easy that boy is," June said.

"He's not always that easy," Kelly said.

"He's been an absolute doll since we've been here," June said. "And I've never seen him jumping like you said he did."

"What do you mean, jumping?" Laura asked.

"It's just that one time I was here, I swear... oh, never mind..." Kelly stammered.

"She thought the boy was flying," June said with a snort.

"Flying?" Tammy asked.

"He wasn't flying. According to Lily, he was going through a phase where he was jumping in his crib. But seriously, when I saw him, I thought he was flying out of that thing," Kelly said.

"Lily never mentioned that." Tammy frowned. "When was this?"

"It was one time when Heather was babysitting, and I stopped by," Kelly explained.

"I'm not comfortable with Heather babysitting Connor," June said. "I don't know why they even use her. From what I understand, Danielle is always willing to look after him, and they have you."

"What about Connor's jumping?" Tammy asked.

"He didn't do it for long. I watched him after that, and he never did it again. Of course, I was careful, terrified he would hurt himself when I was babysitting," Kelly said.

"After Kelly told me about it, I suggested she put pillows around the crib, just in case," June said.

Tammy frowned.

"CONNOR DANIEL BARTLEY," Marie scolded when she material-ized in his bedroom. She had left Connor to his grandmothers but decided to pop in and say goodnight. But instead of sleeping in his crib, he had climbed out and was now crawling toward Rupert, who sat in the cardboard box of toys, waving at the baby coming his way. When Rupert heard Marie's voice, he looked her way sheepishly.

"Rupert?" Marie frowned at the boy ghost.

"We just wanted to play some more," Rupert said.

"You promised," Marie reminded him.

Rupert let out a sigh. "I'm sorry. I was just lonely."

"I'll tell you what, I'll put Connor back in his crib, and then I'll tell you both a story. Would you like that?"

"Yes!" Rupert said, climbing out of the box.

Marie picked up Connor and lifted him to the crib. Just as she was about to set him down on the mattress, she heard a gasp from the open bedroom door.

"Oh dear," Marie muttered. She gently set Connor on the mattress as she looked to the open doorway, where Laura and Kelly stood.

"Is that what you were talking about?" Laura squeaked.

Kelly nodded.

THIRTY-FIVE

Snowflakes floated down from the ceiling. The mediums looked upwards.

"What is it?" Lily asked.

"Eva's on her way," Danielle explained.

"Snowflakes or glitter?" Lily asked.

"Snowflakes," Danielle said.

The next moment Eva materialized, and the snowflakes vanished. "Good, you're all still here! Chris mentioned you were all getting together."

"Danielle, tell Eva what Joe's sister told you," Heather suggested.

After Danielle relayed what Tori had told her, Eva said, "You can't call them the Forgotten Women of Marymoor."

"Why do you say that?" Danielle asked.

While the mediums conversed with Eva, Lily and Ian remained silent, waiting for someone to repeat Eva's words.

"Your friend seems to base that label on the assumption no one knew they were sent to Marymoor. That's not true. Some people were aware of it back then. When Marie and I saw Viola Hawke's photograph at the museum in the Marymoor files, Marie didn't recognize her face, but she did the name. Her father knew they had sent Viola to Marymoor. He told Marie."

"Interesting. Someone told me she died in Paris," Walt said.

"It's possible news of her actual death came out after you died," Eva suggested.

"True," Walt agreed.

"What's true?" Lily asked.

Danielle quickly filled in Lily and Ian.

"Having a family member committed was considered shameful and something commonly hidden. Especially in the families they came from—wealthy, influential members of society," Walt explained.

"Sort of how a pregnant teenager was often sent to live with a relative in another state, when they were really off having a baby," Heather said. "Most people never found out, but some did."

"So Joe came from a wealthy family?" Lily asked.

"Which one was Joe's ancestor?" Eva asked.

After Danielle told Eva, Eva said, "That name is familiar; I'm sure I knew her. Are you saying she was one of the women in those photographs?"

"Yes." Danielle took out her phone and opened her photos app. A moment later, she showed Eva the picture of Joe's ancestor.

Eva studied the photo for a moment and then said, "Yes! I remember now. I didn't recognize her when I saw this picture in the museum. She's much older in that photograph. She was just a girl when I knew her."

"Was her family wealthy?" Danielle asked.

"Yes. When I knew her, she lived in Portland, but they vacationed in Frederickport." Eva looked at Walt. "Don't you remember her?"

Walt took the phone from Danielle and studied the woman's photograph.

"I imagine she was just ten or eleven when we knew her," Eva told Walt.

"I suspect she was in her early twenties when that photo was taken," Danielle said. "According to Tori, she was just twenty-six when she died. I assume they took those photos within a few years of her death."

"Remember, Walt, she had that cute little white dog. It rather liked you," Eva reminded him.

Walt studied the photo a few minutes and then said, "Yes, I do remember her." He handed the phone back to Danielle. "When Danielle told me about her discussion with Joe's sister, I did a little research on the woman. I didn't realize she was the little girl I once knew."

"So Joe's family was wealthy?" Lily said.

"Yes, at one time," Walt said.

"What happened to their money?" Lily asked.

"The money came from her father's side of the family," Walt said. "And now that I think about it, I remember something about her telling us her mother had recently remarried."

"Yes," Eva said. "Her father had died when she was very young, leaving the mother a very wealthy widow. Like me, Caroline was an only child and would someday inherit a fortune."

Danielle repeated what Eva said for Lily and Ian.

"What happened?" Lily asked.

"From what I discovered," Walt said, "just months after her first child was born, her husband died, leaving her a widow. She died relatively young, and that child, a girl, was raised by her mother and stepfather. From what I read, by the time the girl came into her inheritance, there wasn't much left. Apparently, the stepfather mismanaged the estate."

"The stepfather had control of her money?" Heather asked.

"Apparently," Walt said.

"And why was she at Marymoor?" Lily asked.

"After looking closer at some of those documents we copied, it appears she fell apart after her husband's death," Walt explained.

"Or her evil stepfather wanted her out of the way," Heather suggested.

"Just because the man was bad with money does not make him evil," Chris argued.

"According to one document," Walt said, "Randal Snide, who was the head doctor at the sanatorium, evaluated her, and according to the records, that's why she was institutionalized."

"I thought Tori didn't know why she was there?" Lily said.

"There were a lot of files in those boxes," Danielle said. "I suspect she overlooked that one."

KELLY AND LAURA left their parents to babysit Connor while they went to get frozen yogurt. Kelly drove.

"I wish our mothers had seen Connor jump like that," Laura said.

"Tell me about it," Kelly grumbled. "At first Mom believed me, but since they got here, and they haven't seen Connor jumping, she's convinced I imagined it."

"It was pretty freaky. I swear, for a minute there, I seriously thought he was floating over the crib!" Laura said.

"I have to admit, I'm glad you saw it. I was beginning to wonder if I had imagined it."

"Hey, can we drive by the Glandon Foundation office before we go to the yogurt store?" Laura asked.

Kelly glanced briefly at Laura and grinned. "Why?"

Laura returned her grin and shrugged. "Well, I didn't notice Chris coming home from work yet."

"You were watching?" Kelly teased.

Ignoring Kelly's question, Laura said, "And if that poor guy is still working, I thought we could drop by and offer to pick him up a yogurt."

"He really is hot. But Joe's not crazy about him," Kelly said.

Laura laughed. "I imagine most guys aren't. Considering Chris's looks and his money, I'd expect most guys to hate him!"

"Funny thing, he and Walt seem close. Which both Joe and I find odd, considering they used to date before she met Walt," Kelly said.

"My sister told me Chris was Walt's best man at their wedding," Laura said.

"Yeah. That was weird."

"So can we drive by?" Laura asked.

"You sure you just want to *drive by*," Kelly teased.

Laura laughed.

A few minutes later, they turned down a street leading to the Glandon Foundation.

Laura noticed a street sign on a side street that said Beach Drive. "Hey, isn't Beach Drive Lily's street?"

"Yeah. That's where the street ends. But there aren't many houses on that stretch of Beach Drive." Kelly turned down the street to the Glandon Foundation. A few moments later Kelly stopped in front of the foundation offices yet made no attempt to pull over and park.

"That's Ian and Lily's car," Kelly said.

"What are they doing here? And there's Walt's Packard," Laura said.

"They're supposed to be at dinner in Astoria."

Laura frowned. "Let's get out of here. I sure am not going to ask Chris if he wants me to get him some yogurt. It looks like his car, and Heather's here too."

"Dang, the whole Beach Drive gang," Kelly said before stepping on the accelerator.

NO ONE HAD THOUGHT to turn the front porch light on for Ian and Lily when they got home on Wednesday night. As they pulled into the driveway, they noted the house seemed dark except for the dim glow of a lone table lamp in the living room.

"Are they all sitting in the dark?" Lily asked when they opened the front door a few minutes later. Sadie greeted them.

"It's sure quiet," Ian said as he walked inside. "They must have all gone back to Marlow House."

"I hope not all of them," Lily teased as she shut the door behind them.

They walked to the living room and found Laura sitting alone on the sofa, her feet propped up on the coffee table and her arms folded over her chest. She glared at Lily and Ian when they walked in the room, yet she did not greet them.

"Did everyone go back to Dani's?" Lily asked as she tossed her purse on a chair.

"Kelly went home," Laura said stoically, her arms still folded across her chest.

Lily frowned. "Is something wrong, Laura?"

Laura looked at Ian and said, "Can I talk to my sister alone, please?"

"Um… sure…" Ian and Lily exchanged glances. He turned and headed for the hallway.

"What's wrong?" Lily asked as she sat down in a chair across from Laura.

"What is going on, Lily?" Laura asked.

"What are you talking about?"

"Where did you go for dinner tonight?"

Lily didn't answer immediately. After a moment, she mentioned a restaurant in Astoria.

"Really? How long did it take you to get there?"

"What is this about?"

"I saw you, Lily. What is going on? Why did you lie about going to Astoria for dinner?"

"You saw me where?"

"Where were you tonight?" Laura asked. "Because that's where I saw you."

Lily stared at her sister but said nothing.

After a moment, Laura cursed, uncrossed her arms, removed her feet from the coffee table, set them on the floor, and sat up straighter. "Kelly and I went out for frozen yogurt, and we drove by the Glandon Foundation. You were there when you said you were going to be in Astoria. I assume Danielle and Walt were there too since I saw the Packard."

"Why were you driving by the Glandon Foundation? That's not on the way to the yogurt store."

Laura let out a frustrated grunt and said, "Stop changing the subject! What is going on, Lily? You used to tell me everything. Now I feel like Mom."

Lily frowned. "What do you mean you feel like Mom?"

"How you and I used to keep things from her. But we always told each other. Come on, Lily, what is going on?"

"I assume Kelly saw us, too?" Lily asked.

"Yeah." Laura leaned back on the sofa and propped her feet back on the coffee table. "She told me you guys are always keeping secrets from her."

"She said that?"

"Yeah. I know she bugs you sometimes, but I get her. And she's not wrong. You guys are obviously doing something you don't want us to know about."

Lily let out a sigh. "It's complicated."

"I'm your sister, you can tell me," Laura said. "Oh, and I saw Connor do that jumping thing. Kelly didn't imagine that either."

"What do you mean you saw Connor doing a jumping thing?"

Laura told Lily what she had seen in Connor's room earlier that night.

"I haven't seen him do that in a long time," Lily lied.

They sat in silence for a few minutes. Finally, Lily asked, "Did you tell Mom and Dad?"

"You mean about Connor? Yeah."

"I meant about seeing us over at the Glandon Foundation."

"No. I'm not a snitch," Laura said.

"Did Kelly tell her parents?" Lily asked.

"She told me she wasn't going to say anything to them. But it's bugging her. What's going on, Lily?"

Lily studied Laura for a few moments before answering. Finally, she took a deep breath and said, "I need you to just trust me. I'll tell you all about it in a few days. But for right now, please, just keep it to yourself, and ask Kelly to do the same. You will both find out why we were over there in a few days. I promise."

To herself Lily said, I just hope Dani can come up with a good story to tell Laura and Kelly.

THIRTY-SIX

L ily eased Connor's bedroom door open on Friday morning and looked in. She could see her son through the slats of the crib. He slept soundly, his breathing steady.

"Rupert," Lily whispered, "it's time to go. Dani is waiting in the driveway for us." She turned and walked to the kitchen, leaving Connor's bedroom door ajar. She found Ian in the kitchen, making coffee.

"Is Connor still sleeping?" Ian asked when Lily walked into the room.

"Yeah. Dani's out in the driveway, waiting for me. She texted me a few minutes ago."

"Do you have Rupert with you?" Ian stood by the coffeepot, waiting for it to fill.

Lily shrugged. "I think so. I'm not sure." She glanced around the room.

"Let me get you a cup of coffee to take with you." Ian reached in the cupboard and removed a travel mug.

"You are wonderful." Lily stood on her tiptoes and kissed Ian's cheek.

"Does Danielle want one?" Ian asked as he filled the travel mug.

"Probably not."

"Why hasn't she taken a pregnancy test yet?" Ian handed Lily the cup of coffee.

Lily shrugged, accepted the cup, and kissed him again.

"Good luck. Is Walt going with you?" Ian asked.

"No. Just Dani. They didn't feel they should both go, not with our families over there."

Ian walked her to the door. A few minutes later, he stood in the open doorway and watched as Lily climbed into the car with Danielle. He waved to them; they waved back.

"IS RUPERT WITH US?" Lily asked as she hooked her seatbelt.

"Yes. He climbed in the back seat when you got in the car. Good morning, Rupert!"

"Good morning, Danielle," Rupert said.

"Why can't I see him?" Lily asked.

Danielle backed out of the driveway. "You don't normally see ghosts, so I'm not sure why you're asking."

"But I used to see him," Lily grumbled.

"Yeah, and you were a child."

Lily turned and looked in the back seat. It looked empty.

ACROSS THE STREET at Marlow House, Laura got out of bed and stretched. Yawning, she walked to the front window and pulled open the blinds, wanting to check out what the sky looked like today. Would it be clear and sunny or filled with dark clouds?

Motion from across the street caught her eye. She watched as Danielle backed her car from Lily's driveway. Laura frowned. Was that Lily in the passenger seat? Where were they going so early in the morning?

"RUPERT, I'm sorry for everything. I feel like I abandoned my best friend," Lily said.

"Tell Lily it's okay. I understand now," Rupert said.

"He understands, Lily," Danielle said. "It wasn't your fault, and really, it wasn't your mom's or Laura's fault, either. They had no idea your imaginary friend was the spirit of a little boy."

"Oh, Laura," Lily groaned, turning around in the seat. She looked out the front windshield.

"What's wrong?" Danielle asked. ·

"I didn't have a chance to tell you yesterday, but Laura and Kelly saw us at the foundation office. They went out to get frozen yogurt and took a detour."

"Why would they be going over there? It's not on the way to the yogurt shop."

"Why do you think? Laura never said it. She was too busy grilling me. I suspect she wanted to see if Chris was still there. I imagine if she hadn't seen us, she would have stopped by and asked Chris if he wanted to go with them to get yogurt."

"She really likes him, doesn't she?" Danielle asked.

Lily laughed. "She barely knows him. But seriously, Chris is superhot, and he is Chris Glandon. I'm hardly surprised she's shown interest in him. But that's not the point. The point is, she and Kelly both saw us over there when we said we were in Astoria having dinner."

"Just tell them you stopped by the foundation to pick up something on your way to the restaurant. Or on the way home. Depending on when they drove by."

"That would be great, but I don't know when they drove by, to make that plausible. And I didn't want to get in deeper."

"So what did you tell her?" Danielle asked.

"I told her to trust me, and that in a few days I could tell her and Kelly why we were there. She promised to talk to Kelly."

"What are you going to say in a few days?" Danielle asked.

"I don't know, Dani. What should I say?"

Danielle frowned. "Why are you asking me?"

"Because you're the one who always comes up with the plausible excuses. I need to tell her and Kelly something in a couple of days, so think of something! I'm counting on you!"

WHEN THEY PULLED into the parking lot at the Salem cemetery, Lily said, "Thanks for coming with me today. You hate going to cemeteries."

"I don't really mind it as much as I used to." Danielle parked the car and turned off the ignition. "Walt wanted to come with us, but we figured if our guests woke up and found us both gone, they might think aliens abducted us."

Lily laughed. "What are you going to tell them?"

"That you wanted to get a few last-minute things for the birthday party, and I agreed to go with you. Walt's going to tell them you didn't want to ask your mom or Laura to go because you figured they wanted to spend time with Connor."

"Yeah, my flying kid."

Danielle laughed. She had already heard about what Laura has seen in the nursery.

Danielle took her seatbelt off and turned around to face Rupert. "You ready, kiddo?"

"What if it's not my mom?" Rupert asked.

Before coming to the cemetery, they had gone to the church to attend the funeral. It had been a closed casket, and the picture on display showed an older woman whom Rupert did not recognize. They had sat at the back of the church and didn't talk to anyone. While there, Danielle didn't notice a single spirit. She hoped Rupert's mother would show up at the grave site—if she was his mother.

"Then you can come back with us, of course," Danielle said. "Unless you want to try crossing over by yourself."

Rupert shook his head. "I don't want to go alone. What if no one is over there waiting for me? I'll be all alone again."

"Don't worry. We won't leave you," Danielle promised. She then conveyed to Lily Rupert's concerns.

Lily turned to the back seat and smiled. "Rupert, you'll be much happier when you move on with your family. If not today, then later, when you feel comfortable. But until then, you can stay with us. Connor would love having you. Like I did."

THEY STOOD UNDER A LARGE TREE, about six feet from the rest of the mourners, listening to the minister say his final words over the woman being buried. Danielle wondered if the woman's spirit had already moved on.

When the minister finished saying his words and the crowd dispersed, Danielle turned to Lily. She was about to say something to her when a man's voice said, "I noticed you at the church."

Both Danielle and Lily turned to the voice and found an elderly man looking at them.

"Are you family or friends?" the man asked.

"I'm not sure," Danielle said.

"Excuse me?" The man cocked a brow.

"My mother had a very good friend named Mary Peterson in California. I live in Oregon now, and when I read her obituary, I thought it had to be the same person, because the obituary mentioned her son, Rupert. I'm assuming it's the same woman. And if so, I had to come; my mother had been so fond of her," Danielle lied.

"Your mother couldn't make it?" he asked.

"My mother passed away some time ago," Danielle said.

"Oh, I'm sorry. Mary and I were neighbors. I'm Ed Hall." He held out his hand for Danielle. She accepted it and told him her name and introduced Lily.

"I don't imagine you ever knew Rupert. You look too young," Ed said.

"No, but my mother told me about him," Danielle lied.

"I met Mary when she and her husband moved to Oregon. It wasn't long after losing their son. I don't think they ever got over his death."

"I don't imagine any parent does," Lily said.

"True." He nodded.

"When did her husband die?" Danielle asked.

"Several years ago. Was a heart attack. It happened so fast. It's how I'd want to go, but it wasn't easy for Mary. Too sudden, like her son's death. But now, we can have comfort knowing they're finally together."

"Did my mother leave without me?" Rupert asked.

"Rupert!" a woman's voice called out.

Danielle and Rupert turned to the voice. The transparent image of a young woman stood some ten feet away. A shaft of golden light streamed through her. Danielle thought the spirit looked a little like the picture she had seen earlier at the church. Yet a much younger version.

"Mom!" Rupert called out. He ran to his mother, and she gathered him up in her arms.

"Dani, Mr. Hall was saying goodbye," Lily interrupted.

Danielle looked at the man, smiled sheepishly, and said goodbye.

When he turned away, Danielle hastily grabbed Lily's hand and pulled her from the few people still mingling around.

"She's here!" Danielle said.

"Does Rupert know?" Lily asked.

Danielle pointed to a nearby tree. "He's with her, over there."

Lily looked where Danielle pointed. She saw a tree.

"WE NEED to go to your father, he's waiting," Rupert's mother told him.

"I have to say goodbye to Lily," he told her.

"Okay, but then we must go."

Rupert nodded and ran back to Danielle and Lily.

"I have to go now, Lily."

"Remember, she can't see or hear you. But whatever you want to tell her, I'll make sure she understands," Danielle promised.

LILY STARED down at the patch of dirt where she assumed Rupert stood, considering that was where Danielle currently directed her conversation. At first, she thought she was imagining things, her eyes or mind was playing tricks on her. It was as if someone had turned on a floodlight, filling the space before her. It sparked and flickered, making her think of those times Danielle and the others had talked about Eva's glitter and snowflakes.

The next moment Lily gasped when the vision of a little boy appeared in the light—a transparent image of her long-ago imaginary friend. Abruptly, she reached out and grabbed hold of Danielle's hand.

"I can see him!" Lily said.

"You can?" Rupert asked.

"I can hear you too!" Lily said, her grin wide. Without thought she got down on one knee to make herself eye level to the ghost, paying no attention to those around her who might notice her peculiar behavior.

"Really?" Rupert asked in awe.

"Yes! Oh gosh, you look exactly as I remember!" Lily said.

"You look a lot older," Rupert said.

Lily laughed. "I guess I do."

"I have to go with my mom now," Rupert said.

Lily glanced toward the tree, and to her surprise she saw Rupert's mother standing there, waiting for him. Lily had no doubt the woman was his mother, considering her transparent nature.

"Yes, you do," Lily said. "But I want you to understand how much you meant to me. We had so much fun. I remember you used to tell me I was a princess, taken from my kingdom, when Laura would tell me Mom found me after someone left me on the doorstep."

Rupert grinned. "You were a princess. I wish I could stay and get to know Connor better, but I think it's time I go."

"Yes, it is. I love you, Rupert."

"I love you too, Lily."

THIRTY-SEVEN

Danielle and Lily stood together and watched as Rupert ran to his mother and took her hand. The two spirits looked back to them and smiled before fading into the light washing over them. When they were no longer visible, the shaft of light faded, as if some invisible hand slowly turned the knob of a dimmer switch.

"I'm so glad I got to see him one more time," Lily whispered.

Danielle reached over and took one of Lily's hands, giving it a reassuring squeeze.

"In my heart, Rupert was always real to me. Laura would tease me about him. I know she never meant anything, and I understand why she thought the entire thing was so funny. But it wasn't funny to me."

"I understand."

Lily gave Danielle's hand a squeeze. "I imagine you would. Over the years, I convinced myself Rupert was a product of a child's imagination, but there was always a part of me that thought he was real."

Danielle gave Lily's hand a final squeeze and released it.

"Good, I caught you!" a voice boomed out.

Danielle was startled by the sudden intrusion. "Eva! You scared me!"

"Well, I am a ghost in a cemetery," Eva said before breaking into giggles.

"Eva's here?" Lily looked around and saw nothing new.

"Yes, and she's highly amused with herself right now." Danielle chuckled.

Eva finally stopped giggling and said, "I understand Rupert and his mother moved on."

"How did you know?" Danielle asked.

Eva shrugged. "I have my ways. But that's not why I'm here. I've come about Randal."

"Would you ask Eva something for me?" Lily interrupted.

Both Danielle and Eva turned to Lily. "What?" Danielle asked.

"Was all of this planned?" Lily asked.

"Planned?" Eva asked with a frown.

"What do you mean, planned?" Danielle asked.

"The fact that Rupert came to me after all these years, when I'm living in Oregon, and just at the right time to go to his mother's funeral, in Oregon. Walt and Danielle said something like that," Lily explained.

Eva smiled. "I'm not sure if planned is the right word. But stars do align to make opportunities, yet it is up to us to make them happen or not. One thing to remember we all have free will—free will to change the course of our destiny."

Danielle repeated Eva's words.

"Does that mean it was sorta planned?" Lily asked.

"Some things you just need to accept," Eva said.

Danielle repeated Eva's words again. Lily frowned but did not ask another question.

"I stopped at Marlow House and talked to Walt before coming here. It wasn't easy with all those people underfoot," Eva said. "He mentioned you planned to look for Randal's grave while you're here."

"Yes, but I'm not sure we'll be able to find it, and we need to get back to Frederickport," Danielle said. "Not sure there's any point in looking for it."

"Ahh, it's those aligned stars!" Eva said.

Danielle frowned. "I don't understand."

"Like what I said to Lily. I realized it when I stopped in to talk to Walt earlier today," Eva explained.

"You realized what?" Danielle asked.

"That you need to find Randal's grave. That's why you're here," Eva said.

"No, we came here to bring Rupert to his mother," Danielle reminded her.

Eva laughed. "Oh, Danielle, nothing is ever that simple!"

Furrowing her brows, Danielle stared at Eva.

"What is Eva saying?" Lily asked. She glanced around. The other mourners who had gathered for the grave-site service had since dispersed. For a non-medium, it looked as if just Danielle and Lily stood alone.

"I'm not sure. But I think she's suggesting the Universe wants us to talk to Randal," Danielle said.

"And he's here?" Lily asked.

"I think his spirit is." Danielle looked at Eva and asked, "Is it?"

"There is no guarantee. There are no guarantees in life or death." Eva paused a moment and then added with a shrug, "That's not entirely accurate. But hurry, let's find Randal's grave."

THEY LOCATED Randal's grave in the older, desolate section of the cemetery. Eva, Lily, and Danielle stood in front of his standing headstone, reading the inscription. The late morning breeze rustled the leaves in the nearby tree branches overhead. An occasional chirping of a bird added to the sounds of the cemetery.

Lily looked around. "Is he here?"

"I don't see him." Danielle looked at Eva.

"Then why are we here?" Lily asked.

"Patience," Eva said.

The next moment Eva stretched out her arms while the illusion of her body slowly lifted from the ground until it hovered above the headstone, stars shooting from her fingertips.

"What's happening?" Lily asked when she noticed Danielle watching something overhead.

"Eva theatrics," Danielle whispered.

If Eva overheard Danielle's comment, she said nothing. Instead, she called out, "Randal Snide, show yourself! The time for reckoning is now!"

Eva remained hovering above the headstone, her arms still outstretched and her eyes closed. After a moment, she repeated her cry. To Danielle's astonishment, the spirit of a man appeared, standing next to the headstone.

"Okay, I heard you already. Stop screaming," the male ghost grumbled.

Eva opened her eyes, lowered her arms, and slowly floated downward until her feet landed on the grass next to Lily and Danielle.

"I think Randal is here," Danielle whispered to Lily.

"Can you tell him and his ghost buddies to stop haunting Marymoor," Lily whispered back.

"You sound rather grouchy. I assume you are Randal Snide," Eva said.

"Yes. And who are you?" he snapped.

"Eva Thorndike."

His eyes widened. "I've heard about you. Have they sent you to come get me? Do I have to go to hell now?"

"Do you belong in hell?" Eva asked.

"What good would it do for me to lie now?" he asked. "I've been stuck here since they buried my body. Can't leave the cemetery." He looked at Danielle and Lily. "Are you dead too?"

"No, we're not," Danielle said. "I can see and hear you, but my friend Lily can't."

Lily eyed a park bench some twenty feet away. She turned to Danielle and said, "While you guys chat, I think I'll go sit down. Please warn me if I'm about to walk through anyone."

"No, you're good," Danielle said. "Randal is standing over there." Danielle pointed to the spot where the ghost stood. "And Eva is to your left."

Lily nodded and walked away, heading for the park bench.

"This is all very strange," Randal said.

"Confession is good for your soul," Eva said. "Time to confess, Randal."

Randal looked to Eva, studying her for a moment. Finally, he let out a sigh. "After I do, I assume I'll go to hell. But I don't understand, what is the point of keeping me here all these years? Is it extra punishment, making me think about where I'm eventually going? God letting me stew in the anticipation?"

"As my friend Heather says, it is not all about you, Randal. You can't leave because you have unfinished business here. As for going to hell, it is more complicated than that. But for now, let's deal with your unfinished business," Eva said.

"What unfinished business?" he asked.

"The consequences of your actions have paralyzed some souls, making it impossible for them to move on. You terrified them. Your spirit visited them once, didn't it? After you died and before you were trapped here?" Eva asked.

Randal stared at Eva for a moment. Finally, he asked, "Are you talking about when I visited Marymoor after I died, and they were still there? All of them."

Eva nodded. "Now confess your sins, Randal. So others will know what really happened and your victims can finally be free."

"Is she my confessor? Is that why she's here?" While Randal asked the question of Eva, he looked at Danielle.

Instead of answering, Eva said, "Go on. It's time for the truth to come out."

Randal lowered his head and said, "I killed Molly. And then I killed Waylon."

"You killed them? Why?" Danielle blurted.

Randal looked up at Danielle. "Molly knew my secret. She found out, and she confronted me. I didn't plan to kill her, it just happened. And then Waylon walked in on us, and he got scared and ran off. So I blamed him. I told everyone he was the one who killed Molly. When they found him, they brought him back to Marymoor, and I made sure it looked like he committed suicide. I had Sid do it. He always liked Molly, and I convinced him they would never really punish Waylon for his crime because the state would deem him insane, unfit to go to prison. And Waylon's life would not really change after murdering Molly. Sid gladly did it. But afterwards, he felt such guilt. While we were closing Marymoor several weeks later, he went on a drinking binge, ran his car into a tree on the property. Died on impact. I had nothing to do with it. But I suppose I really did."

"What secret did Molly discover?" Danielle asked.

"I had a little side business. If someone needed to get rid of someone, they could pay me to make sure they got committed."

"Like you did with Sean Sullivan?" Danielle asked.

Randal chuckled. "I didn't really make any money off Sullivan. That was a favor. There was a guy on the police force who knew what I was doing. He felt it was in his best interest to stay quiet, because he could call in a favor—like he did with Sean."

"Who else got committed who shouldn't have been there?" Danielle asked.

"Technically speaking, Sean belonged at Marymoor. Oh, he wasn't a real danger, but to my credit I did think he was crazy back then."

"But the others weren't?" Danielle asked.

Randal shook his head. "No. And Molly figured it out."

"Who were they?" Danielle asked.

Randal listed the names—eight names. The names of the women Chris and Heather had seen at the Marymoor property, the women whose photographs had been in the box in the museum storage room. The Forgotten Women of Marymoor.

"According to the death dates of those women, they all died before Marymoor closed. Some of them were very young," Danielle noted.

"I didn't kill them," Randal said. "But I was responsible. I understand that now."

"How do you mean?" Danielle asked.

"Five of them took their own lives. Once they realized why they were really there, that they would never get out, they couldn't face their future," Randal said.

"How did the others die," Danielle asked.

"Influenza," Randal said. "Yet I suppose I'm to blame there, too. Had they not been at Marymoor, they may not have gotten sick."

"Tell us about each woman," Eva told Randal. "Tell us their stories."

"HE'S GONE NOW?" Lily asked Danielle as they walked back to the car.

"Yes. I assume he's moved on in his journey, wherever that may be," Danielle said.

"And Eva?" Lily glanced around.

"She's not here. Said to tell you goodbye."

When Danielle and Lily got into the car, Lily asked, "What now?"

"Now I need to let the Marymoor spirits know it is no longer a secret." Danielle closed her car door and hooked her seatbelt.

"And you think that will get them to move on?" Lily asked.

"Sometimes a spirit just needs the truth acknowledged. It's not so important that the entire world knows, just that the truth is finally released—that someone knows. Someone other than the victims and the guilty parties. But we'll have to see."

"Those poor spirits. Heather was wrong. They are sad, not creepy," Lily noted.

"I suppose most creepy and scary hauntings stem from sad spirits," Danielle said.

"I guess." Lily fastened her seatbelt.

As they drove home, Danielle told Lily all that Randal had confessed to her and Eva.

"What I don't understand, you'd think at an institution like that, it wouldn't be so easy for a patient to commit suicide. If they're watching them closely so they can't escape, how is it they could kill themselves?" Lily asked. "Did a lot of patients at Marymoor commit suicide?"

"No. There was protocol in place to help prevent that. Rules that weren't enforced for those eight women. Apparently, Randal earned a bonus when any of the women died. A bonus paid by the people who paid him to incarcerate the women. That's what got Molly to start asking questions, asking why the rules were lax for those patients. At first, he claimed it was because of who they were. VIP patients who had special privileges."

"Privileges that got them killed."

"Exactly."

"Randal is going to hell," Lily said.

THIRTY-EIGHT

"Hello!" a voice shouted from the back seat.

Startled by the unexpected sound—especially since they were driving on the highway and no one was sitting in the back seat a minute ago—Danielle jerked the wheel to the right, sending her car veering into traffic.

Lily screamed, and Marie took the wheel, bringing the car to the right side of the road and averting an accident.

"Careful, Danielle," Marie scolded from the back seat. "You almost sent Lily and yourself over to my side."

"I wouldn't have done that if you hadn't screamed at me!" Danielle shouted.

"I didn't scream at you!" Lily yelled. "You almost killed us!"

Danielle took a deep breath, told herself to calm down, and said, "I'm sorry, Lily. I was talking to Marie."

"Marie?" Lily frowned.

"I can't see her in the rearview mirror, but I assume she is now sitting in the back seat since she just shouted hello at me," Danielle said.

"Oh, dear," Marie muttered. "I did, didn't I? I'm sorry, Danielle."

Lily turned around and looked in the back seat. It looked empty to her. Yet she knew that meant nothing.

"I know you didn't mean to scare me," Danielle said. "And thank you for taking the wheel. I'm not sure I could have made it."

"Oh, dear, I really need to be more careful. Heather is always telling me not to just pop in like that. But I just wanted to find out if it all worked out with Rupert."

Danielle told Marie about their morning with Rupert. Before she could tell her about Randal, Lily asked, "How's Connor?"

"Tell Lily he's fine. When I left, he was napping."

Danielle conveyed the message, and then she told Marie about seeing Eva and Randal.

"Oh my, you have had a big day. I would have really mucked it up if I'd gotten you killed on the highway," Marie said.

"Well, I suspect that wouldn't be possible if everything Eva says about this is true," Danielle noted.

Lily almost asked Danielle what wouldn't be possible but sat back to wait until later to ask her questions.

Marie let out a sigh. "Please tell Lily I'll stop by after Connor's birthday. With Rupert on his way, she no longer needs me over there, and I think it would be best if I don't interfere. While I might not actually be able to get you killed on the highway, it's enough Laura walked in on me putting Connor back in his crib. She's been watching that boy like a hawk ever since it happened."

INSTEAD OF DROPPING Lily off at her house, Danielle pulled up the alley behind her garage. She clicked the garage door opener, watched the door open, pulled in the garage, parked, turned off the ignition, and shut the garage door. When Lily and Danielle stepped out of the garage into the side yard a few minutes later, they found Laura waiting for them.

"I noticed your car drive by the house," Laura greeted them.

"Hi, Laura," Lily returned.

"So, what did you buy?" Laura looked over her sister's shoulders as if she might see something. Danielle and Lily each carried a purse, yet no shopping bags or packages.

"Um..." Lily stammered, glancing at Danielle.

"Walt said you guys did some last-minute shopping for Connor's party. I would have liked to go. I like to shop. I assume it's still in the car?"

"Trust me, you would rather have stayed here," Danielle said as the three walked toward the house. "We didn't go mall shopping. I heard about a guy who had one of those inflatable kids' funhouse thingies for parties, that he rented for real cheap. We looked at it, and the thing was gross. Lily said no way would she let Connor play on it. So our little ride today was a bust."

"Oh." Laura looked at Lily. "Why didn't you mention it last night?"

"Because she didn't know last night," Danielle answered for Lily. "I called Lily early this morning, asked her if she wanted to drive to Salem with me to check out the funhouse for Connor's birthday. It was sort of a last-minute thing. A stupid one."

"Your heart was in the right place," Lily told Danielle.

Danielle shrugged. "Just one of my stupid ideas."

"What Walt told us, it sounded like you were just shopping," Laura said.

"I was hoping to surprise everyone with the funhouse, so I asked Walt to say we were just picking up some last-minute stuff," Danielle lied.

Lily and Laura said goodbye to Danielle as they continued across the street to Lily's house.

"Now I feel like a jerk," Laura grumbled.

Lily stopped on the sidewalk in front of Marlow House and looked at her sister. "Why?"

Laura stopped next to Lily. She looked at her and shrugged. "I was so annoyed at you not asking me to go with you today. I admit, I get a little jealous of Danielle."

"Why?"

"Seriously, Lily? You guys seem to share all sorts of secrets. I still don't know why you lied to all of us about where you were going the other night. And when I saw you leaving with her this morning, and Walt said you were going shopping, well, it hurt my feelings that you didn't invite me."

"Oh, Laura." Lily sighed. She reached over and hugged her sister. "I'm sorry, I didn't mean to make you feel that way."

When the hug ended, Laura looked at Lily and said, "You have everything. This amazing man who adores you. Connor. All sorts of friends. A house right on the beach. You have this great life, and I just want to be part of it." Tears filled Laura's eyes.

"*Damn*, I am a crappy sister," Lily groaned. She hugged Laura again.

When the second hug ended, Laura sniffled and wiped tears from her eyes. "Oh, don't pay any attention to me. I am PMSing."

Lily laughed and took Laura's hand. Together, they continued across the street to Lily's house.

"IAN'S NOT HERE," Laura told Lily before they entered the house.

"Where is he?" Lily asked.

"He took Sadie to play Frisbee. Mom and June are watching Connor, and Dad and John are over at the lot they bought."

Still standing on the front porch, her hand on the doorknob, getting ready to open it, Lily frowned. "Why did they go over there?"

Laura shrugged. "John can't seem to talk about anything but this new house he wants to build. Not sure if Dad is really interested or just wanted to get out of the house."

Lily smiled. "I think hanging out with Connor all day is more a grandma thing than a grandpa thing."

"Dad did say he was looking forward to when Connor is older so they can do stuff," Laura said.

Lily smiled and opened the door. When she did, she could hear Connor crying. It came from the living room.

When Lily and Laura walked into the living room, June and Tammy sat on the sofa, while Connor sat on the floor with a pile of toys, sobbing.

"I'm glad you're here," Tammy told Lily, looking helplessly at Connor.

Lily walked to her son and picked him up. He wrapped his little arms around her neck, burying his tear-filled eyes in her neck. Absently, she felt his diaper. He seemed to be dry. "What happened?"

"He's been fussy ever since he woke up from his nap," June said. "I think he might be coming down with something."

Lily pressed her face next to Connor's. He was cool.

"As long as we were on the floor playing with him, he was happy as a clam," Tammy said. "But the minute we got up, he would get fussy again."

"I can't sit on the floor that long," June said. "And neither can your mother. When we sat back on the sofa, we tried to take him with us, but he wanted down. We decided to just let him cry."

"We really didn't think he would get this upset," Tammy said.

Lily smiled at her son. "Yeah, well, like I told you before, Connor has his moments. You just experienced one."

IT TOOK little convincing to get the mothers to go back to Marlow House and take a rest. Laura stayed behind with Lily and Connor.

Lily sat on the sofa, watching her sister sitting on the floor with Connor, pushing around toy trucks and making siren sounds.

Laura looked up to Lily and said, "He's not crying now."

Lily laughed. "No. Because you're playing with him. I'm afraid my son is spoiled."

"How can you say that?" Laura smiled lovingly at Connor. "He's been so sweet natured since I've been here. So he had one meltdown, big deal." She leaned over and kissed his forehead.

Lily smiled but didn't comment.

When Ian and Sadie returned to the house fifteen minutes later, Lily stood up and asked Laura, "Can you stay with Connor for a few minutes? I need to talk to Ian about something."

"Sure, no problem."

Ian and Lily retreated to Ian's office, leaving Sadie in the living room with Connor and Laura. Lily shut the door behind her and began telling Ian about their eventful morning.

LAURA GLANCED AT HER WATCH. Lily and Ian had been in the office for about fifteen minutes. Connor no longer wanted to play; he had become fussy again and rubbed his eyes. She suspected he had a wet diaper.

"While diaper changes aren't my thing," Laura muttered, "I guess I need to be a good auntie and change yours."

With a sigh, Laura stood and picked up Connor.

"Dang, you're heavy. How does Lily do it?" Laura grunted as she carried her nephew to his bedroom. Once there, she set him in the crib and changed his diaper. Thinking he needed a nap, she left him in the crib, but was reluctant to leave him alone, considering what she had witnessed the other day.

Laura walked to the large box her mother had brought Lily and sat down next to it. She hadn't had a chance to see what old toys her mother had put in the box. Removing a tattered Cabbage Patch doll from it, she leaned against the wall while examining the doll.

It was then she heard it—voices. Ian and Lily's voices. They came from the nearby heating vent on the floor.

Curious, Laura tossed the doll aside and leaned closer to the vent. The voices became louder and clearer.

"What's the plan?" Ian asked.

Wow, this is like an intercom, Laura thought as she eavesdropped on Lily and Ian's conversation.

"Dani feels we should do this right away. Before anything else happens. If we can get them to go, then your parents can build on the lot, and we don't have to worry. But if something happens in the meantime, your dad might refuse to build, which might not be necessary," Lily said.

"Our dads are over there now."

"Yeah, but since we haven't heard anything yet, that's a good sign," Lily said.

"Who's going to do it?" Ian asked.

"Dani wants to."

"It's not risky for her?" Ian asked.

"Considering everything, she doesn't feel it will be. She and Walt will go over to your parents' lot at sunrise tomorrow morning. The plan is to get back to Marlow House before anyone wakes up."

"Does she really think she can do it that fast?" Ian asked.

"She wants to give it a try," Lily said.

THIRTY-NINE

The only time Laura slept with her watch on was when she needed to get up at a certain time in the morning. Before going to bed on Friday night, she used her smartphone to Google sunrise for Frederickport. She set her watch alarm to go off fifteen minutes prior to sunrise before putting it on.

As it turned out, Laura was already wide awake when she felt her watch vibrate. She had woken up several times during the night and, after the last time, could not fall back to sleep. Turning off her alarm, she rolled out of bed and started to get dressed without turning on a light. She pulled on jogging pants and a long sweatshirt.

After slipping on her running shoes, she headed for the bathroom. Not wanting to wake anyone up, she didn't turn on her bedroom light when she eased open the door. A night-light plugged into a nearby hallway socket partially illuminated the area. She had only opened the door a few inches when she heard steps coming down the attic stairs. *It has to be Walt and Danielle*, she thought, reclosing the door, leaving it open only a sliver.

Standing inside the bedroom, she peered out into the dimly lit hallway. Silently, she watched as Walt and Danielle walked past her door and headed toward the stairs leading to the first floor. She waited until she felt they were downstairs before coming out into the hall.

When initially deciding to follow Walt and Danielle over to the Marymoor property, Laura had considered taking her parents' truck, yet she was afraid they would see her following them. The property wasn't that far away, and the sun was coming up, so Laura decided to walk—or jog. *I need the exercise anyway*, Laura told herself. She remembered Lily telling her how Heather jogged every day on the beach. Laura had tried that once and found it brutal. Jogging on sand was not Laura's thing, but perhaps she could do it on the streets from Marlow House to June and John's property.

Walt and Danielle were still in the garage at Marlow House when Laura took off running, keeping out of sight and in the shadows. Laura had gone a little over a block when she noticed headlights coming up the street in her direction. She assumed they were from Walt and Danielle's car. Breathing heavily, Laura wondered how Heather did this every morning, especially on sand. Needing to take a break and to drop out of sight for a minute, Laura dived into nearby bushes. As she landed with an ungraceful thud, she heard the startled hissing sound of a cat, who ran from the bush, off into the darkness. Fortunately, she had not landed on the cat's body, just its tail.

Breathing heavily and rubbing a hand over her bruised thigh, she noticed her pants were now soaked from the wet ground. A moment later the Packard drove by without seeing her. She groaned and awkwardly got to her feet while wiping mud and dirt from her pants. Instead of jogging the rest of the way, Laura stuck to a fast run, while grateful she had done no actual damage with her geeky jump into the bushes.

When Laura arrived at the property, she found Walt and Danielle sitting in the Packard. Overhead, to the east, the sun peeked over the trees. Laura assumed the Marlows were waiting for someone. Who? That she planned to discover. Creeping closer to the Packard while staying out of sight, Laura hid behind a grouping of bushes some six feet from the car. She cringed at the possibility of Walt and Danielle finding her there. What would she say to them?

Laura didn't have long to consider that thought. The next moment, Walt and Danielle got out of their car. She watched as they approached the open gate leading into the property, just a few feet away. The pair stopped walking.

"Please don't leave," Laura heard Danielle call out. Laura didn't believe Danielle spoke to her, since Danielle's and Walt's backs were to her.

"I have something you need to hear," Danielle said.

Who is she talking to? Laura wondered. She expected someone to come walking out of the shadows. But instead of a person, what looked like a fallen tree branch lifted from the ground and flew toward Walt and Danielle. An instant later the branch froze in midair, hovering overhead a few seconds before falling to the ground. Laura threw a hand over her mouth and gasped.

"PLEASE DON'T DO THAT AGAIN," Danielle asked the spirit standing just inside the gate. He ignored her request, and the next moment a small boulder lifted from the ground and flew in their direction. Walt focused on the incoming missile. It froze in midair, gently vibrating as the competing energy of Walt and Waylon pressed the boulder from opposite sides. And then, like fireworks at Fourth of July, the boulder literally exploded, sending bits of rock in all directions, raining down on them.

"Would you stop that!" Danielle snapped. "Are you Waylon? We just want to talk."

Molly appeared. "Please leave. You're frightening Waylon."

"Waylon is the one throwing trees and boulders at us, not the other way around," Danielle told Molly.

Molly looked at Waylon. "Don't throw things."

"I didn't mean to frighten him," Danielle said. "But we just need to talk to you. We're here to help."

"You can't help us," a third spirit said. The next moment, the spirit attached to the voice appeared. He stood to Molly's right.

"I assume you're Sid? I'm Danielle, and this is my husband, Walt."

"Listen to Molly," Sid said. "You need to leave before Randal comes back."

"I saw Randal yesterday," Danielle said. "He's not coming back. He told me he did some bad things, and he hurt all of you."

"Randal said that?" Sid frowned. "I don't believe you."

"I also need to talk to some of your other patients," Danielle told Molly. She then listed the names of the eight women Chris and Heather had seen.

"Why do you want to talk to them?" Molly asked.

"Because it's time for them to go home. They should never have been sent here. None of them deserved to be sent to Marymoor," Danielle said.

A morning breeze replaced the stillness, sending the leaves overhead fluttering—yet only on the property where Marymoor Sanatorium once stood. Neighboring trees, not on the site, remained motionless. After a few moments the breeze died off, the leaves grew still, and eight transparent apparitions appeared, standing behind Molly, Waylon, and Sid. The Forgotten Women of Marymoor.

"What do you mean we can go home?" one called out. "Is this a trick?"

"It has to be. Randal must have found out we've been working together on a plan to expose him," another one said.

"It's not a trick, and Randal is not coming back," Danielle insisted.

"Where is he?" one woman asked.

"I assume facing the consequences for his actions," Danielle said.

"Do you really know what he did?" another woman asked.

"Yes. Randal confessed his crimes," Danielle said. "Which of you is Caroline?"

"I am. Why do you call my name?" Caroline asked.

"Your father was wealthy, and when he died, your mother remarried. Your stepfather was an evil man. After your husband died, your stepfather committed you to Marymoor, claiming your widow's grief was something more serious, and Randal agreed with him. But he did it for the money your stepfather paid him," Danielle told her.

"They wouldn't let me see my daughter! I begged them!" Caroline sobbed.

"You can see her now," Danielle said softly.

"How can I do that?" Caroline asked.

"Think back, Caroline, do you remember the last time you saw Randal? You didn't feel good that day, you had a bad headache. You wanted to see a doctor. And you just wanted to go home. But Randal said you didn't need to see the doctor, and that you were never leaving Marymoor. He told you to get used to your life, and he locked you in your room."

Caroline frowned.

"Try to remember what happened," Danielle urged.

Caroline closed her eyes, trying to visualize that long-ago day. Finally, she opened her eyes and said, "I was so sick. I was alone for hours. And then my head stopped hurting. But I was still in bed. I watched myself sleep."

"You watched yourself sleep because you stepped out of your body," Danielle explained. "You weren't sleeping. Deep down you know the truth."

Caroline stared at Danielle for a few moments. Finally, she said, "I'm dead."

"And you don't have to stay here anymore. You're free. Free to go to your husband and daughter," Danielle said.

"Are you saying my daughter is dead?" Caroline asked.

"Your daughter lived a long life. She married, had children and grandchildren. But that was many years ago. It was time for her to move on, and now it's time for you to move on.

Caroline smiled at Danielle. "Thank you." The next moment, Caroline vanished.

"Which of you is Viola?" Danielle asked.

"I'm Viola," one of the women said as she took a step forward.

"You married the wrong man. He wanted your money. He told everyone you died in Paris," Danielle said.

"I didn't die in Paris," Viola said.

"No. You died at Marymoor," Danielle whispered.

Viola stared blankly at Danielle. Finally, she said, "I couldn't take it anymore. I had to end it."

"And you did. But now you're free to go. You're no longer bound to Marymoor," Danielle said.

Viola smiled at Danielle and then disappeared.

One by one Danielle called out the Forgotten Women of Marymoor, acknowledging what had happened to each one of them, giving them permission to move on. When only Molly, Sid and Waylon remained, Danielle said, "Molly, you tried to stop it. You found out what was going on. You confronted Randal."

Molly looked down at her hands now covered with blood. "He was so angry. He picked up a knife. And then Waylon walked in." Molly looked to Waylon.

"I was afraid. I should have helped you, but I ran away," Waylon said.

"It was too late to help her," Danielle told him. "There's nothing you could have done."

"I blamed Waylon," Sid said. "He did nothing wrong."

"Like the others, you're no longer trapped here. Randal is gone. He has to deal with the consequences of his own actions."

"Oh, my god, I'm dead!" Molly blurted.

"It's time for you to move on, Molly," Danielle said gently.

Molly looked at Waylon. She held out her hand. "Come, Waylon, it's time to go now." Waylon took Molly's hand, and the two disappeared.

Sid remained. He looked at Danielle. "I'm dead too, aren't I?"

Danielle nodded.

"What's going to happen to me?" Sid asked. "I did something bad. I killed Waylon, didn't I? I remember now. I made it look like a suicide."

"Sid, face the consequences of your actions. It's time for you to move on, too," Danielle urged.

Sid let out a sigh. "I'm tired of this place. I really wanted to get out of here. I thought about killing myself. Now I find out I'm already dead!" He vanished.

Walt took Danielle's hand. The two stood in silence for several minutes, staring at where the spirits had been standing.

"You did good, Danielle," Walt whispered.

"Are they gone?" Danielle asked.

"It certainly feels that way," Walt said.

"Let's go home," Danielle said with a sigh.

Walt and Danielle turned toward their car, and when they did, they saw her.

FORTY

Danielle's eyes widened at the unexpected sight of Laura. Without thinking, she squeezed Walt's hand. They both stared at Laura, neither one saying a word. Walt quietly reached down to loosen Danielle's grip on his other hand, their eyes never leaving Lily's sister.

"Laura," Danielle stammered, no longer squeezing Walt's hand.

Without saying a word, Laura abruptly turned and started running in the opposite direction.

"Crap," Danielle groaned. "What did she hear?"

"What did she see?" Walt asked.

"We'd better tell Lily." Danielle took her cellphone from the pocket of her hoodie. "If we're lucky, she'll go straight to Lily's and not to her parents."

"Why would she go to Lily's first?" Walt asked.

"Because something tells me going back to our house right now is the last thing she wants to do."

LILY OPENED the front door for Laura before she had time to knock. "Dani called, said you were probably coming here. Ian's in the living room, waiting."

"I just want to talk to you," Laura said.

"But—" Lily began, only to be cut off by Laura.

"Just the two of us," Laura reiterated.

Lily let out a sigh and led her sister into the living room. Sadie greeted them while Ian remained on the sofa.

"Can you give us some privacy?" Lily asked.

"Sure." Ian stood up and gave the side of his pant leg a little pat, signaling to Sadie to follow him. They retreated to his study and shut the door.

LAURA SAT on the sofa where Ian had been sitting, while Lily sat in the chair across from her. "Dani called. She said she and Walt saw you over at the lot, and that you ran off before she had a chance to talk to you. Said you seemed upset. What happened?"

Laura stared at her sister. "Didn't she tell you?"

"A little. Why don't you tell me?" Lily urged.

"You'll think I'm crazy."

"No, I won't. Come on, Laura, tell me what happened."

Laura took a deep breath, exhaled, and started talking, telling Lily everything she had seen and heard at the Marymoor site, including exploding boulders and Danielle talking to imaginary people. Lily found herself relaxing because Laura was giving her the opening she needed to give her the explanation Danielle had suggested.

"So you think I'm crazy?" Laura asked when she finished telling what had happened that morning.

Lily smiled softly. "No. And I can probably explain what you saw."

"You can?"

"Yeah, but I imagine you'll think I'm crazy when I'm done."

"Go on," Laura urged in a quiet voice, her gaze locked on Lily.

"It's about the rumors of the property being haunted. That used to be the site of the Marymoor Sanatorium, an insane asylum. None of us really took the stories seriously. After all, who believes in ghosts?" Lily grinned nervously.

"Mom does," Laura said.

Lily let out a sigh. "Yeah, well, perhaps Mom was right. You see, after they bought the property, we saw some strange things over there. Some really strange things."

"Like rocks floating in the air and exploding?" Laura asked in a hesitant tone.

Lily nodded. "When Heather and Chris were over there, they saw some strange stuff. Ian saw some things when he was over there, so did Walt and Danielle. Even Brian Henderson did. But Ian's parents didn't. I don't think Joe and Kelly did. And if we said anything, you all would think we were nuts."

"Why were Walt and Danielle there today?" Laura asked.

"First, I want to explain why we were all over at the Glandon Foundation instead of going out for dinner. We wanted to talk about what some of us had seen. I imagine Kelly told you that when Dani was little, she claimed to see ghosts. I'd be surprised if Joe didn't tell her. And knowing Kelly, I expect she probably told you, especially with all this recent talk of haunted property."

Laura nodded. "Yeah. I knew that."

"Well, I doubt Dani really saw ghosts when she was little, no more than Rupert was real," Lily began. "But over the years, Dani researched the topic and came up with a theory that since we're all made up of energy, and when we die, they say that energy doesn't die, then perhaps those places where some claim to experience hauntings are nothing more than that energy—trapped in some way. Considering the history of Marymoor, we figured trapped negative energy might be the explanation."

"Something was there."

"Yes. I agree. After we all talked on Wednesday night, we decided to investigate the history of Marymoor. Walt came across some information that suggested the head of the sanatorium had been taking bribes to incarcerate women who never should have been sent there. We decided, if anyone might haunt that place, it would be them."

"So Danielle was basically performing an exorcism?"

Lily shrugged. "It sounds nuts. That's why I never said anything. But we had to try something. And Dani and Walt feel it worked."

Laura slumped back on the sofa.

"I hope it worked," Lily muttered under her breath.

The two sisters sat in silence for a few minutes. Finally, Lily said, "I hate telling Kelly all this. It's just going to cause problems between her and Joe. He would never imagine any of this might be possible."

Laura frowned. "Why do you have to tell her?"

"For one reason, I had you tell her not to say anything about seeing us at the Glandon Foundation the other night, and I promised that in a few days I would explain why we were there," Lily said.

"That won't be an issue," Laura said. "All I told her was that I'd find out from you what was going on and suggested she not say anything right now. I didn't tell her I'd already confronted you."

Lily frowned at Laura. "Why didn't you tell her?"

Laura shrugged. "You're my sister. She doesn't need to know everything that goes on between us. My first loyalty is to you."

Lily grinned at Laura. "Um, what time exactly did you guys stop over there the other night?"

BRIAN HENDERSON PULLED his car up in front of the Marymoor property on Saturday afternoon and parked. "You know, Kelly might drive up at any moment," Brian teased after he and Heather got out of his car.

Heather shrugged. "Hey, I decided if you don't care, why should I?"

With a grin, Brian walked around the car and took Heather's hand. "Does this mean you're bored with sneaking around?"

Heather frowned. "Dang, I forgot about that."

Brian laughed, and together they walked hand-in-hand toward the chain-link gate. When they were a few feet away, they stopped and studied the property.

"So they're really gone?" Brian asked, no longer holding Heather's hand.

"I haven't seen anything yet. It doesn't feel creepy," Heather said.

"So Lily didn't tell Laura everything?" Brian asked, his gaze still focused on the vacant lot.

"No. Just what I told you. Danielle thought telling her every-thing—" she paused a moment and glanced at Brian "—like Walt and I did with you, wasn't necessary and frankly would probably cause more problems. This is enough for Laura to take in."

"She believed it?" Brian asked.

"I guess watching that boulder fly up in the air on its own and explode was kinda convincing."

"I'm glad it was Laura and not Kelly."

"Yeah, I'm not sure Joe would believe even if he saw the Forgotten Women of Marymoor himself. And now that Lily has the time frame for when they stopped by the foundation office, Ian can make up a story about how they stopped by after they got back from dinner to pick up something. I guess he's going to somehow work it into a conversation before Kelly comes out and asks him about it."

"Should we check out the temperature?" Brian asked.

Heather gave him a nod and then walked with Brian through the open gate. Once through, they stood there for a moment.

"No temperature change," Heather noted.

"Maybe they are gone."

"Cool. Danielle's exorcism was a success."

Brian grinned and looked over at Heather. "I've been meaning to ask you something."

Heather looked at Brian. "What?"

"Would you like to go to Joe and Kelly's wedding with me?"

LAURA ACCEPTED LILY'S EXPLANATION, and the sisters spent the next three days together, with Laura helping prepare for Connor's birthday party on Wednesday afternoon. Lily didn't feel it necessary to move Connor's party to a Saturday, because most of the guests didn't have jobs to go to—or had the day off—and the party was going to be an afternoon barbecue on the beach, so even Evan and Eddy Junior could attend after school that day.

Since Danielle and Walt's encounter with the spirits of Marymoor on Saturday morning, the mediums—save for Evan—had visited the property, and all agreed the ghosts had moved on. When Eva stopped by the day before Connor's birthday, she confirmed their suspicion.

THE WEATHER on Connor's birthday proved ideal for an outdoor cookout. They brought extra chairs and tables over from Marlow House and from Chris's and Heather's. Family and friends gathered on the patio and beach behind Lily and Ian's house, visiting, playing

Frisbee, and enjoying the refreshments before Ian and Chris started up the grill.

"You think they're really gone?" Adam asked Danielle. He and Melony stood away from the rest of the group with Danielle. She had just given Adam and Melony the same story Lily had told Laura.

"I think so. It feels different over there," Danielle said.

"I could tell by Ian's attitude when we got here; he doesn't seem to have a problem with his parents building on the lot now," Adam said with relief.

"Do you think that's true, what Walt found out about those women?" Melony asked.

"Very possible. But it's only a theory, piecing together the information he found," Danielle said, not able to tell Melony, Randal had been the story's primary source.

An hour later, as the group gathered around the barbecue while Chris and Ian handed out burgers, Brian Henderson showed up at the party. Lily looked at Brian as he walked their way. She flashed him a smile and shouted, "I'm glad you could make it." He had just gotten off work.

Joe and Kelly sat with Laura at a nearby picnic table and looked at Brian. Joe, burger in hand, gave Brian a wave and pointed to the empty spot at their table.

Heather, who sat at the next table over, stood up and walked to Brian. When she reached him, she kissed his cheek. He took her hand, and together they walked toward the group. Joe dumped his burger in the sand. He didn't mean to. But he was too busy watching Brian and Heather.

"Heather and Brian?" Lily whispered to Danielle.

"That's what it looks like," Danielle said before grabbing a chip off Lily's plate and saying, "By the way, I took that pregnancy test this morning."

Lily looked at Danielle. "And?"

Danielle grinned.

THE GHOST AND THE CHURCH LADY

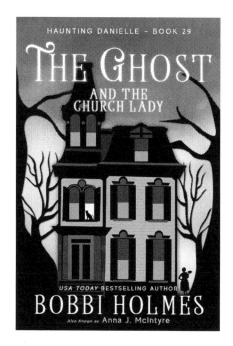

RETURN TO MARLOW HOUSE

THE GHOST AND THE CHURCH LADY

HAUNTING DANIELLE, BOOK 29

When autumn arrives in Frederickport, it brings surprises—some welcomed.

Meanwhile, the residents of Beach Drive learn there are some things more frightening than ghosts.

NON-FICTION BY
BOBBI ANN JOHNSON HOLMES

Havasu Palms, A Hostile Takeover
Where the Road Ends, Recipes & Remembrances
Motherhood, a book of poetry
The Story of the Christmas Village

BOOKS BY ANNA J. MCINTYRE

COULSON FAMILY SAGA

COULSON'S WIFE

COULSON'S CRUCIBLE

COULSON'S LESSONS

COULSON'S SECRET

COULSON'S RECKONING

Now available in Audiobook Format

UNLOCKED ⟨⟩ HEARTS

SUNDERED HEARTS

AFTER SUNDOWN

WHILE SNOWBOUND

SUGAR RUSH

Printed in Great Britain
by Amazon

66122108R00163